PENGUIN MET.

OUR IMPOSSIB

Durjoy Datta was born in New Delhi, and completed a degree in engineering and business management before embarking on a writing career. His first book—*Of Course I Love You . . .*—was published when he was twenty-one years old and was an instant bestseller. His successive novels—*Now That You're Rich . . .*; *She Broke Up, I Didn't! . . .*; *Oh Yes, I'm Single! . . .*; *You Were My Crush . . .*; *If It's Not Forever . . .*; *Till the Last Breath . . .*; *Someone Like You*; *Hold My Hand*; *When Only Love Remains*; *World's Best Boyfriend*; *The Girl of My Dreams*; *The Boy Who Loved*; *The Boy with the Broken Heart*—have also found prominence on various bestseller lists, making him one of the highest-selling authors in India.

Durjoy also has to his credit nine television shows and has written over a thousand episodes for television.

He lives in Mumbai. For more updates, you can follow him on Facebook (www.facebook.com/durjoydatta1) or Twitter (@durjoydatta) or mail him at durjoydatta@gmail.com.

Our Impossible Love

DURJOY DATTA

PENGUIN BOOKS

An imprint of Penguin Random House

PENGUIN METRO READS

USA | Canada | UK | Ireland | Australia
New Zealand | India | South Africa | China

Penguin Metro Reads is part of the Penguin Random House group of companies
whose addresses can be found at global.penguinrandomhouse.com

Published by Penguin Random House India Pvt. Ltd
No: 04-010 to 04-012, 4th Floor, Capital Tower -1,
M G Road, Gurugram -122002, Haryana, India

Penguin
Random House
India

First published in Penguin Metro Reads by Penguin Books India 2015

ISBN 9780143424611

Typeset in Bembo by Manipal Digital Systems, Manipal
Printed at Thomson Press India Ltd, New Delhi

www.penguin.co.in

MIX
Paper
FSC FSC® C010615

Our Impossible Love

1

Aisha Paul

For an average adolescent, I was five years late in getting my period.

And when I finally got it, I created a scene from a slaughterhouse in the bathroom.

'*Maa!*' I howled. I knew my mother would miss her dying daughter's yelps in the blare from the shrilly mothers-in-law in her favourite soap, *Kaahani Kis Kis Ki*, now into its eleventh year.

'*Maa! Switch off the TV! I'm dying!*'

Blood was trickling down my thighs. The pain felt as if I had given birth to a sixteen-wheel trailer. I pulled out the last tissue from the box and dabbed the blood off my thighs and the toilet seat. The bathroom still looked like a slaughterhouse. I felt every bit like an injured Rambo cauterizing his wounds, except I was mewing and not grunting.

'*Maa! Your daughter is dying. Like right now!*'

Finally, I heard the title track play out. My mother was a complete sucker for the show. But thankfully, she'd heard me and came running to the bathroom.

'Were you calling me?' she asked sweetly; I could imagine her pressing her ear to the bathroom door. God. Yes. She's a sweet woman, like Mother Teresa Home Version 2.0 and I love her more than life itself. I used to wish her illnesses on me—and then mine on my brother—and I still do sometimes, but I know better. It doesn't work like that. God doesn't cut deals with seventeen-year-olds. He's too busy engineering genocides in his name.

'I'm dead, Maa.'

She knocked on the door. *Perfect*. I had locked it from inside. I scampered to the door on tiptoes, like Bambi, around the little pools of my blood as if they were toxic waste. I opened the door.

'What . . .' Words ran dry, my mother looked around the bathroom like the air had been kicked out of her. But then she smiled. 'Aisha! *Amar bachha!*' she shouted and she pulled me close and hugged me, enveloping me in her arms, blood and all, and cried in joy. 'I knew Dr Roy's medicines will work. *Ami jaantam.*' She was crying now, kissing me all over my face, even as I doubled up in pain in her arms. I imagine this is what it would have been like when I was born—bloody, disgusting, painful, and joyous. That is if I'm not adopted like my brother once claimed I was.

'Are you in pain?' she asked.

Duh.

'Okay, Aisha. Nothing to be scared of.' She made me sit on the toilet seat, and cleaned me without once scrunching up her nose. In fact, she smiled throughout it all, while I was like, 'Can't I just die instead?' Once done, she gave me a medicine for the pain.

She taught me, like how she had taught me many other things before, to use a sanitary pad not knowing that I had practised wearing one quite a few times. In fact, I had once worn it to school for an entire week in the hope of invoking the God of Period.

'You're a woman now,' said my mother, looking at my reflection in the mirror, peering in to see if anything had changed in me since a few minutes back and made me more *woman-like*. Quite ironical because puberty was still coming at me from all corners of the ring, hitting me with whiteheads, acne and weight gain in the strangest of places.

And then she started to cry, and I cried with her. Our tear glands are hardwired. She cries. I cry.

It was a big day for her, and I thought it would be a big day for me as well. After all I had been waiting for this day since I was twelve—the first of my friends, Megha, got her period then and for the next few months, till someone else got it, she was supposedly superior and more grown up than her prepubescent friends. But, now that I finally got my period, I didn't feel much different. If I were to say this to the fourteen-year-old Aisha, who was obsessed about getting her period and spent over five thousand hours reading about PCOS (Polycystic Ovary Syndrome), whose variant I suffered from, she would have smacked my face.

How can spilt blood make me a woman?

Outside, my mother was crying into the phone to Dad while lighting incense sticks and murmuring little prayers from time to time. Over the past five years, the problem of my delayed period had been troubling them emotionally and financially. At last count, I had visited twelve specialists, some of whom charged a limb for advising us to wait patiently. A few had prescribed medicines which were rather discomforting but I did everything without so much as a word of complaint even though I saw through their deception. My parents were stressed out and I could not add to their anxiety by being a rebel.

Later that night, we went out to celebrate my becoming a woman. My dad couldn't join us because, like always, he was in a city different from where his family was. He worked in a nationalized bank and took every transfer that came his way, sometimes for a raise as low as Rs 200 a day. That seemingly measly extra four thousand two hundred a month went a long way to provide relief to our extenuating circumstances. My dad's sacrifice game on a scale of 0 to 10 was Jesus. I loved him, though not as much as I loved Mom because she was a goddamn fairy. But I loved him enough and we loved each other in the way fathers and daughters love each other—a little on the shy side. I never jumped up and sat on his lap like I did with Mom or hugged him when trying to sleep. Nor would he kiss me all over. But he would forgo food for a month if it meant a new uniform for me or my brother.

Sarthak and I were both scholarship students, and we skimped on lunches, wore worn-out clothes, but there was never too much to go around. *Four more years*, we used to tell ourselves every time we killed a desire. 'I will buy you everything!' I used to tell my mother. 'Buy everything you need first,' my mom would answer, a little guilty at how much her medical bills cost the family.

So, the celebration.

The restaurant was clearly beyond our means but thank God it was a buffet and we had with us a human vacuum cleaner of food—my eighteen-year-old brother, Sarthak. He's only a year older and really, really quiet. He went to a boarding school once. I think that did it—made him serious and broody and ripped. Initially, we would also move with each of Dad's transfers, which made both my brother and me lose a couple of school years, which in turn made us the oldest in our classes. So Sarthak, eighteen, was literally the oldest guy in our school.

'Thank you,' he said to me while loading his plate with portions rivalling a UN food aid package to Kenya.

'What?' I feigned innocence because that's what we do as siblings. Discussions around period, lingerie and masturbation, or any sexual reference for that matter, was out of bounds.

'And congratulations,' he said.

Why was he talking to me? Of all the times, he found today to be a supportive big brother!

'If you need anything, let me know,' he said.

Stop talking to me. I nodded and walked as far away from him as possible.

It had taken me three months to teach my mother how to use Skype and she had used this recent knowhow to surprise me—Dad was on the table as well, watching us eat. I think he was crying. I didn't look at him because I would have cried too. We cry a lot as a family, my brother excluded, who just stares into his books and reads.

And so we *celebrated*.

Because now I was like all the other girls and I could have kids when I grew older. All this when I had just about started to like being different—the girl with a faulty uterus suffering from something as unpronounceable as primary amenorrhoea.

But now, I was just another girl.

My mother hugged me to sleep that night and kissed me more times on my back than any of my future lovers would ever kiss me.

I'm sure I smiled in my dreams.

2

Danish Roy

They keep telling you, you're unique, you're different, you have a calling, a talent, a miracle inside of you. I had bought into this theory for a really long time. But no more. I was ordinary and there was no point waiting for that hidden genius in me to bubble to the surface. I would not discover my yet unexplored talent for painting, or interpreting ancient languages, or being a horse whisperer, or interpreting foreign policy at thirty.

And I think I would have been okay with it, or at least as okay as everyone else is with their ordinariness, had it not been for my overachieving little brother, my parents' favourite, who was wrecking corporate hierarchies like he was born to do so. Only last year, he got into the top 30 under 30 (at 21) in *Forbes* magazine for being a start-up prodigy. Fresh out of IIT Delhi, his crazy idea of sending high packets of data over Bluetooth in a matter of seconds sent potential investors in a tizzy. He was always in a tie-suit now, carrying leather folders and taking late night flights to meetings where capital flow, structural accounting and other terrifying things are discussed.

I'm two years older than him and I hadn't even won a spoon race in my life.

Quite understandably, I was a bit of an embarrassment to my parents—my father was a high-ranking official in the education ministry, and my mother, a tenured physics lecturer at Delhi University. It's not that they didn't love me, of course they did, but it was only because I was their son and they were programmed to love me more than themselves. But yeah, they loved Ankit more, and I didn't blame them.

Even I loved him more.

I was still struggling to complete my graduation in psychology (a subject my parents had chosen for me) from a college no one knew about, including the government, I presume. I was twenty-three and I had never been employed, a situation that didn't look like would change in the near future. It was more likely I would flunk my final exams too. Flunking exams by ridiculous margins was my superpower!

I was the most self-aware dumb person I had ever met.

Throw me a Suduko and you could study human behaviour in hostage situations. Medieval torture had nothing on me but keep a mathematics exam paper in front of me and I would start shitting bricks.

Today I was in bed, faking an illness, because my father had invited all his colleagues for an *informal* dinner where he would talk endlessly about my brother's million-dollar seed funding, shove in their faces little cut-outs of my brother's articles, while my mother would half-heartedly ask him to stop. We had been an upper-middle-class family, living in a duplex, with two cars, an AC and a television in every room, but there we were, talking in millions with dollar signs at the end of it. It wasn't hard cash but it still was money!

I had no business in such get-togethers where parents update each other about their sons' and daughters' acquired trophies, college admissions, jobs and citizenships, in the US. No, thank you. I was not jealous of them or my brother. I was merely embarrassed. Okay, maybe it was more than mere embarrassment; I could do without feeling suicidal about my failures.

'But do I need to stay in the house?' I asked my mother who looked beautiful in her green saree and the jewellery she had made my father get from the bank's locker.

'Yes, you do. They will think we are hiding you.'

'Why would they think that?'

The stupidity of the question immediately hit me. Obviously, I needed to be hidden, like an old mentally unstable uncle who roams around naked, slapping his head. 'Can I at least pretend that I'm sick and not come out?'

'You can,' said my mother after a pause. 'But you have to greet everyone as they arrive. After that you can go to your room. Touch everyone's feet, okay?'

I nodded and walked back to my room on the second floor, where Ankit and I lived in adjacent rooms, curled up inside my blanket and practised the sick routine I had perfected over the years of usage against unit tests, PTA meetings, annual functions etc. I was just getting into the groove when the covers were pulled off me.

'*Bhai*. Get up. It's time. Everyone must be coming,' said my brother, looking quite dapper in a crumpled cotton jacket and jeans. His hair was slick and wet like a gangster's, his face smooth as a baby's bottom and his eyes were twinkling. He was the better-looking brother—the one with the high metabolism, finer hair, and even straighter posture. The gene pool had been quite partial. Maybe I came from a contaminated test tube.

'I'm sick,' I groaned.

A look of pure horror came over his face and he rushed to touch my face. 'You seem okay? Have you told Maa? You want a Flexon?'

I should have hated him but I loved him, quite a lot, that beautiful, overachieving brat of a younger sibling whose brotherly love for me was sickening and claustrophobic. 'I had asked you to get the AC shifted to the other corner.'

'I'm not sick, Ankit,' I said. 'I just don't want to go outside and socialize.'

'And I wouldn't have pestered you but the Khannas' daughters are joining their parents. You might want to meet them.' He thrust the cell phone in my face and started to flick through their pictures. I was tempted but not enough to walk into the minefield of questions, humiliation, sideways glances and smirks.

'Today is your day, Ankit,' I said.

'I want you as my wingman. I like the younger one a lot and without you, how am I going to separate the two? Please?' He made that face. Fucking prick.

'Fine, I will be the untalented, boring brother and take the ugly sister away. Years of practice,' I said.

'You're not that bad, brother,' he said, shook my hand and left the room.

'Of course I am.'

3

Aisha Paul

So now I was like everyone else. I missed my pre-period self. These past few years had always been about me not getting my period.

Who am I if not the girl who's waiting to get her period and finally be a woman?

The last time I felt this uneasiness in my chest was when I was in the seventh standard and someone remarked at my boobs, or rather about the lack of them. *Was I my boobs?* I had asked myself then.

But God! The year before my breasts sprouted was torture! 'Have they come yet?' asked the boys in class one day, then giggled and scampered away like little mice. And believe you me, following that day I had slept clutching my chest every night, hoping they would *sprout* the next morning. As if being left out in the period-race wasn't enough, my chest was in no mood to comply with my prayers.

'I will take good care of them! Even small, perky boobs will do,' I used to say.

This was also the time I discovered masturbation, the pastime of the gods. Touching myself, thinking of a naked Michael Douglas, was fun, tingly, and sent me to sleep quicker. I never shared about this secret pleasure-giving pastime with my friends, not even with Megha, whose boobs had come at the same time as her period, because I thought it was dirty.

But my relationship with my fingers didn't last long.

I started getting acne and I thought it was just punishment for having touched myself. My face was suddenly a battleground

10

of red hills and craters. I rallied with my entire arsenal of toothpastes, creams, face washes and Dettol but the acnes emerged victorious.

And I still didn't have boobs.

In the eighth standard, slowly and thankfully, my chest started to grow and quite soon I needed a bra the size of two salad bowls. The boys shut up. Now they would keep staring at my tremendous chest, which was a victory of sorts in the beginning. I would strut about proudly, the buttons of my shirt tested for strain.

But soon it started to feel like an invasion of privacy. True, the eyes were theirs but these were my boobs—the results of my prayers.

Just stop looking, will you!

With the sprouting of the twins, my popularity rose. Rumour mills worked overtime.

'She has sex all the time. That's why the big boobs!' the girls would say in hushed tones.

Sometimes it made me want to take my prayers back and just be a *normal* size again. But that never happens, does it?

'You're like an Indian Beyonce,' my mother used to say.

'Easy for you to say! You're so fair and cute!'

I'd got my complexion, my height, my thick thighs and muscular calves from my father, and absolutely nothing from my mother who was a little, plump, aged-out brunette Barbie.

To distract people from my breasts and my face, the hemline of my skirt kept riding up.

I was popular but also hated, I used to be stared at (strictly below my face though) and ignored, talked politely to but also often subjected to vicious rumours about my sex life—which didn't exist. I had friends to talk to but never really had *friends* who I could *talk* to.

I slowly learned to enjoy the attention, and weed out the bad parts.

Though the questions still haunted me.

Am I my boobs? Am I my pimples? Am I my unfertilized eggs? Why am I even thinking about this?

I checked online if I were insane and found nothing.

After I got my period, the uneasiness returned. Like where do I go from here as a woman? Like where was the manual for that?

Life was much easier before the *incident* that changed everything. Before the incident all I wanted to be was to magically turn into my mother some day but then everything changed. Now all I wanted was to find and be my own woman.

I grappled with the questions for days on end . . . And then it struck me. I knew the *first* step.

I had to lose my virginity.

Later that night, standing in front of a mirror, naked and inspecting my body, I called up Megha. 'What do you think about sex? Like do you think it makes you into a different person?'

'I don't get you.'

'If I'm sexually wanted by a man, wouldn't that be like the final frontier for my womanhood?'

'Do you have a boyfriend?' asked Megha, her voice suddenly gleeful.

'No.'

'Then, why are you asking? And moreover, sex is not the last step in womanhood. The last step is getting married and having kids. That's what defines you finally. That's what being a woman is about. Like our mothers.'

'That doesn't sound exciting at all,' I said. I disconnected the phone soon after. Regardless of what Megha had said,

I decided to go ahead with my plan of ticking off sex from my checklist.

But what if not being a virgin any more didn't make me a woman, too? I knew of a few girls who had supposedly had sex with their boyfriends and they didn't quite look or behave any different. Maybe it was more of an internalized change, something only the girl could feel herself. But, of course, I wouldn't know that for certain till the time I actually lost my virginity to a man who deserved it.

So I started compiling a checklist of qualities I would want in the man (it had to be a man not a boy from my class who would gloat about having sex with me) who I would want to lose it to, and since I wanted to gloat about it, the list started with the words *rich* and *successful*.

4

Danish Roy

Two years ago, my brother had personally overseen the civil work of the duplex we now live in. The two of us had the entire first floor to ourselves, complete with a separate entry from the main gate and a floor thick enough to block out the din of a jackhammer. That night my parents slept soundly on the ground floor after knocking themselves out on Panadol Night while my brother engaged in a rather loud late-night cardio session on the first floor.

My brother was sleeping with the younger of the Khannas' daughters and I could tell from the noises that he was pretty good at it. (Unless screaming, 'Call me a bitch!' periodically is a sign of bad sex.) Also we are brothers and I was used to seeing him walking around naked in the house till he was about eleven and it didn't become the most awkward thing ever, so I know he's hung like a horse. Again, the dice of fate had rolled in his favour.

I wouldn't know at the time if size mattered; of course, I know now it does because I was still a virgin at twenty-three and I was sufficiently ashamed of it. My brother didn't know that, because I never told him. I think he thought of me as more of an arrogant snob who was picky about his sexual encounters.

In the party the night before, the elder of the Khanna sisters got bored after the first five minutes of my unsuccessful attempts to be charming, and she stared intently into her phone for the rest of the party to avoid any conversation with me. Truth be told, I was quite relieved. The elder sister was hot (by my standards, which you know by now didn't exist)

14

and if the conversation led to sex I wouldn't know what to do, except maybe prematurely ejaculate.

Worse still, my brother would know I had underperformed in bed. Being the brother with a smaller dick was enough humiliation for a lifetime. I had to make sure the venn diagram of the women I would sleep with and the women who could tell my brother how bad I was in bed never intersected.

But being small, sexless and foreseeably bad in bed were the least of my issues. What troubled me that morning were the impending final exam results of my course, while my parents were actually looking forward, as well as terribly scared, to their son being a graduate and hence employable.

'Aren't the results available online?' asked my mother when she was leaving for college that morning.

'The website is down,' I answered, hiding myself behind my Kindle. I was re-reading *The Lord of the Rings*. If only textbooks were as interesting.

My mother wasn't a fool. She knew I was a compulsive liar and a pro at hiding exam results, so she tried to check the website of my college in her phone. Good thing she was also stingy and relied on Wi-fi and never bought a 3G plan.

'I think the Wi-fi isn't working,' she said.

Of course it wasn't. I had switched it off. 'Let me know whenever the results are out?' I nodded. 'And ask Ankit to have his breakfast before he leaves.'

As if on cue, my brother walked out into the living room and hugged my mother before she left. She pointed out the little dark circles he had going on underneath his eyes and asked him to stop straining himself so much. If only he wasn't a god in bed, he would have got some sleep and would be blessed with as smooth under-eye skin as mine.

'So, a graduate today, haan?' my brother said, piling bananas, apples and oranges on his plate. The girl must be starving after the extensive cardio session my brother had put her through.

'Keeping my fingers crossed,' I said.

'You will make it,' he said and squeezed my shoulder. So naïve of him despite his intelligence! A little later, I could hear the girl screaming again while I took my shower. It was sex like that which gives women quintuplets, I guessed. His *Forbes* article had made him quite desirable and I'm sure my parents knew he sometimes got girls home but I was never too sure about it.

I left the house, nervous, and trying not to feel bad about myself.

*

I would have been surprised had I passed the exams but fate has a funny way of not surprising me ever. I wasn't the only one who had failed, thank God for that, but I had failed quite miserably, even by my standards.

'How did it happen?' asked Raman. 'You read so many books!'

'Fiction doesn't count,' I said, surprised that he had got through.

'So what will you do now?' asked Raman.

'It's a toss-up between hanging myself and drowning. And you don't have to sit here. It's your day. You should go dance,' I said, pointing to our classmates who were celebrating their success. Yes, I had friends. I wasn't some lonely sociopath who just wallowed in his inferiorities all day long. But how valuable a friend I was to any one of them was a different matter. There's always this guy in a group who's not funny or resourceful or kind or good-looking or rich but still is a part of the group for no understandable reason. The guy who only sits and listens and hopes some day they will talk about their favourite authors and he will be the one who will have the most to say.

They could have done without me.

I left the party without informing any of them and no one bothered to text me to ask where I was. I wouldn't hang out with me as well—I was a bit of a drag.

I sat on the pavement scrolling through my social media timeline, liking all the statuses, 'Finally a graduate', '64 per cent, yay!' and the like when my phone rang.

'Hello, baba!' said my mother. 'Where are you? Come home right now!'

'In college, why? What happened? Why are you so frantic?' I asked, fearing that she knew about my college results and wanted me back home so that she could slap me and ground me for three weeks. But that hadn't happened in like seven years now. And she actually sounded sprightly and happy. Had she lost her mind because her son had failed yet again? Was this the final straw before her dementia set in?

'*TIME* is interviewing your brother today. They want a picture with the entire family! I'm so happy! I will be home by 3.30. I have to pick up something to wear from Nalli. I hope your suit still fits.'

'Yes, it does.'

'Okay, go home right now. Don't be late! And please shave. It's a big day for Ankit. He has made all of us so proud!' She would cry any moment.

'I will be there on time.'

'And oh? I just forgot. How were your results?'

'I passed. 49 per cent,' I said.

'Oh,' her voice trailed. 'Never mind, you can still get a few jobs. Your father will put in a good word.' She disconnected the call.

5

Aisha Paul

Women's magazines are expensive and depressing.

I always assumed they were written by women for women to guide them, like self-help books. Quite the contrary.

'How to impress your man in ten ways'

'How to drive your guy crazy'

'How to save your relationship'

'How to find out if he's satisfied in bed'

'How to make him lust for you again'

After reading about twenty of them, I had a rough idea that sex was about understanding the man's needs and making him happy. Also that virginity was a big deal and is to be only lost to a worthy man. The boys' virginity didn't really seem to matter. In fact these magazines encouraged you to sleep with someone with *experience!*

Armed with all the knowledge about what's expected of a woman, I was sure to knock sex out of the park. But, of course, I had to get into shape first. I stood naked in front of the mirror, and used my two fingers to poke and flick the fat beneath my arms and on my thighs just as they had instructed. 'If it jiggles, it's fat,' they said, and 'Why be fat when you can be skinny and fabulous?'

For the next few days, I was depressed.

Megha and I went jogging every day at five in the morning and then at six in the evening. She mostly sat on a bench and Snapchatted risqué pictures to her *not really my boyfriend* who didn't think she was fat at all. He must be blind. He should have seen the last three cover models of *Vogue*, all of whom could have passed through the eye of a needle.

'You can't match up to them,' said Megha, foolishly. 'And moreover, it's all Photoshopping and airbrushing.'

'Of course I know it's airbrushing. I'm not a fool. But that's how we are supposed to look, otherwise why would they shrink their waists in the first place?'

Megha had no answer to that, instead she asked me something else. 'So have you decided who you want to have sex with?'

'I have given it some thought.'

'Aren't you scared?'

I shook my head. I was *terrified*. Not about how my first time would be, but about how the subsequent times will be. The magazines had made me believe that not all women come during sex.

Then what's the point! What if I never come?

That would be a travesty.

I had to find other ways to satisfy myself in case the mystical man, who would wrest away my virginity, fails to make me orgasm. It was time to indulge in that once shameful activity—masturbation—and see if I was self-sufficient.

6

Danish Roy

There was no celebration or a casual gathering of people in my house in honour of my graduation though my parents did whip up a meal more extravagant than usual. They had bought my lie hook, line and sinker. For the first time, they were talking about my career, how I should be very careful while making my choices and playing my cards from here on.

Late one night, I saw my father working out a list of places he could get me a job in, and that's when the possibility of my lie being caught hit me squarely on the face.

Like a true boy transitioning into a responsible man, I told my father I wouldn't accept any job if it required his help to get it.

My father took off his spectacles, a little dramatically, and said, 'I'm proud of you.' Luckily, he didn't cry or I would have felt like shit for lying to him.

'So are you looking for opportunities?' asked my father.

'Yes, I am,' I said, looking into my phone, planning my exit strategy from the room, which primarily comprised answering in monosyllables.

'Where?'

'Still looking.'

'Do I get a list?' asked my father, his kind demeanour quickly morphing into the taskmaster he always has been.

'Soon.'

'How soon? Date?'

'Next Thursday.'

'Thursday,' he said and marked it in his organizer.

'Do well. We have told all our relatives about your graduation. They are expecting great things out of you. Don't disappoint us,' he said, his words thorny but coated with a smile.

Why did they have to have any expectations from me? The only thing I share with them is a strand of DNA, which I share with another million people who don't care.

'I won't.'

Satisfied, he picked up the newspaper and started reading. I slunk out of the room, the thought of the impending Thursday tightening around my neck like a noose.

It was three in the morning, my search for jobs having led me nowhere, when there was a knock on my door.

'What?' I asked.

The knocking persisted. I opened the door and Ankit stumbled in, drunk out of his wits, looking like shit. He stumbled across the bedroom to the bathroom where he spilt out his guts into the toilet and a fair bit outside.

'Fuck. Why would you do that?'

He was too busy having an epileptic fit to answer. I walked outside and closed all the windows and deleted the browser history for you can never be too sure. Fifteen minutes later, he walked out and slumped on the bed like a log.

'Social drinking will kill me some day,' he murmured.

'That doesn't seem like a fair explanation for why you just wrecked my bathroom.'

'There's a girl in my room. I needed to keep that bathroom clean.'

'But—'

'Mom and Dad are too zonked out on their sleeping pills. I came through the back door,' he said and lay flat out on the bed. Then he changed the topic. 'What's happening with your job search? You'd better find one before Dad does.'

I looked at him blankly.

'C'mon. I know you failed. It's okay.'

'H . . . how?'

'I had your roll number. I checked it online,' he said.

'You knew it all this while?' I asked, shocked, my heart in my mouth.

'Of course I did,' he said getting up slightly and looking at me. 'It's not a big deal! Degrees never got anyone anywhere.' He smiled his charming smile at me. The one that gets him all the investments (of course his massive brain helps) and gets him laid all the time. 'You will get a job, don't worry.' His confidence in my non-existent abilities was quite heart-breaking, like I was the only subject the brainiac couldn't solve. I was Bella to his Edward in a parallel creepy universe.

Next morning, the bathroom was all cleaned up and my brother had left a note, '*Sorry for the mess. Best of luck. Mailed you the contacts of a few firms that are looking for psychology grads. Go for it!*'

7

Aisha Paul

I cried for two whole hours before leaving home. If it were up to me, I would crawl back into my mother's womb and never leave.

'I will miss you.'

'Stop it, Aisha! School will end in another six hours and you will be back home,' said my mother, tired of me lungeing at her and kissing her all over. In times like these I wondered if my brother was right about my adoption.

The summer vacations had ended too soon, as if the two months had rammed and packed into a neat box of day and a half. I returned to school in my little skirt and rolled down socks.

But I hadn't wasted the time.

I had spent it carefully working on myself. *Quite literally.* And after spending weeks locked up in my room, learning the tricks to self-satisfaction, I wasn't going to let my knowledge go waste. I would pass on my knowledge to other girls and I would guide them through the wondrous and dirty and fabulous world of earth-shattering, toe-curling orgasms.

It wasn't easy to begin with.

It took me two-hour long showers for a week to find the exact rhythm to transport myself to a place that's hot and blinding and blank and extraordinary. Now if I concentrate hard enough I can finish myself up in about three and half minutes. I was extremely good in bed with myself. Men should be able to take out three and half minutes of their time to learn to love the women they are with.

*

I distinctly remember the first time I orgasmed. It's still the smuttiest, sexiest thing I have ever done, and it took me fifteen days to plan the entire operation.

I had read in one of the issues of *Cosmopolitan* about this little shop tucked in one corner of Palika Bazaar—a dark, dank, strange place—which sold sex toys, whips, handcuffs, porn CDs and the like.

I would swiftly walk past the shop a dozen times every day for a couple of weeks—scrunching up my face like I didn't belong there—sizing up and categorizing the different dildos kept in little glass cabinets by shape, girth, length and texture. I finally chose a big red one, complete with big red balls—it was veinous, curved to the right, about nine inches in length and as thick as my forearm. It was love at first sight and I was just denying it for the longest time trying to like some other average, safer ones. Just thinking about it made me feel kinky and wrong and wonderful.

But then came the difficult part. There was no way in hell I could have casually walked into the shop in my school uniform and gone like, *Hey, can you pack that dildo real quick, yeah? I will pay by cash, can you make it quick, I really have to go now.* I strategized and I waited for me to be united with my *lover*.

The next Sunday I reached Palika Bazaar before it opened and stood guard at the entrance, looking for someone with similar *needs*. Three hours and ten Diet Cokes later, four giggly girls, dressed top to bottom in overpriced brands, distinctly drunk, teetered through the entrance. They were up to something naughty; I could see that in the furtive glances they threw at the shops. I followed them around as they enquired about what they needed. Fifteen minutes and many awkward stares later, they were in the toy shop flicking through the *goods*. One of the girls dared to lay hands on my *boy* but backed off before I lunged and ripped her head clean off her shoulders. Little later, they left happy and scandalized with a pair of handcuffs and a whip and small vibrator.

I waited for them to exit.

I closed my eyes and calmed my nerves. My heart thumped. I felt hot, like both sweaty, nervous hot, and hot, like sexy hot. I walked into the shop as if I belonged there.

'Hey, I was just here with my friends. And that girl? The one whose bachelorette we are celebrating? We want to gift her that dildo as well,' I said, pointing to my lover on the shelf. 'How much? Three thousand? We just bought so much right now. It's not our first time, okay. Don't fleece us. It's not that you have any customers anyway.'

I closed the deal at a thousand. The blow-up sex doll in the corner smiled at me. Clutching my man close to my chest, I rushed back home feeling super dirty. I closed the door and drew the curtains. I took a quick bath, shaved my legs and my nether regions, to put it politely, put on an oversized T-shirt, and jumped into bed under my blanket. My panties were drenched at this point in time. With trembling hands, I took the dildo out from the brown paper bag, and wrapped my fingers around all nine inches of red, glorious plastic.

I can't believe I have a dildo in my hands! I'm so kinky. It's mine! It's in my bedroom!

I took off my T-shirt slowly, the way a boy would have, and started feeling myself all over. If I had to fuck myself, I had to be insanely good at it. I grabbed at my breasts and clutched them. My body felt like Christmas. I guided the dildo below. Oh. My. God. It reached a few inches below my navel and my body flooded with warmth. I started to sweat. I pulled the blanket off me and watched myself in the mirror as I made out with myself. I didn't know when my fingers found themselves playing with my tongue, and when I grabbed my breasts and kissed them, and when I alternately guided my fingers and dildo inside of me. It was hot and weird and kinky and my red lover was incredible. I thought I would shatter the windows with my screams so I bit my tongue and let out a hoarse cry instead. My heart raced and found it hard to keep up with all the sensations my body was throwing at it.

Ten minutes of panting, heaving, wetness, grabbing, clutching, licking later, my body convulsed like I had just been exorcized and I felt a whiteness take over. My toes curled, my body spasmed, and I was suddenly aware of every cell of my being. I floated away somewhere and I could feel colours and taste sounds and ride unicorns and feel the sun in my palms. I touched myself a little more and accumulated a little more of that incredible blankness before I collapsed and felt enlightened.

Later I hid my lover deep behind the cupboard, wrapped in all my clothes I didn't wear any longer. Every few days, he would come and visit me and I would indulge in a little space travel with him. I named him Hellboy after the comic book character.

*

The more I masturbated, the less I felt the need to lose my virginity. Why would I need a man when I could give myself so much pleasure? I didn't need a fleshy, unreliable appendage when I had shampoo bottles, hair brushes and rolling pins, and of course, *Hellboy*. These things I'm sure were made by women, for I don't know what they are if not symbols of women empowerment hiding in plain sight! Imagine a rolling pin used to make chappatis setting a woman free of her man.

Brilliant, just brilliant.

'So did you find anyone?' Megha asked me in the washroom while fixing her hair, and pulling up her skirt and dropping her shirt over the belt. She looked quite cute if you ask me. She had the whole Punjabi sharp features, clear complexion thing going on for her. She still looked twelve though. Her father had a huge jewellery shop bang in the middle of Rajouri Garden, and a driver use to pick and drop her to school every day. Money was never a problem for her so she never really understood why I never put any make-up on. Or why I didn't hang out after school that much. Or why I never changed my uniforms on time. But we still talked out of habit. I knew she was a little toxic, fuelling rumours about me from time to time, and to be fair I had had made fun of her exam results quite often, but we remained friends or whatever you call it. Sometimes you get into relationships you don't want to be in but don't know how to get out of them. Megha and I shared a similar bond. We had nothing in common, nothing whatsoever, but we had started talking when we were really young and comparatively stupid, and now it was inertia more than anything else that was the reason why we still talked. She was into clothes and Bollywood, and I was into books and academics. We were poles apart.

Megha and I were seat partners back in the day when our bodies were changing. Suddenly, the two of us were thrust into the limelight because we looked more womanly than others—she was cute and I was busty—and we enjoyed it. We were like two mean girls who didn't love each other but only maybe hated each other a little less. The little popularity we had got us heady and we knew we had to work together to selfishly hold on to it. So we stayed together to concoct gossip about other girls and boys to pull them down. It was all fun and games. But we had done nothing worse than what I had done to Namrata, my classmate for five years now, the girl I secretly admired and hated at the same time. Megha now knew too many of my secrets, so that was another reason why we had to continue to be friends.

I could stop talking to her from the next day and not feel the loss and I could say the same for her. But for some reason we dragged on with our relationship since no one between the two of us was brave enough to walk out, say no, we are not meant to be, this is over, and never look back. We do waste a lot time in relationships that only ask and not give anything back.

'I don't think I need a man to know what sex feels like!' I said, hoping to impress her by my revelation.

'You have had sex, isn't it? That's why you're deflecting,' she said quite convinced. 'Tell me about it!'

'I haven't but I shagged. And it's the most beautiful thing ever!'

'If you don't want to tell, it's fine, you don't have to lie about it,' said she and walked out angrily. It was quite strange of Megha to believe more easily that I had had sex with someone than trusting what I told her about being a compulsive masturbator.

Between her walking off from the washroom and the sixth period, the news had travelled of my having regular sex with a boy from outside school.

'He's a college guy,' one girl whispered.

'I heard they are just fucking. No relationship,' said another.

It was clear soon enough that I needed to be a little ashamed of myself, and by the end of the day, I was called to the principal's office.

'Sit, Aisha,' he said. 'I have been hearing things about you in the school. You're a brilliant student and I don't want you to be mixing with the wrong people.'

'They are rumours, sir. I'm still a virgin. There was a time I thought I should have sex with someone but the feeling has passed. I'm looking for something else now.'

The principal looked at me like I had admitted to heroin abuse. 'I don't understand.'

'I don't understand it either. I'm still looking for what I'm looking for,' I said, smiling widely at him. 'For now I'm quite satisfied with masturbation.'

He was quite aghast to hear this despite having three kids himself—the babies couldn't have been possible without him being sexually active as well, right?

'Look, Aisha, I know you're going through a lot,' he said, barely able to meet my eye. 'I understand that. But I will have to recommend you to our counsellor.'

'Counsellor? Why? Because I masturbate?'

'I will appreciate if you don't use that word around here or in front of other kids in school. If you continue to do so, I will have no choice but to notify your parents about this.'

'But students use far worse words! They cuss all the time!'

'You're not in a position to argue, Aisha. You will have to spend an hour every second day with the school counsellor or I go with this to your parents.'

At this point I must mention that with my tales of getting my period and masturbation stories, I missed an important detail of my life, which people often blame for my slow descent into madness. A few years ago, my mother woke up to a crippling pain in her lower back. A battery of tests later, she was told she had a weak kidney and would have to rely on dialysis for the rest of her life. No one tells me how long she would be alive but I have a gnawing premonition that it wouldn't be long.

And so, I didn't plan to give her any more pain than she was already in.

'I will attend counselling.'

8

Danish Roy

I'm beginning to think I'm quite the antithesis of the stereotypical boy or man. I'm not brave, or honourable, or intelligent, or rich, or charming; neither am I too strong, nor do I have an enviable reproductive organ. If the remains of our civilization are unearthed billions of years later and my fossilized history is used to represent homo sapiens, I should probably apologize to all you 'men' for painting our kind in a bad light.

As a boy I harboured many wishes which I thought would make me into a man, but none of them had been granted. Just like any jobless man with limitless time on his hands, let me count the things I have been wanting to be ever since I have memories.

I was nine years old.

The seating arrangement of my class had been reshuffled and Manisha, a girl with golden yellow skin and a voice as sweet as candy, had been assigned the seat next to mine. It was my first brush with symptoms closely associated with a cardiac arrest. All I wanted was to be charming, and by that I mean have a tongue and enunciate words and have her smile at me. Instead, what I did reflexively was to yank out my belt during lunch breaks and fight with classmates, shouting out expletives I had just learnt. Evolution had missed me. I was marking my territory and it would have worked if she were a scratching, hairy ape looking for someone who threw hot turds at encroachers. Charm eluded me. As I grew bigger, hairier and smellier it became tougher for me to have a normal conversation with anyone from the opposite sex. It would usually start with sweaty palms and palpitations and end with me insulting the girl somehow.

I had figured out quite early in life that being hated was always preferred to not being liked. All that hate I garnered in those few years balled up into an avalanche of bitterness that wouldn't leave me until many years later.

I was twelve.

My hormones had started raging mini battles, mostly around the groin area and I had finally figured out why God bothered to make women—to give young boys something to think about while they shagged in bathroom stalls. Apart from wishing shorter skirts for all the girls in my class, I really wanted to be taller. I stood at 124 cm and a lot of my classmates, including girls, towered above me. I was convinced I would never grow any more and would have to spend the rest of my life as a dwarf in a little home staring at people's chins. Because why on earth would God make someone so much shorter than others? It made no sense! And why me?

I glugged milk and ate like a refugee on food aid and still I didn't grow; I would hang from the football post till my eyes teared up and my arms threatened to rip right off, but I still remained short. I prayed, and threatened God with dire consequences, hoping he would look into more important matters than saving the world from complete ruin and such. He didn't. Slowly, I just learned to accept my physical form.

At fourteen I finally had a growth spurt which took me to 178 cm for which I was grateful—not that it helped me build a fulfilling friendship that lasted decades. So, yeah, I would not be attending any of my school reunions.

But what I really wanted at fourteen was a huge cock. When I say huge I'm talking in terms of biblical proportions, something which would require special underwear, or linings in trousers to accommodate the sheer size of the thing. I wanted to walk out of changing rooms during my swimming class and be greeted by gasps from the girls of my class. I wanted my organ to be an object of fear and envy, like a weapon of vaginal destruction. I wanted to it big, veiny and monstrous, the length of an arm and the girth of a little baby, a bit godly. I would have bequeathed it to medical research teams after my death. *Was wanting a museum-worthy dick too much to ask for?* Seems like it was. No penis enlargement exercises worked for me and I was stuck with an average-sized dick. Did I mention my brother was embarrassingly huge? Yes, I did.

Once I realized that no temples would be built to worship my schlong, naturally I wanted the next best thing. Big cars and money—otherwise known as penile extensions. I wanted to blind women folk with so much glitz they wouldn't know what my dick size was. Having entered the eleventh standard my parents, too, expected me to be serious about my aspirations and chalk out my future plans. How was I otherwise going to support my family and be a man of the house? I tried harder than I had ever tried before. I stayed awake all night mugging up macro and microeconomics, redoing maths sums early into the morning, and yet, all my knowledge eluded me when it came to the actual exams. No matter how hard I tried I couldn't dig myself out of the trench of my low IQ and non-existent attention span. It became clear I wasn't going to be rich or famous. Report cards don't lie. A below average college and a shady future stared back at me like Orcs from Mordor. I was destined to live a life with all my shortcomings. But I wasn't going to let go of my aspirations.

Soon, I wanted to be a hero. Now, I wasn't a brave fellow. I'm not the one who picks up a baseball bat or a .47 Magnum and charges howling and threatening towards an intruder in the middle of the night. I'm the one who locks the door and tries climbing out of the window and begs the intruder to do his business and leave quietly. Maybe even make him a cup of coffee and write him a cheque. I would never willingly risk my life, disfigurement, or mutilation of my body. I would never be a willing hero. Though I waited for the day I would accidentally run over a terrorist, or a save a plane from crashing, and be caught on camera doing so. It happened all the time in the movies and there was no reason why it couldn't happen to me.

However, none of the aforementioned things ever happened to me. I could vanish one day and it wouldn't matter to the world. My parents would probably wail for a few days because, after all, I am their flesh and blood and parental instinct is hardwired, not acquired. My brother would be crushed, but other than that no one would really miss me if I were to step in front of a train and die.

9

Aisha Paul

My mother was diagnosed with the kidney disorder when I was all of eleven years old, waiting for my period and my bust, and all the guidance my mother could offer when I needed her. She was a bit like superglue. She made the rest of the family stick together and a little whiff of her maternal superpower got us high. I always thought some day she would whip off her saree and show us her Wonder Woman costume. She was my answer to the question, 'What would you want to be when you grow up?' I wanted a husband, a kitchen, two kids and a dog. My mother would laugh so hard listening to my answer from harrowed class teachers. 'It's just a phase,' she would tell them, and then tell me, 'I was married when I was eighteen and although I love your father and you and your brother, I still wish I had a few years to myself when I was young.'

'But—'

'You have to be more than me, Aisha,' she used to say, her eyes twinkling with innocent hope. 'And you will have boyfriends and a career and you will make stupid decisions.' Clearly introducing her to the joy of Bridget Jones movies wasn't one of my brightest ideas.

'I want you to be more than what I was and will ever be,' she would say.

'But all I want is to be you,' I would snap and she would smile at my naivety.

And then it all came crashing down.

All these years, she had been slowly withering away inside. My mother was diagnosed with Chronic Kidney Disease.

While it is not an uncommon disease, fatal only in a small percentage of people, it is an extremely expensive ailment. You would be surprised how easily people say, *at least she will live*, and not realize how things will never be the same again.

'Will you die?' I had asked my mother.

'Of course not!' my father had said and pulled me close to him. My mother laughed and brought us some pakodas she had been frying. Sarthak continued to play Fury on his computer like nothing had happened.

But slowly my mother's appearance began to deteriorate— her eyes were constantly puffy, her skin lost its lustre and she was always tired. And though her smile never faded, an unmistakeable exhaustion had crept into it. For the first few months, she spent more time in hospitals than in her beloved kitchen, undergoing a battery of tests. Father broke FDs, encashed LTAs and put it all into doctors and hospitals, flying her from Delhi to Bangalore to Mumbai to Chennai for a second, third and a fourth opinion. The answer was pretty simple—regular dialysis for the rest of her life and prayers that her kidneys don't give up.

After that we all resumed our lives, getting used to living with and loving an older, MS DOS version of our mother. Then the first cracks began to appear. Regular dialysis meant an additional expense of 8 lakhs a year (in addition to the visits to many doctors), which meant all my parents' savings were gone within the first two and half years. We moved into a tiny, one-bedroom apartment. Sarthak and I would sleep in the bedroom and my mother would sleep on the sofa in the living room.

My father started working overtime and still wouldn't earn anything to save for a rainy day, so we just hoped there wouldn't be any. My mother's illness, no matter how hard she tried, wasn't only hers to carry. It was ours as well.

My shoes were worn out, Sarthak's bag was torn and tattered, and my father's shirts kept ripping off from where my mother had darned them.

Sometimes late into the night I would watch my mother staring at her medical reports and bills, crying, drinking bottle after bottle of water because the doctors had told her it helps the kidneys. She would sit in front of the TV, out of habit, but not switch it on. She would lie sweating beneath the still fan to save on the electricity bill. My father would flick newspapers from colleagues' desks after they were done and read it in the night. Unnecessary furniture was sold off. My parents even went off tea for an entire year. We never ate out. No picnics. No fetes. There was a sadness but we were never unhappy.

Days passed and things never looked up financially. There was never enough to go around. Sarthak and I garnered whatever scholarships, cash prizes, and the like we could get to help with the expenses. We would scribble on newspapers to save paper, slyly eat out of other's lunches to keep from eating a lot at home, and steal from the library. Sarthak even got a scholarship to a boarding school and left for a few months, leaving us richer but quite miserable without him. But he didn't last long and came scampering back.

My mother, my beautiful, smiling mother started to break down, one smile at a time and one day, when I was just fifteen, I found her in the bathroom, naked and in a pool of blood. My mother had tried to kill herself. She was still conscious when I found her. I had shouted and pulled her away from the shower, and dragged her limp body on to the sofa in the bedroom.

She had turned on the shower so that I didn't have to clean up later, she told me afterwards.

I called the doctors who stitched my mom up (she refused to go to any hospitals so they made our bedroom into a makeshift hospital bed), and called me brave and whatnot. Sarthak and my father were visiting relatives in Raipur.

She made me promised not to tell my brother and father about the little incident. *It's our secret*, she told me.

'Why did you do it?' I asked, crying, thinking of what my life would be like if she had died in the shower. The thought was unbearable, it was like a physical pain, like someone had reached down my throat and was clawing at my internal organs. I howled.

'I . . . I didn't want to be a burden any more, Aisha . . .'

'You're not a burden!' I shouted and hit my mother repeatedly. I thought of her being dead, burnt, ashes, nowhere, nothingness. I would be so lost.

'Yes, I am, Aisha. You could have such a better life without me. You would be fine without me,' she said.

I wanted to slap my mother really hard, like really hard. How would my life make sense if I couldn't share it with my beautiful mother? She was my only friend! How could she say that? Was she insane? I wiped my tears on the end of her saree and said in as serious a voice as I could muster, 'If you ever try this again, I swear on you, no, not on you—that wouldn't work—I swear on my father I will kill myself.' And with that I jerked the cannula off my mother's hand and jammed it into my wrist. God! That hurt!

My mother gasped and pulled the needle out, little puddles of tears in her eyes, as she rubbed the blood off my wrist and asked me if it was paining.

'Do I make myself clear, Mom?' I asked, trying not to wince since I was making a strong point here.

My mother tearfully nodded. She cleaned up the wound on my wrist and covered it with a Band-Aid.

'But Aisha, promise me something?'

'What?'

'You will not grow up to be like me.'

Now that was confusing. 'Who should I grow up to be like then?'

'Find that out yourself. Find out what kind of woman you would want to be. Just don't be me.'

'Why?'

'Didn't I almost leave you alone in this world? Didn't I just fail?'

That she had. Her selfless act was pretty selfish after all. Her love for me and for us was flawed after all, and beneath the saree there was no shield, and no star-spangled Wonder Woman costume.

'But I love you,' I said and hugged my mother.

Since that day, following my mother's instructions, I started my search to find a different *me*, one different from Mom.

I had to be someone better. I had to become my own woman.

It was three months after the *incident* that my father's overtimes resulted in a promotion that loosened the noose around our necks but by then I knew I didn't want to be my mother any more.

10

Danish Roy

While my career plans had come to a screeching halt, Ankit, like a true supportive brother had asked me to join him for a celebratory party thrown in his honour by the rich, smug bastards who would fund and overwork him.

Before we left for the party, I was suitably drunk on my father's twenty-year-old single malt—it was my revenge for his and my mother's lop-sided genetic transfer of intelligence and charm.

'It's going to be a great party!' exclaimed my brother as we slipped into the BMW the organizers had sent for him. There was a little icebox with miniatures of Grey Goose and Black Label. Like a true unemployed person, I transferred them into my pocket before we left the car.

The party was the fakest thing I had ever been to. Drunk and totally out of my wits, I stumbled from one conversation to another, being nasty with everyone who would talk to me.

'So you work with your brother?' a girl asked me, clearly hoping to network.

'Yes, I manage his whores. Do you want to sign up?'

Another fledgling female entrepreneur walked up to me when she saw me and my brother together. 'So, your brother is quite the rage here, isn't he?'

'Sure, he and his ten-inch big cock. Bet you can fit two of those in though, can't you?'

I was an angry disappointing fucking loser who couldn't do one thing right in his life amongst these overachievers.

Before I could be sued for sexual harassment and be an even bigger embarrassment to my brother and my family, I plonked myself on the bar stool, and decided to drink myself to nothingness.

Three hours and four hundred drinks later, my brother was literally dragging me across the floor, trying to wake me up because it was time to go home. I know this because my head bumped into tables twice but I was too hammered to regain control of my limbs. I was a paralysed octopus. Too many limbs. Not enough head.

Outside, he sat me down and turned my head towards a flower pot where I vomited for the next twenty minutes. He had ordered a cab. In my blurry, post-alcohol vision, I could see a girl in his arms, not the entire girl, just a pair of the longest, glittery legs I had ever seen.

'Hey,' said Ankit, slapping my face gently, 'hey, I'm just going inside. She will be with you. Be okay, okay?' He thrust a plastic cup of lemonade in my hand. Seemed like a perfect waste of a good buzz but I sipped at it, and after fifteen minutes I was better enough to hear my brother's newest girl talk.

'I run couponcode.com. I started it when I was nineteen,' she said.

'I was still watching xnxx.com fifteen hours a day when I was nineteen,' I replied.

'You're funny,' she said.

That must have been the sweetest thing anyone had ever said to me in the longest time.

'So you're planning to sleep with my brother tonight?' I asked, my social charm again failing me. She thought I was joking, again. I wasn't. Did I mention I couldn't talk to girls without insulting them?

As we waited on, a Mahindra Scorpio came to a screeching halt a few yards away in front a cigarette stall, and two boys jumped out, raucous and more drunken than I was. Suddenly put into a protective role, I told the girl, 'Let's go inside. It's not safe.'

'Why? Why should we go inside? They should get into their car and leave,' she said.

'This is Delhi, not a feminism rally,' I slurred.

The boys were now looking at us while dragging on their cigarettes. They weren't doing anything, just staring lecherously, licking their lips, blasting songs from their stereo, laughing rowdily, making their muscled pecs dance. But I was scared shit. They could rip me apart limb by limb and take this girl away. Nobody can say I didn't warn her.

'Let's just go inside. Don't be foolish. I want to live.'

'I'm not going anywhere,' said the girl. She refused to budge.

'Don't be stupid. They are drunken men, they can do anything! If something happens, you will be to blame!' I almost screamed but I was too afraid to say out anything louder than a whisper.

'What!'

'Who is what?' asked my brother who appeared from behind.

'Those men are staring at my legs and your brother here feels I should go inside and hide. He thinks if anything happens to me it would be my fault and not theirs. Because they are drunken men and they can do anything!' she exclaimed.

'You don't have to put it like that. You make me sound like—'

'What?' the girl snapped. 'A patriarchal, medieval boy who burns women for dowry? Yes, probably you're that.'

And even as we were talking, my brother, the hero, had walked up to the men and asked, 'You can leave if you have bought your cigarettes.'

The girl's eyes which were like embers were trying to burn through my soul, searing on my conscience that I was a regressive, scared piece of shit. Suddenly she turned dove-like and fluttered near my brother.

'You should leave,' she said to the men who, I could tell, were counting the number of cricket bats they had hidden in the trunk.

And before I could make sense of what was happening, as it often happens in Delhi, blows were being exchanged and my brother was getting pummelled left, right and centre.

This was my spot in the limelight.

It was one of those moments where a man's character is tested, one solitary moment which defines the good in a person, one selfless act of bravery that obscures everything else he might have done in his life.

But . . .

There wasn't even a shred of bravery in all 178 cm of me. Zilch. Nothing. Nada.

My feet were bolted to the ground and I shrieked like a little kitten on seeing my brother getting smashed.

The girl came running to me and pulled my arm and pushed me towards the battlefield. *'Fuck you, Danish. Go help your brother!'*

'Yes,' I murmured and said a little prayer. For someone whose facial beauty is comparable to a dead rat's, I didn't want them to break my nose.

Finally, I gathered my senses and got into the thick of things, wildly throwing punches, cursing and shouting, missing everything and everybody while trying to pull my brother out of their way.

The last thing I remember was following the last seconds of the trajectory of a head of a hockey stick coming in my direction.

Blank.

*

I woke up later with a bitch of a headache in the backseat of a car the nice girl was driving.

'Your brother really ditched you back there. Isn't he older than you? Shouldn't he be protecting you?'

'He was just a little rattled, that's all,' Ankit said.

'He's a coward, that's what he is. He asked me to go inside. Can you believe it? How do you stand him?'

'He's my brother and I love him,' Ankit said.

'He's a shit brother to have.'

'He's still my brother,' Ankit said, grinding his teeth.

'He's a disappointment and you know that,' she said.

Ankit didn't reply to that. A little later, the car stopped in front of our house and Ankit pulled me out from the backseat. He dragged me through the front gate of our house.

'Where are you going?' Ankit asked the girl as she started to get out of the car.

'I thought . . .'

'I'm not sleeping with someone who insults my brother.'

And that was the end of the nice girl for that night, who was rather truthful I must add.

*

'What happened!' my mother shrieked the moment she saw blood coming out of both our faces.

'I got into a fight and Ankit tried to save me,' I said before Ankit could utter a word. 'It was totally my fault. I'm sorry.'

My father charged at me and it seemed like he would almost hit me before my mother came between us.

'I told you not to take him!' my father shouted at Ankit.

'But—'

'He's a disgrace, Ankit. *Disgrace!*'

He threw the newspaper he was carrying to the ground for dramatic effect and stormed off. My father wasn't finished though. A little later, he emerged from his room with an envelope in hand. He had that look on his face I have so clearly etched in my memory, that look which was an indication that he had found out about another one of my lies.

He threw the envelope on my face. Inside, was an application for the registration for my second attempt at graduation. It had reached him that morning. He knew I had failed.

'*He failed his final year.* He lied to us. He lied to you!' he shouted at my mother who looked at me as if I had committed genocide. '*He will amount to nothing in life.*' He charged at me again, angry. 'What will we say to our relatives now?' He almost hit me again but stopped short and thrust a finger in my front of my face instead. Then probably seeing his spawn drunk and bleeding evoked pity in his cold heart. 'I will find you a job and you will do it regardless of what you think about it. I will not have you sitting at home being a burden on this family. Get it?' he shouted and worked himself up enough to finally slap me. He walked away and slammed the door behind him.

11

Aisha Paul

One of the worst things about my school life was what my elder brother had to endure because of me. Poor boy went through hell and back for me. It started when the boob gods started being benevolent on me and gave me a 34B when they should have stopped at something like a 32A. Even Megha wrote in her diary which I chanced upon (I was surprised she wrote one): *Aisha is not even pretty! She's so dark! And her pimples. Oh God. All she has are her boobs.*

No one cared about my unwaxed legs, or the pimples, or my bad hair or my crooked teeth or shabby shirts, it was like suddenly my boobs were the epicentre of all gossip.

Sample these rumours:

Aisha and an eleventh grader were behind a dumpster and he had his hands up her shirt.

Aisha uses a massage oil that gets them really big. She kneads them like dough every morning. Sometimes she gets boys to do it!

Aisha is quite the nymphomaniac. That's why they grew so big!

Her boobs might be big but they have ugly moles on them.

She has ugly nipples. A friend sucked on them. He's in college. Of course, she's into college guys.

It was sweet of Sarthak to never confront me. I knew it was hard for him. He must have been struggling with his own adolescent sexuality. To top that, he was dealing with the repercussions from mine. Every time a rumour cropped up, he just curled into his own space like a little snail and totally cut me off.

We were quite thick before my damn boobs grew out.

It was like he was standing at the junction of a forked road for people who had to decide whether to be an introvert or an extrovert. He chose the former because people kept reminding him of a sister who had boobs, which of course, made him vulnerable to attacks and humiliation.

If only I had been a boy, my brother would have been a different person altogether. He wouldn't have spent the last four years of his school trying to block out all the voices of the hormonally charged boys who wanted to flick my nipples or look up my skirt. If he were not the nicest person in the world, he would have slapped me and told me to wear loose clothes, stay away from boys, and maybe even have asked me to shift to a girls' school but he didn't, and that made him the only kind of man I like in the world. However, I wouldn't want to wish any brother in the world a sister like me.

We waited for the bus together that day. His cycle had broken down. He stood away from me, like I had leprosy. When we got on to the bus, I got away from my friends for a change and sat next to him on the last seat. He flinched. Just what a girl needs from her big brother.

'Why don't you sit with your friends?'

He stared into his phone like he always did. I had never seen him hang out with people, or go on boys' night outs, but he was always on his phone, scrolling through social media feeds, reading up articles, and catching up with world news. He knew *everything*.

'I wouldn't really call them my friends. I know them and I talk to them but they are not really my *friends* friends. I don't think I have found a *real* friend yet. You?'

He looked outside waiting for me to leave but I was stubborn. He would have known that if he knew me better.

Finally, he spoke, 'Is what everyone saying in school true? Did you . . . ?'

'Lose my virgi—'

'Shhh!'

'No, I haven't! Where did you hear that?'

The bus stopped outside the gate of our school and the kids poured out. Sarthak, literally, jumped over me and walked away before he could catch my infection. Grabbing my bag from my seat, I ran after him to get my answer.

'Tell me. Who told you, Sarthak?'

He stopped, turned at me, furious as he seldom was, and said, his spit flying angrily all over, 'Everyone, okay! The boys in my class are taking bets about who will be the next one who sleeps with you!'

'But—'

'I know it's not your fault but that's what it is! And I'm sorry for shouting right now but I can't help it.'

'I'm sorry.'

'It's better we don't talk.'

'But—'

'Look, Aisha, what you do is your own business. I won't stop you. But don't expect anything more. That's how it is.'

'But you're my brother.'

'I know, Aisha. You deserve a better brother.'

It sounded more like a plea for me to leave him alone. I obliged and let him walk away into the crowd.

I sat through mathematics and physics and chemistry and English thinking if I were at fault, discovering masturbation, wanting to have sex, getting my boobs. They should have been my little high points in life. Then why did people find some way to ruin it all for me? The last time I had truly laughed with my brother was when I was in the seventh standard and a new school year was about to begin. We'd shoplifted brown covering paper from our neighbourhood stationery shop. Usually we stuck to pencils and gel pens, so wrapping paper was a bit of a stretch, and we almost thought we'd get caught as we cycled away from the sprinting shopkeeper. We spent hours laughing that night as we wrapped our copies with brown papers, stuck labels on them and wrote our names neatly with our flicked pens.

'Are you looking forward to the counselling session today?' asked Megha in the middle of the chemistry class.

'I would rather throw myself in a blender.'

'Oh! I forgot to tell you! I have a date with Dhruv today after school. We are going to this new pub and a movie afterwards.'

'Are you planning to drink?'

'Of course,' said Megha. 'How dowdy will it be to not drink in a pub.'

'Then he will probably slide his hand under your skirt.'

'What?' she exclaimed.

'I mean he might.'

'How do you know?'

'I read books,' I said.

'*Fifty Shades of Grey*?' she asked.

I rolled my eyes at the poor, ignorant girl. She had taken my copy but her parents got hold of it, read a few pages, and branded me as a slut. They asked her never to talk to me. I hadn't even enjoyed the book! It was stolen and I'd later exchanged it for a copy of *Eleanor and Park*.

Why do I even talk to her?

'Okay, but what should I do if he does that?'

'I think you should stop him,' I said. 'If you're not ready.'

'Am I ready?'

'I don't think so. You don't even touch yourself. How can you allow him to do so? Plus he won't know what to do. Your nether region is like an archery target. You have to be totally precise!'

She crinkled her brow. 'What if I'm ready and I don't know if I'm ready. I think I will stay quiet.'

'I think you should say *No*.'

'What if he doesn't listen? I don't want to be uptight with him.'

'You should say *No*.'

'What if he still doesn't stop?'

'If you think that's a possibility, you should not go out with him and tell all your friends not to go out with him as well!' I said with authority.

'C'mon!' she said, exasperatedly. 'I should just give him what he wants. He might begin to date me after all.' She shrugged her shoulders excitedly as if free candy was on offer.

I decided to be happy about the fact that I wasn't the kind of woman who was happy that a boy was ready to date her. Nor was I a woman who wouldn't shame a boy trying to get into her pants, even after she said *No*.

The classes ended and I was instructed to wait outside the counsellor's room, who was running late by an hour, and so I waited, drawing love handles on the skinny women in the newspapers.

Along with me were three boys—one was caught smoking weed, another had set off fireworks in the washroom, and the third had abused a teacher.

I was the last one in the line.

The stoner, hardly thirteen, looked at me and asked, 'Are you the one who mast—'

'Yes, I do!' I snapped.

'That's only like the coolest thing ever.'

'You think so?'

'I know so,' whispered the boy. 'I just discovered it. It's awesome!'

'I know, right?'

'So you are here for that?' I nodded in response. 'You're so screwed. So are you going to deny it? Stop doing it? What?'

'Of course not. I'm in love with it. I'm *never* stopping.'

'You're like the coolest girl ever, bro,' he said.

12

Danish Roy

I was not corrupt.

I was not the one hollowing out this country's fortunes, taking horrendous decisions that affected real people, and from that perspective I was much better than my father who got me a job at a fancy school as a counsellor to young boys and girls. Anyone with an elementary level education would know why this was such a bad decision. I made a quick stop at the local liquor store and picked up a bottle of white wine and drained it into a bottle of Sprite. Don't get me wrong, I'm not an alcoholic. It's too expensive an addiction to have. But there was no way I was getting through this sober.

The principal met me at the reception. 'You come highly recommended. Your father told me you have quite a lot of experience working with young people. I don't need to tell you what to do,' he said, smiled widely and shook my hand with both of his. A firm, tendon-snapping handshake. His confidence in me gave me nausea.

Coming back to a school may flood some with nostalgia but to me it felt like someone had thrust an umbrella up my ass and opened it. At least there was hope when I was young, now there was just disappointment. But I felt shamefully proud when I was shown my room which had a top-of-the-line Mac desktop, a nameplate, letterheads, a printer and a personal peon who would bring me whatever I asked for.

'Should I send the first person in?' asked the peon.

There were already four students waiting outside whom I had to counsel, and my knees shook like fucking tongs.

'Yes, please do.'

I decided I would sit like psychiatrist, nod my head seriously, scratch my forehead from time to time, and pray they didn't look for guidance or comfort or whatever the hell they were here for.

The first boy was Aryan, thirteen, who had been caught smoking weed in the school premises after it set off a smoke alarm. I kind of expected that a rich boy would waltz in, spit on my face, wave his middle finger, and tell me how powerful his father was. Instead, a rather shy boy with round, Harry Potter glasses walked in with his gap-toothed, shy smile.

'Hello sir,' he said.

I nodded. I didn't know what to say so I just let him talk. Every time he would stop complaining about something I asked him if there was something else he would like to talk about.

Depressed. Sad. Tired. Alienated. Rejected. Alone. Lonely. He used words which were expected from an investment banker going through a nervous breakdown.

In thirty minutes, he had cried, apologized, lost his temper twice, called the counselling session a sham, abused his friends, realized he was hurting his parents, and that he did really have two friends, not popular kids but friends nonetheless, and that right now he would rather be on his PlayStation with them, and then he told me he would never smoke weed again.

'I'm writing in your report that it was a one-time mistake, okay?'

'But it isn't.'

'We can all catch a break sometimes, can't we?'

He smiled and left the room.

Then the second kid came in. The Sprite bottle lay untouched. All I had to do was listen and make them talk.

These were smart kids who knew what they were doing. It was a cry for help, an appeal for someone to listen. They weren't twisted, just lost. I had been scared for no reason. There were times when I wanted to jump out of my seat and tell them how I felt the *exact* same things when I was growing up, how I felt so terrible myself. But I didn't.

I called the next kid in.

'Hi.'

I doubled checked her file that lay on the table. Seventeen? When I was seventeen, girls had unibrows and sideburns that could put John Travolta to shame. This girl was . . . a woman.

'Come in.'

She took her seat, poured herself some water in a glass and drank from it. A pall of silence fell between us.

'Are you nervous?' she asked when she saw me with my fingers resting under my chin—a pose I thought exuded confidence. 'I would be nervous too if it were my first day.'

'I . . . I'm not nervous. *You* should be nervous.'

Wow, Danish. What a comeback!

'I am.'

I took my serious thinking pose again. 'Why are you nervous?'

'For Megha, she's my friend, well she's not really my *friend*, but we've known each other since the second standard and we go for movies sometimes, and sometimes our cycles match, so yeah.'

'You missed the part where you should tell me why you are nervous about Megha.'

'Oh yes. That. Megha is going out with a guy. I'm not sure he likes her a lot. But he will try to get his hands under her skirt.'

'Oh, shouldn't you have stopped her?'

'I told her what I could. It's up to her now.'

'So let's talk about why you are here. Do you want to tell me yourself?'

'There was a misunderstanding. The principal thought I have started having sex with people, while all I admitted to was being a compulsive masturbator.'

'You what?'

'I'm sorry.'

'Umm . . . you don't have to be sorry,' I said reflexively.

'But the principal thinks I should be and that's why he has sent me here. To talk to you. You will set me right, he said.'

'I don't think there's anything wrong with . . . umm—'

'Masturbating?'

'Yes, that's perfectly normal.'

'That's what I tried to tell him. The boy outside? Aryan? He told me he does it too. Every boy does it, he said. Then why did the principal call me out?'

I shrugged my shoulders.

She continued. 'You would have such a long day if every boy who masturbated was sent to you, right?' She chuckled. 'I think even my brother masturbates. Sometimes he spends too much time in the washroom. But why isn't he sitting here? He's in the same school, by the way. And we hardly ever talk.'

There has to be a handbook on how to tackle such questions from precocious teenagers. What right did she have to be so straightforward and . . . confident? Like, why? She was seventeen. A kid!

Finally, I came up with a question which seemed most appropriate and I said it in my most serious voice. I asked, 'I'm just trying to get where you're coming from, Aisha. Also because I have to file this report, so don't get me wrong, but you have told people you're a compulsive masturbator. Like why is it a compulsive habit?'

'Why do *you* masturbate?'

'What?'

'I read in the book *Student Careers and Counselling* that therapy sessions should be a two-way conversation,' she said, 'so I thought I can ask you the same question.' She waited for my answer with a bright smile. She was screwing with me.

'But that's inappropriate.'

'Why?'

'Umm . . . because you're seventeen.'

'I will ask you next month then,' she said. 'I'm turning eighteen.'

And just then, the peon walked in and informed us that the principal wanted to introduce me to the rest of the faculty and saved me from the most embarrassing conversation ever.

'See you tomorrow?'

'Sure.'

13

Aisha Paul

OH.MY.GOD. That man-child in that counselling room was cute!

I would have shared this important piece of information with Megha had she bothered to breathe in between her hour-long-minute-by-minute report of her boring but safe date with the boy.

'He drove at 120 mph! Imagine! It was the best thing ever!' she exclaimed.

'That he can drive fast? That's the best thing ever? Does he wear a bracelet as well? Middle-parted long hair?' I asked, a little pissed off.

I wanted to tell her about the awkward, super funny conversation I had had with my cutely fidgety counsellor, tell her how he went so red in the face when I intentionally embarrassed him, but the moment was gone now and I didn't want to say it any more.

'How did your counselling go? Was he cute?'

'Why would it matter whether he was cute or not?'

I just wanted to be angry at her for ignoring me for so long. How was her date more important than my therapy session? 'Of course it does. So tell me, was he cute?' She rested her chin on her knuckles and leaned forward.

'I don't know.'

'But the entire school is saying he's cute!'

'*I don't know*, Megha.'

'Stop being such a spoilsport.'

'*I am not!*'

'Kritika was telling me that he has the most amazing hair, and a light stubble like the one that actor keeps? What's his name? Arjun Kapoor! Yes. So does he look like him? I bet he's cute. You're just not telling me.'

'Why would I not tell you if he was cute?'

'I don't know, you tell me.'

'Megha, I don't know if he was cute or not.'

'How can you not know if he was cute or not, Aisha? It's the *first* thing you notice!'

'I didn't notice it, okay?'

'How can you not notice it?' she grumbled.

'Because he's a lot many other things than just being cute!'

'Like what? Like what did you notice that was so important that you didn't care about his looks?'

'I can't tell you that right now,' I snapped.

I hadn't bothered to find out. I had straightaway, like everyone else in school, had put him in a little box—*cute*—and nothing else mattered. He would now be cute forever. Not necessarily a bad thing, but that's what kids in my school feel about my big breasts. *She's the girl with the big boobs and an active sex life.* Not necessarily a bad thing, but you might just lose a brother because of it.

'You will not call him cute.'

'Why?' protested Megha.

'Because you don't know him.'

'So what?' she said.

'The first thing you know about a person can't be his cuteness! That's just wrong. Who defines what cute is anyway? What if he doesn't want to be cute? What if he wants to be something else? What if he wants smaller breasts?'

'What?'

'Sorry. But don't call him cute. You can't judge people on the most basic thing about them—how they look! You can't do that. It can hurt them.'

'How can calling someone cute hurt them?'

'It can! And it can also hurt people who aren't called cute! Have you thought about people who are *not* cute?'

'What about them?' she shrugged. 'They already know they are *not* cute.'

'Whatever.'

'What whatever, Aisha. You always judge people by how they look. If you can tell me one other aspect that you would rather notice, I will agree to what you're saying,' said Megha.

'Ummm . . . what if like, like . . . like a person walks by and he has a halo over his head?'

'Good luck with that, Aisha!'

We didn't talk for the rest of the day. I decided I wouldn't be the kind of woman who puts people into boxes like cute or big breasts or thick legs. But what about those whom I had already judged, and put into little boxes with no holes? Were they still breathing? Over the years, I had been on the receiving end of many vicious rumours. But I would be lying if I didn't tell you that I had done the same to many others as well. But none worse than Namrata, that nice, intelligent girl in my class.

I needed to talk to Danish about this.

This counsellor was already working for me. He was good for me—yes, that's the first thing I would tell people about him, not that he was cute, but that he was good for me.

My mother served paneer and rice that night. I told her about the counselling session.

'What do you need counselling for?' she asked.

'Nothing major. Just like that.'

She was too busy making little rice balls and feeding me to pursue that line of questioning and asked, 'Is he good?'

'Yes, he's very good. He's nice. I think it's his first time as a counsellor. But he's good. I'm seeing him again tomorrow.'

'Don't trouble him.'

'What makes you think I will trouble my counsellor?'

It was at times like these that I felt my mother knew everything. How did she know that I had enquired about his motivation to wank?

'Eat.'

'Where's Sarthak?' I asked.

'He's eating in the room. He has some assignments to complete.'

'Mom?'

'Yes, *bachha*?'

'Do you remember Namrata?'

'Yes, of course I do,' she said, stuffing my mouth with another oddly shaped rice ball.

'You do?'

'Wasn't she the new girl who'd joined a few years back? Scored more than you in SST and science? God! How many tantrums you threw in those days!'

My mother laughed, reminding me of how I tore up my answer sheets and my science textbook because she had edged me out by five marks. My mother had spent the entire night putting the torn pages in order and then stapling them together. She asked, 'What happened to her?'

'I might have troubled her a little in the past.'

'What did you do?'

'More paneer?'

My mother left to get the paneer. I couldn't stomach what my mother would think of me if I told her what I did to Namrata all those years back.

14

Danish Roy

I was inappropriately happy on the second day of my new job. The first day had gone off smoothly, apart from that one moment where the girl, Aisha, made me want to crawl beneath the desk and stay there for a really long time. Today, will be better, I told myself. Last night, I had spent a few hours on the Internet and read up manuals on how to tackle sexual queries from young people (without making an utter fool of myself). My highlighted notes lay securely in my duffle bag. All I needed was a little revision and I would whoop some ass today. I reached on time and found Aisha waiting on the bench.

'Hi, sir.'

'Aren't you supposed to come later in the day?' I asked.

'I needed to talk to you about something. I can do that, right?' she asked, innocently.

'Of course, just give me a few moments.' I entered my room, closed my eyes and took a few deep breaths.

Calm down. You can do this, Danish. She's just a little girl. Just be confident and straightforward.

I placed my pad on the desk and found myself fixing my hair in the reflection of my computer screen. *Now why would I do that?*

'Sir, may I come in?' she said from outside the door.

'Come in.'

She came in, closed the door behind her, and sat in front of me.

'So, tell me, what's the problem?'

'Umm . . . It's not so much a problem. It's more of a question really,' she said.

'Go on?'

'I wanted to tell Megha that you were really cute. But—'

'Excuse me?'

'I'm sorry. But that's what I wanted to talk to you about. But before I could tell her that I found you cute, she told me the entire college had started calling you cute.'

She waited for me to say something.

'So?'

'You're okay with that?'

Okay? This was the best day of my life. What if they were half a decade younger than I was?

'Can you tell me clearly what's bothering you?'

'I will try,' she said. 'So like you are cute to the entire school now, you will forever be only that. People won't talk about how happy that eighth standard guy was when you let him off the hook with the weed-smoking incident but they will talk about your cuteness. And that can be sort of a good thing and a bad thing.'

'Okay. So?'

I dreaded a loaded question at the end of it all.

'But what if people thought about you as a pervert? Like what if I had started telling people you had hit on me when you really hadn't?'

'What! But I didn't—' I panicked.

'Of course, you didn't,' she smiled. 'Okay, let me give you another analogy. What if there was a rumour that a student committed suicide just after he attended your session? Now there might be no correlation between your cuteness and the student taking his life but then everything you did before or will do after that would be looked through that lens of you being cute, right?

Like people will say you're *cute*, but clearly you're not that great a counsellor because that kid died. Or like what do you expect out of him? He's too busy being *cute*! Or like it's okay if you just look at him, but don't expect any counselling from him. And those two things have nothing to do with each other!'

'You're kind of right.'

'And whose fault will be that?'

'Whoever talked about it first, labelled me as just cute,' I said. 'Not my fault, necessarily. The best I could do is to try to move past it.'

'Fuck.'

'Language, Aisha. And can you tell me what really happened?'

'You're going to judge me.'

'Of course I will judge you if you did something wrong. But I will also forgive you if you do something to undo it,' I said.

'So, I did something to a girl years back and I don't think she has moved past it yet.'

'What did you do?'

'I put her in a little box like I was about to do to you. Only it wasn't labelled as *cute*, it was labelled *slut*.'

Aisha told me about Namrata, a girl who had joined this school a few years ago. A nice, talented girl whose life Aisha had single-handedly destroyed by labelling her as a slut.

'So what are you going to do about this?

'I don't know.'

'Talk to me again only once you finish talking to her,' I said.

'But . . .'

'You can go now.'

'See, you're judging me?'

'I am. I now think you're the kind of person who has the courage to accept she did something wrong and will prove to me that she has it in herself to apologize. You can leave now.'

15

Aisha Paul

I waited outside the class for Namrata to show up. I knew her schedule. She was the first one to enter and leave every class; her entries and exits were carefully timed to maintain a distance from her my classmates—especially me.

Years ago, when I was fourteen and in the seventh standard and growing breasts the size of pumpkins—and was famous for them too—I felt *powerful*. *Everyone* talked about me. I was poor and my mother was dying but at least I had the school by its balls, academically and otherwise, and I was not going to let that go. I could spread gossip through my influence on the girls who hung out with me, and get boys to do anything I wanted. I had quite a time. It faded away slowly as rumours of my non-existent promiscuity started making the rounds, but during the few months it lasted, I was pretty mean to some people and one of them was Namrata.

She was a new student on a full scholarship in our school, freshly transferred from Ryan International, and had taken the school by storm! Now normally I wouldn't have minded but it was *my* time. I was doing well in my studies, led the march past for my house, had a permanent first row spot in the choir, and was a probable candidate for the House Captain. But this girl had rained on my parade. She made it to the dramatics team and the shot-put team and charmed everyone. My dizzying fame was slipping like sand through a closed fist.

'What are you going to do?' Megha had asked. 'I heard she's nominating herself for the House Captain position.'

'No one cares about her. She's *so fat*! She's disgusting,' I had said, quite cruelly. 'And everyone will see that.'

A fat, ugly girl wasn't going to take away my thunder. Though I should probably mention here that I, too, wasn't beautiful as per conventional standards but I had the height (I was 5'3" when I was in the seventh standard), the breasts and the thighs of an adult, and *that* obscured everything else.

Late one afternoon, after a physical education period, I found Namrata changing in the washroom, and I struck up a conversation. We talked about her old school, the friends she'd left behind, and whether she liked my school. She was a nice girl and even liked *Room on the Roof*, my favourite book of all time, but I had a reputation to protect, and one to destroy. So while she talked and laughed, thinking I was her friend, I slyly recorded a video of her changing into her uniform, her naked chest on blatant display.

'What bra do you use?' I had asked innocently.

The funny girl had cradled her breasts and said, 'Nothing that gravity can't beat!'

The next day, a grainy clip, minus the audio, of Namrata's saggy, cellulite-ridden chest was on every other phone. Since my voice could not be heard, everyone thought Namrata had sneaked in a boy to the changing room and was stripping for him.

'Did you see that video? Namrata was changing in front of a boy! Such a slut!' Megha exclaimed.

'I feel sorry for the boy. I would rather claw my eyes out than see that,' I said.

Someone else had added. 'Look at those breasts. Those are ugly!'

'I know, right!' I had said. 'And those love handles. God. She should stop eating men for lunch. I heard she got kicked out from the last school because she slept with someone in the classroom.'

And then the shaming began. She was the ugly, fat slut from Ryan International.

The video never got out of the school or Namrata and I both would have been in trouble. Namrata never confronted me. She missed school for a month, her grades dipped, she dropped out of the shot-put and the dramatics team, her scholarship was taken away, and by the time we got to our eighth standard, she was a nobody.

It had been four years. I knew what I had done to her. I would always sidestep whenever I saw her walking in the corridors. I shirked and shifted the blame on to her, thinking that she should have fought the rumour. But, of course, deep inside of me, I knew I had destroyed her when I passed on that video and firmly tagged her as a fat, ugly slut. And now, I had to make amends. No more tags. No more labelling people on how they looked.

When she finally showed up that day, I walked up to her, smiled my widest and said, 'Hey, I need to talk to you.' I had hoped in my heart that all had been forgiven already, that time had healed her.

'No, you don't,' she said and walked right out of the class.

Clearly time was lazy!

'Hey, listen,' I ran after her, collecting my things. 'I really need to say something to you.'

She turned and asked, 'What?'

'About earlier?'

'What's there to talk about?' she snapped, her eyes already little pools of tears.

'Plenty.'

'I'm waiting,' she said.

'Namrata, I'm sorry for what I did all those years back. I shouldn't have done—'

And the next second my face stung with a resounding slap. I stumbled backwards and lost my hearing for a few seconds. She deserved to be in the shot-put team. People stopped in the corridor and stared. 'I'm okay, I'm okay,' I told the people who had rushed to help me.

She had made her way through the crowd by the time the tinny sound in my ears abated. I ran after her.

'What did you do that for?' I asked, almost crying. 'It hurt.'

'Because that's what you deserve, Aisha! That and much more.'

'I'm sorry, I said I'm sorry,' I said, crying.

'I'm never forgiving you for ruining my life. I had almost killed myself because of you!' she said.

'But—'

'Listen, Aisha. It took me years to be happy again. Please don't come anywhere near me, okay? I hate you!' she said and ran away.

I walked into the girls' washroom, locked myself in the stall and cried my heart out for three hours, hoping to feel the pain I had made the girl go through. Since I couldn't completely comprehend her pain, I recalled the face of my mother as she lay in that pool of blood, and I started howling.

16

Danish Roy

'How's it going?' asked my brother dressed in grey sweats when he joined me at the breakfast table.

'It's okay. Quite strange actually, all we got in our school were slaps from our teachers. This is different,' I said.

'True that! Remember that time you didn't polish your shoes and they made you run ten laps and you fainted? I really thought Dad would sue the school or something,' he said.

'Instead he slapped me. Good memories. Thank you for reminding me.'

He chuckled. 'Come, I will drop you to school today.'

'There's no need for that.'

'Oh, shut up!' he said, pulling me by my arm and dragging me to the driveway.

'Fuck!' I shrieked.

In the driveway, behind our eight-year-old Innova and the three-year-old Honda City, stood a two-seater Mercedes SLK!

I tried to feel happy for my brother but all I felt was envy piercing through my veins. I started to calculate how much it would have cost him, how much he must be earning, and how many years, if not lifetimes, it would take me to have the same car sitting in my driveway. Will I ever have a driveway?

I forced a smile.

'It's a gift from the investors. It's not mine,' he said, sensing my mood. 'But I can drive it around till the time I can buy one myself.'

'Congratulations, man!' I said and hugged him so he couldn't see how jealous I was. I thought about money a lot those days. My brother was successful, a paper millionaire, and would be rich for the rest of his life and beyond. When I will be forty, he will be buying cars more expensive than my house, and my kids will hate me because their cousins will always have better phones/PlayStations/clothes, and my wife will wish she'd married him.

I thought about this a lot. About the power and the feeling of superiority money brings which I didn't have and in all probability never would. A lot of my fellows from schooldays were already in big jobs, married to powerful women, settled abroad, people I wouldn't want to meet ever again in life.

He dropped me to school and wished me luck for the day. As he looked at the school while driving away to his meetings held in glass cabins inside buildings that rose up to the clouds, I wondered what he thought of his big brother.

'Hey,' I said. 'How are you doing today?' The girl was waiting outside my room. I unlocked the door and took my seat.

'She's not forgiving me. And I feel like killing myself right now,' she said in a matter-of-fact way. Then suddenly, she said, 'Don't worry, I wouldn't do that because I will not be like my mother.'

'Your mother?'

'She tried killing herself. It's a long story. But don't tell anyone.'

'I won't.'

'You can't, there is client–patient confidentiality.'

'No, there's not. I'm a counsellor not a psychiatrist.'

'Oh.'

'Don't worry, I won't.'

'You need to talk to Namrata. You can make her forgive me. It's pulling me back. Unless she forgives me, how will I be the woman I want to be!'

'And what is that woman you want to be?' I asked.

'I'm still figuring that out, sir.' Just then, the bell rang. She waited for it to stop before she spoke again. 'I need to go for my class now. Mr Sharma will mark me absent even if I am a minute late. I'm counting on you, sir.'

For the next hour, I downloaded and read articles about forgiveness, and how to move on if people refuse to forgive you. Frankly, the essays were a whole lot of bullshit. I had to do something for the girl, and it wasn't only for her, it was for me. My job had started to make me feel important and needed, as if I could make a difference, like my existence wasn't a total waste.

So I got up and started to look for Namrata in the school records. Twenty minutes later, the peon explained to me that I didn't have to look for students, and if I wanted a student to come, he or she would have to report to me—no questions asked. A bit like a dictator. I liked that. I called for Namrata.

'Can I come in, sir?'

'Yes, yes, come in,' I said. I had a book in my hand, a thick one which I had picked up moments before Namrata had walked in, to look smart and knowledgeable, so she would take me seriously.

'Is it something I did, sir?' she asked nervously.

Never had people been nervous in front of me. It was always the other way around. Even salespeople in stores and fast food joints made me anxious.

'No, it's, in fact, about what someone else did,' I said. 'Aisha. Do you know her?'

'Yes, I do, sir. She's the worst person I have ever met in my entire life. I'm not going to forgive her.'

'Namrata, you—'

'I can forgive Dolores Umbridge but not her!' she said, throwing a Harry Potter reference at me. She clutched the sides of her chair as if trying to grind them to dust.

'But Dumbledore would have wanted to you to forgive her. Remember how he asked Potter to let Pettigrew go?'

'But it was Pettigrew. Aisha is like Bellatrix Lestrange! She killed Dobby!'

'Look. She's trying to change and I can sense that. In my history of dealing with people like her I have noticed that a single apology from someone they have wronged goes a long way in helping them become better people.'

'I don't care about her! She destroyed me!' she shrieked, spitting all over my face. I felt like those little kids in Jurassic Park who turn and find a baby T-Rex baring its fangs, dripping slush over their faces.

'She's trying to make amends. Give her a chance. Draw her away from the *dark* side,' I said. If Harry Potter references is what worked with her, why not?

'But—'

'I understand she must have been really mean to you. But it's your chance to be a bigger person and forgive her. Think about what she did to you and if you would want to weigh yourself down by holding a grudge against her for the rest of your life. Meet her halfway?'

And within seconds, Namrata dissolved into a sentient puddle of tears.

17

Aisha Paul

I rushed to the washroom.

I ruffled my hair and quickly applied some mascara and smudged it. I had to look sufficiently bereaved for Namrata to forgive me. Now don't think I wasn't sad, it's just that I wasn't sad enough to cry at a moment's notice. I had done my crying for the day earlier that morning and had fixed myself post that.

'May I come in?' I asked, head hung low.

'Come in.'

I was asked to sit right in front of Namrata who looked like she had just stopped crying.

'You two need to talk,' Danish said and leaned back in his chair. His casual demeanour told me that he knew what he was doing and there was nothing to worry about. That gave me a little confidence.

'I told you. I don't want to talk to her. She made me want to die, sir. I don't want to be here,' she said.

I don't blame her. It's a surprise she was still sitting there. Then I spoke, 'Namrata, I'm really sorry for what I did.'

'There's no way your apologies can justify what you did to me, Aisha. I lost *everydamnthing*!'

'I know. It's just that I was threatened when you joined the school and it was really bad of me to do what I did,' I said. 'I'm sorry . . .'

'You were threatened? By me?'

'Of course, I was.'

'*Why!*'

'Because you were smart and you were funny! The teachers loved you. The boys thought you were charming. I was losing my grip on the school.'

'But . . . but you were the one who everyone cared about! You were tall and hot, and the boys were in love with you,' she said, shocked.

'No one was ever in love with me. They just wanted to get inside my skirt. I didn't want that. I wanted to be what you were. I wanted to be funny, I wanted people to want to talk to me because I was interesting, not because I had breasts, or because I wore short skirts. I wanted to make people laugh like you did. I wanted people to want being around me. I envied you so much . . .' I said. The tears came and I held her hand and cried.

'But Aisha . . .'

'I really wished to be you. I never wanted to hurt you. Please trust me. I would do anything to undo—'

'It's okay, stop crying.'

'But I'm so—'

'It's okay,' She put her arms around me and I cried into her chest.

'I'm so so sor—'

'It's okay, Aisha.'

'I know it's not. I destroyed you—'

'That you did,' she said.

'I should have never . . . I'm so bad—'

'It's okay. Now stop crying, it's okay,' she said. 'Don't spoil your face. You're too beautiful.'

'You're beautiful,' I said.

'Well, you both are,' said Danish with a relaxed air, a smirk on his face, like he had planned this all along.

I started to see him like this scientist in front of the huge electric circuit board monitoring the emotion circuitry.

I decided to like him. He looked at both of us and said, 'Beauty was devised by someone very insecure to rob others of the happiness he or she couldn't feel. It was a dick move, to be honest.'

I needed to write that down. When I become a woman, these are the kind of sentences I wished to say to engross people with my intelligence and warmth.

'I am still a little confused about something though,' Namrata said. 'There's another boy who joined the school with me. Norbu? He was smarter and funnier and everyone loved him too. You didn't do anything to him. Didn't he make you jealous?'

No, he didn't. I remembered that boy. A teacher's pet, he was now the Head Boy, the captain of the table tennis team, and the centre forward of our school, quite the charmer. Why didn't I take him down? I scrambled for an answer.

'Aisha?' she asked.

'Because he was a boy,' I spat out

'So?' asked Danish. 'Why leave out the boy?'

'I . . . I didn't mind him being better than me,' I said.

'Because he was a boy?' asked Danish.

If I were a turtle I would have crawled inside my shell and waited out for everyone to die before coming out.

'I guess so,' I said.

'And you went after me because I was a girl?' asked Namrata.

I nodded shamefully. 'I'm sorry. I was stupid.'

'Okay, okay, don't cry again,' said Namrata before I started to use her shirt as a tissue.

Danish knew I was drowning in there and he thanked Namrata for forgiving me and told her he needed some time with me.

'Are we friends?' I asked Namrata while she was leaving. 'Because I have never cried so much in front of anyone other than my mother and she's like my friend.'

She smiled. 'We can be if you like Harry Potter.'

'I will draw a scar on my forehead.'

She laughed. Namrata shook my hand again and told me she had forgiven me and hoped I wouldn't repeat the same stuff with anyone else.

'So, it wasn't that tough, right?' said Danish and smiled at me. His smile enough was therapy though it made me cry a little more.

'But why didn't I do the same to Norbu?'

'Ummm . . .' Of course he had something to say. He was a professional and he had just worked his magic, reducing two women to tears in a matter of seconds. I waited for his theory. 'He was a boy, and you thought boys are supposed to be better than girls so you weren't surprised.'

'But boys aren't—'

'Exactly.'

'Shit.'

I had screwed up. Of course it made sense: boys are better than us. Had someone asked me, I wouldn't have accepted it but deep down inside that's what I had grown up believing.

'Yes! You are right! When last year, our senior, a girl, made it to IIT, I was like how can she make it? Wow! But I never said anything about the boys who did. Like it was expected they would. Same with the girl who almost beat Norbu in a track and field event. I called her muscular! I bitched about her and pulled her down. And when a girl partnered with Norbu in the practical exam and aced it, I was like she must have cheated. I have been pulling girls down all this time. *God!* How many people I need to apologize to!'

Danish smiled smugly, that sparkling brilliance lighting up his eyes.

'I have decided something today,' I said.

'And what is that?'

'I won't be the kind of girl who pulls another girl down,' I said and as soon as I said it I felt a little halo crop up behind my head.

'Good,' he said.

And just then the bell rang and Danish asked to me go attend my classes though I really wanted him to ask me to stay. He was making me a better woman. These counselling sessions were great. In fact, I had a bit of a crush on him, and I decided if I had to lose my virginity to anyone it would be him. It would be memorable, fun, tender and everything it's supposed to be. I walked out of his room wondering what our after-sex pillow talk would be like.

18

Danish Roy

I had decimated that one!

The metro had reached the last station and I had missed my station by a margin of fifteen minutes because I was still stupidly smiling, replaying in my head the wise words that had escaped my mouth involuntarily. It was nothing like driving a Mercedes SLK. But it was something and it had filled my heart with so much joy that I wanted to celebrate it with Ankit.

'Hey, when are you coming home?' I asked him over the phone.

'Got back early today. Already home!' he said. He sounded a little buzzed. Good. That was good. Getting high is exactly how I was going to celebrate my first personal victory.

I barged into Ankit's room and found him under a bedsheet grunting and laughing with the girl from that party the other day. I could only see the girl's face, which exuded a joy associated with enlightenment.

'Fuck,' he said, pulled out and rolled over.

'*Get out!*' the girl shouted. I ran out, embarrassed.

When outside, I heard my brother laugh wildly while the girl cursed and shouted and called me names. My brother kept saying between laughs, *he didn't know, he didn't know, he didn't see anything*.

'What's up, bhai!' Ankit came out, still inebriated. My unannounced arrival hadn't startled him at all, and why would anything startle my brother?

'I just thought . . . we should celebrate,' I said.

Suddenly celebrating my workplace victory with him seemed so small. He dealt with hundreds of thousands of dollars in investments every day. Telling him about a little conversation with two troubled teenage girls felt silly.

'Celebrate what?'

'*Your car!* Your new car, Ankit. What else?' I said and he broke out into a huge smile.

The girl came out and Ankit put an arm around her. 'You two know each other, right? She's the girl from the party, remember? Yeah, we have made up again. She apologized.'

The girl rolled her eyes. 'I didn't.'

'Of course, you did. You said *okay* when I asked you to come over and get drunk with me. That's like an apology only, right?'

'Whatever,' said the girl.

'C'mon now, you two, shake hands and be friends. C'mon now, shake hands.' And like a parent, he pushed the girl towards me and made us shake hands.

'Danish.'

'Smriti.'

'I know. I Googled you.'

'Why?'

'I didn't.'

Smriti rolled her eyes. But I *had* Googled her. I Googled everyone. I checked two things about them: 1) what they were doing when they were my age (if they are older) and 2) how much they earned every month. As you know by now, none of these searches ever yielded any happy results. The girl was a young corporate shark.

A little later, all of us were drinking rum and coke and deciding whether drinking and driving the Mercedes was a good idea. Our seventy years of combined experience notwithstanding, we decided a short drive wouldn't hurt anyone. But luckily, we couldn't find the keys and so we deposited ourselves on the sofa and let the alcohol take its due course.

Smriti had become much kinder to me once drunk. 'So, Danish, what exactly do you do as a student counsellor?'

'I counsel.'

'That's like saying I entreprenuerate as an entrepreneur! What exactly do you do?'

'I help students be themselves.'

'Now what does that mean?'

While my brain grew frenzied looking for an answer, my hormones raged seeing Ankit neck Smriti right in front of my eyes. I had never kissed anyone and of late, even insect sex turned me on. There should be a government facility holding perverts like me. I looked away.

'I solve their problems,' I said.

'Like how to get rid of their zits, whether pubic hair is okay, how to wax, etc.?' Smriti laughed.

Ha. Ha. Alcohol makes everyone into the next big stand-up comic. She looked at Ankit who had no interest in her jokes and was busy burrowing a hole into her neck, using his tongue.

'Yes, that. That's exactly what I do. Wow. You're so intelligent,' I said.

There was no point fighting with her. I flicked through the TV channels while Ankit and Smriti made out on the couch, necking, grabbing each other, turning my celebration into theirs.

'*Hey!*' Ankit said suddenly, pushing Smriti away. 'Smriti! Don't you have that cousin who just broke up? What's her name? Kanika, right? Why don't you make her meet Danish? I'm sure they will hit it off! She's a lecturer or something, right? They are both in the same field!'

Smriti, offended at the sudden break in the lovemaking, sat up straight, adjusted her shirt and said, 'She's not over the guy yet. He really used to pamper her.'

'So will Danish!'

'*But*—' I protested though it didn't register.

'She's not into men from the same field. That guy ran a business,' argued Smriti.

'So what, Danish is charming, he will sweep her off her feet! What say, Danish?' Ankit said.

'By saying what? He handles teenage problems? I don't think that's going to cut it. All her exes have been really successful people. She's into that,' said Smriti.

'So what—'

I interrupted Ankit. 'I have to leave. You two can continue this conversation about whether I'm successful enough to date your cousin or not. But I wanted to tell you that I'm already dating and the girl doesn't care whether I'm more successful than her or not.'

'*What!*' Ankit jumped up from the couch. 'You never told me! Fuck. Congratulations, man. What's her name?'

'Aisha,' I said and stormed out.

19

Sarthak Paul

I'm never going to see these people again . . . I'm never going to see these people again . . . I'm never going to see these people again . . . That's what I kept telling myself every time the rumour mills started to work overtime to cook up something about my sister Aisha.

Her apparent beauty is my curse, and my only identity in this school. I'm her brother. I love my sister but I don't like her any more. It's not something she has done but what people around me make me go through because she *exists*.

There were days I wished she were a boy. No one cares about the boy who has an allegedly promiscuous, outspoken, slightly strange brother. Unless of course, he's gay, then that's even worse. Femininity in anyone is a curse. If our creator was so smart couldn't he just have created an androgynous being, and made gender superfluous? Surely, there are other species which are genderless. Why aren't humans? Why can't we have sex with everyone around us regardless of gender?

Years have passed since we had a proper conversation. She prefers to dwell in her own little world of books and her friends and her rumours and the little troubles she constantly finds herself in. I prefer to bury myself in my textbooks, hoping to emerge from the other side of the world.

I should shoulder some of the blame for our strained relationship, too. I was young and thought I could run away from the rumours, that they will stop being a bother, after all, how hard could it be? Quite hard, as it turned out. It was hard to listen to people talk shit about her and not feel every vein in my body burst. I didn't fight any of them. That would have just made all of what they said true. I waged a silent battle against all of them, some I lost, and some I won. I was her brother after all, her protector, and I loved her to bits. I remember when she was small (though she was only a year younger), I used to stand guard outside the school playground and pummel every boy who used to trouble her. She used to be known as my little sister—the girl not to be harmed, my precious girl. But then she grew up and became a woman and things went downhill.

Here's a list of things I had done against the rumour-mongers who were after my sister as if they were being paid for it:

- Poisoned Samrat's food with copper sulphate every day till his appendix burst and he spent a month recovering at home.
- Stole Mrs Batra's phone and placed it in Amit's bag. He was expelled, of course. Yes, that was me.
- Tore off supplement sheets from Kritika's final exam paper. She failed the year and left the school.
- Nudged Namit off the stairs. He broke his leg and was replaced as the cricket team captain etc.
- Set off the fire alarm and left the ID cards of Abhinav, Sumit and Kanika inside the washroom. All three of them were suspended.
- Put porn CDs in Samridhi's bag and got her slapped by her parents and expelled.

But all this is coming to an end now. It was a losing battle; they had too many on their side and I was alone. I had to give up some time or the other. Planning and taking down one person after another was wearing me down

Running away from the entire situation was the easiest thing to do. School would begin and she would start dating someone and the rumours would just keep getting more vicious. I wasn't ready for that. I had played my role of being the vindictive brother for five years now and I had had enough. I loved her, but the resentment people made me feel for her was eating me from inside.

Nine months ago, I had applied to all the universities across the globe which offered scholarships for undergraduate programmes. My destiny lay in a quaint little college in Poland that promised a full waiver on the tuition fee, and a little calculation told me I would be able to pay off the living expenses from the on-campus jobs. Who knows, I might even be able to send a little money back for my mother's treatment? I hadn't told anyone about the acceptance letter. My family has a penchant for drama and I can't handle the tears or afford any change in plans. Also, I didn't want to feel guilty for leaving.

*

'Thank you so much for doing this,' I said and shook Vibhor's hand. Vibhor was helping me throw a big party for my sister's eighteenth birthday. It was sort of a *'Sorry for leaving you and probably being a bad brother'* farewell gift.

'Shut up, man. It's your sister, after all! Okay, how many people are you expecting?'

'I haven't told her yet.'

'Fine, let me know. I will get those massive JBL speakers. It's going to be crazy!' said Vibhor, rubbing his rather large hands in obvious delight. Vibhor was every bit the giant a football goalkeeper is expected to be; and he was every defender's wet dream. It had been six years we had been playing together. And we weren't friends. He was more like God to me. He was rich and effortlessly charming, and every girl in our school fawned over him without much luck. He only dated college girls. He was the *hottest* guy I had ever seen.

But on the field we were brothers, we shed blood and sweat together, our partnership was talked about in football circles all around the city. We were inseparable.

He was the only guy I could go to for planning this party, and he was ecstatic. '*Bro! Parties are my thing! Why didn't you come to me earlier?*' He hugged me like I was the FIFA trophy and I fractured a rib or two. 'Where's the smile, bro? This is going to be the best party ever,' said Vibhor and punched me on my arm.

'Of course I'm happy,' I said and smiled weakly.

It crushed me to leave my sister behind but she hadn't left me any choice.

20

Aisha Paul

My eighteenth birthday was approaching and people around me were making it a big deal.

I *obviously* didn't care about it. Like what's so different about being seventeen or eighteen? It's just another day after all. Will it make me smarter? I would have bought into the concept if it meant a ten-point hike in my IQ but of course that wouldn't happen now, would it? I was the kind of girl who didn't make much of these media-propagated important dates.

Also, I was lying.

Inside, I hoped for balloons, cake, a huge party, a thousand guests, and maybe a little alcohol since everyone else's birthday had that. But where was the money to celebrate? So instead, I put up a brave face and kept telling people that eighteenth-birthday celebrations were for kids and that I was a grown-up. Already eighteen. Done and dusted. A celebration shouldn't make one nervous and anxious. My impending eighteenth birthday made me want to crawl into a hole and die.

'Are you sure you don't want a party?' asked Namrata. 'Not even a small one?'

She was turning out to be my best friend these days. Namrata had swooped in and replaced Megha in a matter of days. She was what people defined as *my type*. Her parents were college professors, English and Sanskrit, and so she was like a walking-talking Goodreads recommendation list, and had a library at home which could put the one at our school to shame. Also, she had little twin sisters, Dhriti and

85

Dhisti, who were fat and cute and edible, and they called me *Agha* whenever I went to her house. I would curse myself regularly for losing all those years of a potentially fulfilling friendship.

Our affair started in the library where we found out we loved the same authors and had often issued the same books in the past. Things were really awkward at first but there's nothing that fifty flavours of Baskin Robbins can't cure. We used to spend hours after school at the outlet nearby eating out of a single cup.

Then we discussed our favourite TV shows, debated aggressively about whether Geoffrey, the chef, was more vile or Gordon Ramsay, watched episodes of *Modern Family* together, admitted that we liked Zayn Malik's hair and Justin Bieber's songs at one point in time, and that we masturbated every alternate night. Finally! I'd got someone to talk to about it without feeling like a complete pervert. We exchanged pointers on what turned us on. Fictional men in books > Porn.

She was just a great person.

She was kind and compassionate, and brought great food from her home, and I was falling in love with her.

'No, I don't want a party. It's all a sham, really,' I lied. *I so wanted a huge party.*

'Norbu has promised me that he will throw me a massive party when I turn eighteen,' she said, blushing.

'Yes, I will,' said Norbu who walked into the library just at that moment. They made quite a pair. He was the ~~cute boy from. . . .~~ No, that's what I had decided, I wouldn't describe people first by how they looked.

Norbu's parents were both IAS officers and the brain gene has carried on in their only child. He was brilliant with words. And yes, he was damn cute. His skin glowed like spring, eyes twinkled like Christmas. I could pack him up, take him home and keep him by my bedside and hug him to sleep every day but Namrata wouldn't have been too happy about it.

It was Norbu who had kept Namrata loved and sane all these years.

'I will make it your best day ever,' said Norbu, holding her hand, and somewhere I cried. They looked so good together. In love. Just perfect.

Maybe that's what I needed. A boyfriend. Someone who treated me like Norbu treated Namrata, someone who would hold my hand and look into my eyes and not at my pimples, someone who wouldn't call my emotions melodrama, who would know what I needed for my eighteenth birthday was a big ass party and not a mature thought.

I needed a boyfriend.

*

I reached home to find my mother cooking chicken that smelled wonderful. It was a luxury and it wasn't my birthday yet. Was my mother losing her mind again? I threw my bag on the couch and barged into the kitchen to enquire why my birthday chicken was being wasted days before the actual date.

'Your brother's friend is coming,' said my mother. I took the chopping board from her and cut a few onions.

'But he doesn't have any friends!' I said. My mother shot me a look. 'Not any I know of,' I added.

Sarthak's friendlessness was legendary and we never talked about it. I remembered Googling about whether my brother was bipolar or depressed or suffered from a mental illness.

I came up with naught.

My brother just didn't talk to *anyone*. It had been years since my mother, my father or I had had a proper conversation with him. He was so shut off. At least I talked about the weather and the food and about my pimples and the hot water running out.

He was a body.

'Is the friend a boy?' I asked.

'Of course, it's a boy!' snapped my mother.

As if on cue the bell rang and I was asked to get it.

'Hi,' said my brother as I opened the door for him and his friend. Hi? We never said Hi to each other? What was Hi? My mother walked into the living room to greet Sarthak's friend and offered him water. His friend was introduced as Vibhor.

She pulled me into the kitchen and asked me to change out of my skirt.

'Why? He studies in my school! He sees me like this every day.'

'It doesn't seem right to wear a skirt in front of a boy inside the house. Go! Change!'

Reluctantly, I changed. I had no clothes. Not like my cupboard was full and I was being a diva. I literally had no good clothes to wear so I changed into my sweatpants and my brother's T-shirt and reminded myself of how little outer appearances matter.

I went to the living room with the tray my mother handed me. Vibhor helped me to keep the teetering tray on the table. Quite chivalrous. Now that I had a good thing to say about him, I can tell you he was gorgeous, delectable, a piece of art even. He was tall, like freakishly tall, he filled up the entire room when he walked in with his muscled biceps and his crew cut. Screw chicken. I could have had him instead!

'So why are you here? Since when have you been friends?' I asked him.

He looked at my brother strangely. 'Umm . . .'

'Go to your room,' said Sarthak.

'Hey? You're the goalkeeper, right?'

Vibhor nodded.

'I knew it. Girls are crazy for you!'

He smiled. Must be totally not embarrassing for him. I felt a little sorry for him now. I needed to shut up.

'We have work,' said Sarthak.

'What work?' I asked him, but still looking at the chivalrous, shy Vibhor.

'*Mom!*' Sarthak shouted.

That was my cue. I ran to my room and bolted the door before Mom could say anything. I stayed put and held my pee for an hour because our bedroom didn't have an attached bathroom. Outside, they tapped furiously on the laptop and talked in hushed whispers. My brother had a nice voice. It would have been great to hear more of it. I pinned my ears to the bedroom door to hear what they were talking about.

Later before leaving, Vibhor knocked on the bedroom door and casually asked for my number. 'If you don't mind,' he added at the end of the sentence.

Yes, he did that.

I blushed and stammered and managed to blurt out the entire number in the sixth attempt.

'Are you sure you just asked for my number? Or is it in my head?'

'I did. And I just texted you.'

I scrambled for my phone. *Hi*, the text message said.

'I will call you?' he asked. 'If it's okay with you?'

'Of course, it is. I need to shut up, right?'

'No, not really but I have to go,' he said and closed the door.

I called him on his number. 'Hey?'

'You're calling me from behind the door?'

'Yes, I am. Does my brother know you just took my number?'

'Don't worry about him,' he said and I could sense him smiling that devilish smile.

Now it seemed like my birthday was approaching. The gods were listening. I might not get a huge party or presents but at least I had a real chance at getting a huge, chivalrous boyfriend. Hellboy finally might have a competitor.

21

Danish Roy

I didn't know why I said that name—Aisha—I didn't really mean it. Maybe because I'd liked the name. Otherwise it was just plain creepy. She was only *seventeen*—over five years younger than me. It sounds like right out of *Lolita* but only more perverse because it's 2015 and they have laws against that kind of stuff. And she wasn't even that pretty. Well, that's just a lie. Let me try and describe her in the most innocuous, legal way possible. She was quite tall, around 5'9" and very fit, not that I noticed or anything. God. *She was only seventeen!* Her eyes had a certain curiosity, like they were questioning everything, me, the room, herself, the universe. *Did I tell you she was only seventeen?* She was dark-skinned in the most beautiful way possible. The pimples on her skin almost suited her, only made her more human. She was always a little lost, like she'd forgotten to walk or breathe sometimes. She was always thinking, always thinking, always thinking . . .

I wanted to get inside her mind and know what she was thinking about.

But I took that name just because I had to take a name.

*

That day, she strode inside the room and almost stumbled over the chair before she could sit on it, her smile so warm it felt like she had dragged the sun in with her.

'Hi!'

'You seem happy today.'

'So happy!' she said. 'I think I might have a boyfriend! This is the best day of my life!'

Thank God, she got one.

'You don't seem to share my enthusiasm. My counsellor should think his job is half done if the student is happy and feeling on top of the world!' she said, her finger pointing towards the sky.

'I didn't take you for a girl who would celebrate getting a boyfriend. That's undermining your worth,' I said.

Gold. Pure gold. I was getting better under pressure. I knew where it was coming from. The rejection of not even being considered for Smriti's cousin's prospective boyfriend still stung. I was happy for her and her new boyfriend, but not happy with the concept of happiness and having a boyfriend/girlfriend being so closely strung together.

'Of course. Yes. Hmmm. Okay. Umm? So I shouldn't be happy about it?'

'Sure. You can be happy. But I don't think it qualifies for the *best* day of your life.'

'So I'm not happy about my new boyfriend, like not very happy, only averagely happy. I'm not really sure if he's yet my boyfriend or anything. So, yes, I shouldn't be *very* happy about that. Because he's a boy and he's also getting to date me. So it's not like it's a one-way street.'

She looked really confused now. Her eyes were staring at the ceiling and then at me and then at her fingers, trying to make sense of what she had just said.

'But what if he's better than I am? Like a better person? Shouldn't I be celebrating even then?'

'Do you know if he's a better person than you are?'

'I don't but he seems nice.'

'What did he do?'

'He helped me with a tray and asked if he could have my number,' she said.

'That's it?'

'Okay, I get it. But then how should I behave? Like he's lucky to have me? Or should I show him some attitude? I want to bring my A game to this thing. So counsel me! How should I act?' she asked, throwing her hair back.

'Like nothing has changed.'

She nodded her head sadly. 'But can I be happy about the party my brother is throwing for my eighteenth birthday?'

'Yes! That's the kind of thing you should celebrate! Brothers are great,' I said.

The last party my brother threw me was when I got through the graduate programme. It was a noble gesture and the party was great but I got drunk too early because I was scared I wouldn't be funny enough without the alcohol. By the time everyone arrived, I was already dunking my head in the commode and puking. My brother charmed everyone in the party and soon they forgot what they were celebrating.

'You aren't kicked about it? ' I asked.

'I am. Of course I am.'

'No, you aren't,' I said, my Spidey-senses working overtime.

'No, I'm not. I know I'm supposed to be happy and this is a great surprise. It must have taken him a lot to plan it. But I feel guilty now.' She looked at her feet.

'And why is that?'

'Like we don't have a relationship. We don't talk and yet he's doing this for me. How am I supposed to take that?'

'Have you tried talking to him?'

'We don't talk any more. He looks through me like I don't exist.'

'Why?'

'We just grew apart. He retreated into a little world of his own and never came out.'

'And you never tried to wrench open that world of his?'

'I'm his little sister! He should have looked out for me! Not the other way round!' she protested.

'You're not a little girl any more,' I said.

These sagely words I said made me feel ancient and my faint liking towards this girl felt even more wrong.

'I should talk to him? I don't know what to say.'

'He's your brother. You can always talk to your brother.'

She smiled. 'Do you have a brother?'

'Yeah. And I love that bastard more than life itself.'

'That's so sweet.'

The bell rang and it was time for her to leave. I spent the rest of the day walking about listlessly in the corridors, watching the happy kids mill around, one among them being Aisha and her prospective new boyfriend, the tall, handsome tree—Vibhor.

22

Aisha Paul

I was starting to realize why first crushes and loves are legendary.

It makes you aware of the intricate workings of your heart's auricles and ventricles. When Vibhor casually asked me out on a date, I felt the world spin around me; it felt like I was on a carousel from one of the *Final Destination* movies and it was a surprise I didn't faint or throw up. He held my hand in the empty corridor, looked deep into my eyes like he was born for this and this purpose only, and asked me if I wanted to meet this Sunday. Sure. Done. Why not? I will go. And hence, I was going.

It was important for me to kick this out of the park, have a check mark in the box in front of the words 'first date', and move on to achieve great heights from there. I might have been too late for a first date but had I got there quicker than my mother, so that's something.

Despite what everyone thought of me—I'm often the guide for other girls' first dates—I had never been on a date so I Googled dating etiquettes for girls. It required me to tease but not give in, wear a nice dress but not expose too much lest I wanted to come across as slutty. Talk but not talk too much, be interested in him and smile and acknowledge his achievements, his job, etc., try and pay the bill but don't try too hard . . . there were way too many rules!

There was absolutely no chance of me following those rules because a) they didn't seem to make any sense and b) how would I remember all of them?

So like every person with a sane mind, I did the next logical thing—I decided to go on a test date to see if these rules made any sense. I called up my student counsellor and asked him if he would meet me for I had to talk to him urgently. It's an emergency, I told him. Reluctantly, he agreed.

I waited for him in the mall, hiding near the washroom because I didn't want to be there before time. 'It reeks of desperation,' the dating manual had said. Though we had decided to meet at the TGIF, I knew I wouldn't be able to pay if I ordered anything more than a basic salad without chicken. The dating rules said the boy should pay, which seemed cute and wrong at the same time.

He was there at the precise time, hands in pocket, chewing gum, in his track pants, making me feel immensely overdressed in my only little black dress. I almost made up my mind to go back home to change into a pair of jeans and T-shirt.

I waited for ten minutes after he took his seat near the window and then entered the restaurant, just like what the dating doctor had ordered.

'Hi!' I said, brightly, as if it was a surprise he was there.

'Hi.' He seemed rather anxious. 'What happened? Anything serious?' He looked me up and down and up, confused. 'You said you wanted to talk. And why are you so dressed up?'

'That's what people do on dates, right?' I said, as I sat down and smiled. I didn't want to freak him out or anything.

'What? What are you talking about?'

'This is a date,' I said, and smiled again though it didn't seem to put him at ease at all. 'No! Don't go! It's not that kind of date, sir. It's only a practice date, just to get my basics right before an *actual* date.' His jaw was still open and he was still standing.

'What's happening here? Is this a prank or something? Is someone recording this?'

'Actually, Vibhor has asked me out and I have never been out on a date. So I need firsthand experience. I need to be smashing good at it. So I thought who better to guide me through it than you! You know? Guidance? You're my guidance—'

'I know the words, Aisha.'

'Okay! Then it's a date.'

'Give me your home number,' he said.

'No, no. Don't call my mom.'

'School rules say if I decide to meet a student outside school, the parents need to know.'

'*No they don't!* The school is stupid. You know that, of course.'

'Give me the number,' he said sternly.

'Remember, I told you my mother tried killing herself once,' I said instinctively.

'Yes, you did, but you never told me why.'

'It's a long story.'

'You either tell me the story or I'm calling your mother.'

I looked down and told him about the *incident*. I decided to fake cry to elicit sympathy but real tears flowed abundantly and soon I was sobbing loudly, attracting a lot of attention. Just the way any first date should go. *Perfect.*

He quietened me down. Like he just sat there and made a sorry face and said nothing. Much better than people telling me that it's going to be okay as if they studied medicine and they have a cure for my mother.

'I'm sorry. I just meant to tell you the real story and then fake my tears so you don't call her.'

He laughed and then so did I.

'I'm sorry. I didn't mean to laugh,' he said.

'It's okay.'

Once I shut up and wiped my face, he said, 'Give me your mother's email ID. I will mail her notifying about this. I hope she doesn't check her mail?'

This man was brilliant. I smiled, and not the creepy psychopath smile I had been assaulting him with before. He typed out a mail and hit 'send'. Next, he buried himself in the menu and ordered himself a salad and a vodka. Clearly, I was not paying for this date.

'I will have the same,' I said to the waiter.

'Without the vodka,' he said and waved the waiter away. 'You're too young for that. And this isn't a date. Don't call it that. You're seventeen.'

'So?'

'That's illegal.'

'Bella was seventeen and Edward was a hundred years old!' I protested.

'I'm not an undead, sparkly vampire.'

'Fine. But you still need to tell me what exactly people do on dates? Like how's it different? Like what do they do?' I said.

'They talk.'

'About what?'

'Depends on who they are talking to,' he said. 'If they really like the person, they open up, otherwise they gossip, talk about pubs and movies they went to, their annoying friends, take selfies and look into their phones and text people who are not sitting in front of them.'

I was taking notes. He was rather knowledgeable about these things. This was a good idea.

23

Danish Roy

I had no idea what I was doing there.

One moment I was sleeping in my pyjamas and the next moment I was apparently on a date with my underage student. It was welcome in a way. My parents were home with my uncle's family, complete with their annoying twin sons, and it was only a matter of time when I would have had to leave my bedroom fortress and sit with them.

I ate my salad and gulped my vodka. And then ordered some more. It made life a little better and I felt less guilty about finding Aisha absolutely stunning.

'Eat,' I said. 'That's also what people do on dates.'

This girl was bat-shit crazy. She had just told me a real story about a sad incident and had intended to act sad but had instead starting bawling in the middle of the restaurant, shouting, *I would have died had my mother died that day*. It was embarrassing and cute at the same time.

And post that, she kept looking at me like things were going to happen, like dates were supposed to be these magic times where every few seconds a bunny appears and amuses the participants. Dates for me had always been boring. I never knew what to say or what to do and the girls always seemed to be in physical pain while being with me.

'That's your fourth vodka,' she said. 'Are you drunk?'

'Me? No.'

'So what do we do after we eat?' she asked.

'I don't know yet.'

'Is that also a part of being on dates? Doing things spontaneously? Then why wasn't it in any of the manuals? I knew they were a sham.'

She rubbed her hands and pushed away the plate in front of her. She had hardly eaten. The salad was quite a disappointment. I felt like having biryani now.

I waved for the bill and studied it intently when it came. 'No happy hours,' the waiter said as he waited for me to clear the bill. I nodded and slipped in my debit card. She protested that we should go dutch on the bill and even fumbled with her handbag but I turned her down. I couldn't have let a kid pay for my alcohol.

'So, what now?' she asked once we left TGIF.

'There,' I said and pointed to the games arcade. The fourth vodka had worn off my inhibitions, making me more inclined towards taking stupid decisions.

Now a games arcade might not feature among top-rated things to do while on a date, but they are certainly top-rated things to do in life. Xboxes and PlayStations would never replace the feeling of standing in a crowd of screaming rowdy boys under the flickering tubelight of a shady video game parlour—your sweaty fingers wrapped around little red controllers—egging you on to beat the shit out of your opponent. It was the closest you could get to being in a fight to death.

'What?'

'Tekken 3 and Street Fighter,' I said. 'You vs me. Okay, let me tell you something. If you beat me, I will grant you permission to skip the counselling sessions!'

'Done!' she said.

We bought eleven coins. I picked the blonde-haired Paul and she picked Katarina.

'You're so dead,' I said as I snapped my fingers, took hold of the controllers and gave them a nice spin. She inserted the coins. 'I should warn you that I was an arcade game samurai in my times. My name was feared.'

She rolled her eyes in a mocking attitude. 'We shall see.'

The first fight started. She started pressing all the buttons at once and howled at the top of her voice as if it would help. I was shaky at first but slowly it came back to me and I knocked her out quite easily. The second and the third fights were even easier. I was the king of this world.

'I'm new at this,' she said. I laughed. 'What? Give me a little room. Let's make it best out of three?'

'Fine,' I said. We had extra coins and there was no way she was beating me. I decimated her again.

'Can we make it a best out of five?' she asked. And then it became a best of seven, and then best of nine, and best out of eleven.

'Give up, already,' I said.

She scrunched up her face and turned away from me in mock disappointment. 'It's a stupid game for boys.'

'You think so? I shouldn't probably tell you that you are one of the fastest learners I had ever seen.'

We resumed the game. By the eleventh game, she had stopped banging on the buttons and learnt the three punch-flying kick combos, which she used cleverly.

'Really?' she screamed and lunged at me. I lost my footing and she landed awkwardly on me, her elbow jammed in my groin.

'Ow.'

'I'm so sorry, I'm so sorry,' she said as she rolled away and got up. I doubled up in pain on the ground, clutching my insufficient tools of reproduction. 'Are you okay?'

'Yes,' I mumbled. 'I just need to lie down here for a little while.'

And she laughed. Not like a little snicker. She laughed with her mouth open, and she mumbled little apologies, but she kept laughing till her eyes teared up.

And then, I laughed too.

When I felt slightly better, we shifted to ice hockey and a shooting game, both of which ended in draws because neither of us wanted to lose so we started cheating. We were thrown out of the arcade when Aisha took the ice hockey puck and flung it outside the window after a self-goal.

Later, we watched three movies for the price of one. We had first row (really uncomfortable) tickets for *Avengers: Age of Ultron* where she shrieked every time Hulk landed a punch. During a crucial scene between Iron Man in a Hulk Buster suit smashing up Hulk in a crowded street, she stood up on her chair and hurled expletives and popcorn on the screen.

'*Sit down!*' a little boy in the row behind ours shouted. She threw a fistful of popcorn at him.

The boy's mother looked at me. I shrugged. 'She's not with me,' I said.

She kept jumping on the seat till the usher held her by her hand and asked her to step down. During the interval, she begged me to walk into another hall which was playing *Margarita with a Straw*, a film about a girl with cerebral palsy exploring her sexuality. She cried like a little child and flung herself in my arms. She stormed out of the movie hall, cursing and accusing the director of emotional manipulation. Finally, we sneaked into the theatre playing *Rio 3*, a happy animated movie and she and I giggled like our life depended on it.

Later, I drove her home and she slept with her mouth open in the backseat of my mother's car.

'We are here,' I said.

'Huh?' She woke up with a start and wiped the drool off her face. 'Thanks.' She stepped out of the car and stretched like a little poodle and rubbed her eyes. 'It was a great date.'

'Yeah, it was.'

'I'm going to knock my date with Vibhor out of the park!' she squealed.

'Best of luck.'

I drove back home. I missed her already.

24

Aisha Paul

I walked towards my house as a new woman.

My practice date was great, and if dating was this easy, I should write a book about it and fleece millions of unsuspecting girls.

I used my key to let myself in. My brother was on the couch watching *Masterchef India*. Without meeting my eye, he asked, 'Where were you?'

'Nothing. Nowhere. Why? I went nowhere.'

'I saw that teacher dropping you home,' he said.

'Oh.'

'Where were you?'

My brain never processed information and situations fast enough to come up with a believable lie. And even if it did, my face would contort and twitch and no one would believe me.

'It was a guidance session,' I said.

'What guidance session?'

'He's not a teacher. He's a guidance counsellor. I was appointed one after I misbehaved in class. Mom knows. And if you don't believe me, he has mailed Mom too about today's session. I needed to ask him a few things.'

He nodded and his eyebrows settled. I went and sat next to him.

'Thank you,' I said.

'For?'

'For asking where I was. And for the birthday party next week.'

'You have thanked me before,' he said, his tone still angry as if I had done something wrong. I sat there and watched *Masterchef* with him.

'Is something wrong?' he asked.

'No.'

'You can tell—'

'Why are you throwing this party for me?' I asked, pointblank, almost like a cop.

'It's your eighteenth birthday, Aisha. You will be a grown up after this. You deserve it.'

It only made me angrier. All these years, I needed my brother and he was nowhere to be seen, and now he was planning to get away with it with just a party. Despite my irritation I wouldn't do anything to jeopardise the party though. It was the best thing to have ever happened to me!

'You don't talk to me, bhaiya. And then you throw this party? Why?' I asked.

'There's nothing to talk about,' he said and increased the volume of the television. I took the remote from him and switched it off.

'I'm talking to you, bhaiya.'

'And I answered you.'

He snatched the remote from me. I snatched it back and threw it on the table. The Sellotape holding the remote ripped off and the batteries spilled out.

'What the hell is your problem?' growled my brother and stormed off.

*

Later that evening, Namrata came over and my brother had to open the door. We shared the room so whoever had a better reason to occupy the room would have it to himself or herself.

'No, Aunty, we are good,' Namrata implored, and waved to tell my mother she didn't need another sandwich. Despite my mother's condition, she always took it on herself to make sure everyone who entered our house was full till half-digested food bubbled up at the back of their throats.

The good thing about being friends with a nerd (I mean that in a good way) are:

1.   They the most genuine people. They are so worried about their marks and about learning that they don't think about playing games in relationships. Nerds rock.
2.   They make you learn things. Once a non-nerd makes friends with a nerd, the nerd makes you learn everything they know. Well, at first they are a little shocked to see how dumb you are.

The world would be a better place if every mean, dumb person was paired up with a book-devouring, number-crunching, equation-solving nerd. They love you unconditionally. Unless you lose their notes—then they don't.

Right now, Namrata was making me read all her favourite books. We started with Enid Blyton, then Roald Dahl and Ruskin Bond, and then we worked through John Grisham and David Baldacci, before moving on to Arundhati Roy, Manu Joseph and J.M. Coetzee. We also sprinkled quite a few young adult authors in our reading list. She made me read widely and deeply.

But that day we weren't having a conversation about books, we were having a conversation about blowjobs. Namrata's parents were leaving for Panipat for a day and she was sneaking Norbu in.

'Norbu asked for one?' I almost exclaimed.

'No. He just mentioned it in some context a few times. So I guessed—'

'You don't know how to give a blowjob, do you?'

'I think I can. Like I used to think it's gross but right now I'm a little confused. Of all the boys you have dated, you haven't given it anyone?'

I blushed. The old Aisha would have lied, but not the new one. The new Aisha doesn't lie to her friend. Friendship should mean not having to lie.

'I haven't dated a single boy yet.'

She laughed.

She saw me not react and her laughter trailed off. 'What? You? Aisha? Not one? None?'

No. And then I started to cry for no reason whatsoever. She didn't know what to do so I just crawled up to her and put my head on her lap and cried. She patted my head, not knowing what to make of it.

'Why are you crying?'

'I don't know.'

'What do you mean, you don't know? Stop making a habit of crying. You give us girls a bad name,' she chuckled.

'Sorry, sorry.'

'Stop crying!'

'Fine.'

'You're beautiful, Aisha! If someone doesn't date you, it's their fault not yours.'

'It's so unfair. I don't have a problem with not dating anyone. But it sucks when everyone thinks you are and you aren't!'

'Yeah, tell me about it. I didn't strip for a boy and people thought I did. Wonder how that happened?'

'I'm sorry again.'

'It's okay, I was just kidding,' said Namrata.

'See, you're smart and funny and adorable and understanding, and you have this cute face I could kiss all day. No wonder Norbu loves you! Why would anyone love me? I'm just big breasts.'

'Girls would kill for that,' she said.

'And a face full of pimples!'

'Not *completely* full,' said Namrata and laughed. She hugged me. 'You will find someone truly deserving of you who will love you as much as you want, Aisha.'

I smiled and sat up. I wiped my face on her sleeve and said, 'Vibhor is taking me out on a date.'

'Uff! Why are you such a drama queen? Why were you crying right now then? What's wrong with you?' she said excitedly.

'Hehe. I think I forgot that with all our blowjob talk.'

'Hmmm . . . I'm thinking of not giving one now.'

'Why?'

'Men always have it a little too easy. Blowjobs shouldn't be doled out just like that. Norbu will need to work for it. He won't win so easily.'

'Blowjobs mean the man is winning?' I asked.

'Ummm . . . If I don't feel like it, then I think it's him who's winning.'

'And sex too shouldn't be about men winning, right? We should make a poster out of that,' I said.

'I'm not sure if I want to be counselled like you,' Namrata winked at me.

'You would love to be counselled by Danish.'

'Wait? Why are you smiling? Do you have a crush on him?'

'*No*. I don't. I have a date with Vibhor,' I said.

She didn't believe me. We spent the rest of the night arguing who out of David Nichols and Nick Hornby is a better writer, and it was so much better a conversation than talking about other people's lives and clothes, and gossiping. I loved the woman I was becoming. Also, I learnt an important lesson. As she slept, I thought about how men pumped their fists after having sex for the first time, while the girls shied away, ashamed.

And so I Googled the entire night about sexuality, virginity, and learned of how sex—supposedly a spectacular thing to do with one's body—was often an instrument of oppression for women. Like it wasn't fun any more, it was something dirty, something to be gossiped about, some taboo, to be snatched, or stolen, or cheated for. Why would they do that to poor sex?

So I decided that sex shouldn't be about men winning. Sex should be like chess, a sport where gender is irrelevant. Winners should be based on who performed better regardless of gender.

They should make a poster out of this. Sex is chess.

25

Sarthak Paul

It would be unfair to blame it all on Aisha.

She wasn't the only reason why rumours about her bothered me so much, and why I wanted to hide from it all. I had always been a bright student. Students who score great marks without even trying? I was one of them—hated, envied, idolized. Maths, physics, chemistry, even Hindi and Sanskrit, give me a question and I would solve it. It was a lucky break for the entire family when I aced the entrance examination to one of the toughest boarding schools in India. The scholarship covered everything and would save us thousands of rupees a year which we could use to pay off the loans Dad had taken. My parents were beaming for weeks after the result.

'Stupid scholarship,' Aisha used to say as she clung to my leg, begging me not to leave.

It took us five times the duration we thought it would for us to pack my stuff into three suitcases. Every night when we used to sleep, Aisha sneaked out and unpacked the suitcases and hid my clothes and books around the house. She would have this look on her face, this cute weasel look, as if to say she didn't know who did it, and that maybe it was a sign from God telling me not to go. I hated to have to leave her behind. But I was a young boy and I wanted to experience life in a boarding school as well. I had heard that they had great boxing coaches and an unbeaten soccer team. That's something that really excited me.

'I will miss you,' Aisha had hugged me and cried on the day I was supposed to leave. She hung on to me for her dear life. I would have changed my mind but the fees had been paid by the scholarship trust and I had to go. Leaving my little sister behind made me sick in the stomach.

The first few days in the boarding school was horrendous, I would cut classes and fake illnesses so I could call Aisha and we would talk for hours; whatever little money I had would be spent on long STD calls. If I could have, I would have gone back in a heartbeat and never let go of my sister's hand ever again. She was the love of my life.

Slowly, the homesickness wore off and I started to enjoy my time at the boarding school. It was everything a young boy could have hoped for. I was good at sports, great at academics and the teachers loved me, already forecasting my rise to the Head Boy position when the right time came. And then slowly everything came down like a house of cards.

I was thirteen when I realized I liked boys. There I said it. I can already sense the derision in your eyes, the coldness that's creeping up on you, the sense of hatred and disgust taking over whatever else you know about me. It doesn't matter if I was a good son or a good brother or a good student, it just matters that I am gay.

I tried denying it at first, forced myself to talk to girls, objectifying them, hoping I would feel something for them, thinking it was just a phase everyone goes through in their life. No. I am gay, gay for life and there was no escaping that.

I started to hate myself. Sooner or later, I knew it was all going to blow up in my face. I was a disgrace, an anomaly, something to be mocked and stereotyped and laughed at in Sajid Khan movies. Luckily for me, I wasn't feminine. Funny, how people make fun of men who are effeminate. Aren't their mothers feminine? Aren't the girls who laugh at feminine gay men themselves feminine? And who the fuck decides what's feminine and masculine? And look at me, I'm tagging all gay men as feminine even though a lot of them aren't.

My grades started to drop, I started being sick a lot, like physically sick, like my body was revolting, as if it was disgusted by how my brain worked. Every night I would sleep wishing the next morning would be different, that I would be like everyone else, but nothing changed. I wanted to eat all the time but I couldn't keep it down and would throw up. Knowing myself better made me nauseous and sick and hateful and vile.

It took me months to accept it. I knew things would never quite be easy for me for the rest of my life. We evolve but do it rather slowly. I was sure homosexuality wouldn't be a part of our culture during my lifetime, which I often hoped would be short.

But things turned for the better again. On the boxing team was another boy. Big. Strong. And quite popular. Karan and I struck up a friendship and even though I never told him about my 'condition', it seemed he knew. Weeks later, I broke down in his arms and told him who I was or what I was or whatever and he said it was okay. He said it was okay! And then, in the changing room of our boxing gym, he had kissed me. That was not the only place we would kiss in. Post that, we started hanging out quite often in dark corridors, deserted changing rooms, and shower cubicles. But soon enough, the jig was up.

Someone started a rumour about the two of us, and it was vicious. It was the half-truth anyway. Karan was the popular one and he controlled the narrative of the rumour. He told people I had begged him to allow me to suck his dick and he had conceded after weeks of trying, that too, just to see how it felt. Which was as big a lie as saying I was straight. People bought it hook, line and sinker, and from then on began the daily crucifixion of Sarthak Paul, the gay boy who begs people to fuck in his mouth. My classmates revelled in my misery.

What followed sometimes seemed worse than death. The students of my class literally would chase me across corridors, laughing, pointing fingers, mocking me; they would draw me (or what they thought looked like me) on the classroom boards with a dick in my mouth, and for two months it looked like nothing else happened in the school. I was hit, slapped, punched, kicked, humiliated, spat on. I was flashed dicks in the dorm rooms, made to parade naked in the locker room and asked to shag in front of the entire class in the hostel.

Nothing happened to that boy, Karan. Because, of course, he was the *man* in the lie. I was the one on my knees, supposedly begging. I was the woman in the relationship that never existed, and aren't the women always the ones who are at the butt end of everything. If they fuck when they want to they are sluts, if they don't they are prudes. But why was it happening to me? *I was a man.* And to think of it, all the abuses hurled at me were misogynistic. But the girls stood watching and even laughed and called me a pussy.

I started spending days on the roof of the faculty building, legs dangling over the edge, thinking of jumping off and ending it all. What had I done? It wasn't my fault. If it were up to me, I would be the straightest person in all of history. I would be Ghengis Khan and father a billion children. If there was an active God and if this were against religion why would he create me? What did I do in my mother's womb that pissed him off so much that he made me gay? And what do people think? We are so attracted to a certain gender that we pick a life full of relentless hatred? Does our attraction, or choice, mean so much? Of course not! Because it's not a *choice*. It's not in our hands. We don't fight for our right to be attracted to the person of the same sex, we fight for our right to exist.

Soon enough I started to think of ways I could die. The only thing that kept me alive was the face my sister, Aisha, how she could cry and bawl at seeing my face crushed against the pavement.

I even wrote an impassioned suicide note. I hoped to God I was the only fourteen-year-old who had to do that because he was made a certain way. And I addressed it to Aisha. My scholarship was rescinded because of my low marks. I survived the year somehow and came back home to join our old school.

I had never been so happy to see Aisha. In the one year I had been away, she had grown into a wonderful woman, while I had been told by my peers that I was no longer a man.

But then the rumours about Aisha started, and I had to step away from her. I would have fought the world for her but I was tried and defeated. I had no strength left. I had done my fighting. I couldn't take it any more; no matter how much I loved her, I had to step away. I was done being humiliated and laughed at. Call me a coward but I wouldn't have survived it.

I would have jumped off the roof.

26

Danish Roy

'Thank you for doing this. This is going to be awesome!' my brother said as he drove his Mercedes through the choc-a-bloc traffic in Central Delhi like only he can. I suspected he was a trained spy on the side.

I had told my brother I was back on the market and I wanted a shot at Smriti's cousin, Kanika. He said he would take care of it without making me sound like a complete loser in front of Smriti. This date had nothing to do with Aisha going on her date with Vibhor today. Absolutely nothing.

'You picked this? Of all the places, you picked this?'

He flicked the keys towards the valet outside the most expensive club in Delhi. It had only been weeks since Verve opened and only rich kids and Bollywood stars and businessmen in gleaming Bentleys visited the jaunt. Well, my brother was one of them now but I was still a lowly school teacher of sorts. And as if he was listening to the monologue in my head, he slipped his black American Express card into my back pocket. He smiled, and shameless as I was, I didn't protest.

About half an hour later, Smriti walked in with Kanika, and I have to say it took all my restraint to not drool. If Smriti was a strong seven, Kanika was a ten and a half, and I'm saying it despite being vehemently against marking women.

'Hi,' said Ankit, and greeted both of them by hugging them.

I smiled at Smriti and did what could be called an awkward cross between a handshake and a hug. Same with

Kanika who smelt of fresh roses. Why do women smell so nice all the time?

'Nice place,' she said to me.

'He's paying. He comes here often so they usually have a table for him,' Ankit butted in and nudged me. Kanika flashed a shameless smile at me.

A quick scan through the alcohol and the food menu was enough to know that our bill would be upwards of fifteen thousand. I felt my back pocket to check if I still had my brother's card. Four beers later Smriti and Ankit were snogging shamelessly. Kanika and I were yet to exchange a single word other than guessing the next song by the opening music piece.

It was time I made my opening move. I had to have something to share when Aisha would narrate to me how her date went in the next counselling session.

'So I heard you were a lecturer? How's that? It's fun? You always wanted to be that?'

'Yes, it is fun,' she said and didn't say anything for a while. She sat there, swaying her head to the music, scrutinizing every girl on the dance floor, silently judging them.

'Do you like it?'

'It's a job,' she said. 'You like yours? Talking teenagers out of drugs and sex?'

I could sense the condescension in her voice. 'I like it. They need guidance.'

'Teenagers are teenagers. They won't listen to you.' I shrugged and said otherwise.

'So you plan to do this your entire life?' she asked half-heartedly while she tweeted 'Having a good time at Verve' with six hashtags dedicated to the good life.

'I can't think of anything better. So what do you like to do? Other than teaching?'

'Nothing. Just go out. Eat. Party once in a while.'

Silence again. She looked into her phone and liked a bunch of Instagram pictures of curtain patterns, baby animals, and watched a couple of vines. So I started the conversation again. 'So, you just broke up, right? Dealing with it well?'

'Yes.'

'Any recent books you might have read?'

'No.'

'Movies?'

'Yeah, watched one. Don't remember the name though.'

She refreshed her Twitter account and tweeted 'drunkkkkk, biatches, Sachurday Nite!'

'Did you win a spelling bee contest when you were young?'

'No.'

'You couldn't have.'

'What?'

'Nothing,' I said. 'So what do your folks do? Do you have siblings? I love the dress you're wearing. Where did you get it from? What kind of music are you into?' I wanted to see if anything mattered to her at all.

'Huh? What were you saying? I just saw this on Facebook. It's a slow motion window of a cat yawning!' she said and thrust the phone in my face.

'That's probably the most enlightening thing I have seen this month.'

She got back to her phone. She wasn't even listening to what I was saying.

'You're a slut!' I shouted.

'What?'

'Not for you. I was just saying the lyrics of the song aloud.'

'Oh, okay.'

I chugged another beer to make this conversation more bearable. This was the reason why I had hardly ever dated. I don't have the requisite charm to make anyone talk. She was looking into her phone again, this time laughing at GIFs of cute pandas falling asleep.

She would take breaks from looking into her phone to deride a random girl making out on the dance floor, or tell me about a dress she wanted to buy, or how she really liked a new club that opened in GK, or how much she hated people from East Delhi, or how a friend of hers is a total slut, and how a guy friend got a terrible haircut. I still knew nothing about her. She wasn't talking to me. She was talking at me. Like you shout at the television. They were just bits and pieces of information about other people. How was I supposed to know her better? By which new store had opened in a new mall? Or by listening to her story of how her friend was dating an ugly guy? Or how desperately she needed to change her car? It was boring. She was like a tabloid newspaper. Maybe I was expecting more out of this dating thing.

A little later, my brother and Smriti dragged us to the dance floor. And suddenly, it was as if Kanika had been pumped with an adrenaline shot. She danced, and sang, and gyrated, and updated her phone thrice, clicked fifteen pictures, visited the washroom thrice to fix her hair, and danced a little more. She asked me to charge her phone, and then had five shots. I wondered how Aisha was faring in her date.

The night almost over, all four of us went back to our table, and the cheque arrived. It was for 18,000 rupees. Ankit passed on the cheque to me and I took out my own card instead of his. I wanted to pay because I wanted this to be a reminder to myself about spending time with women who couldn't do me the simple courtesy of answering my questions. Now, I might not be smart, or funny, or charming, or even worth talking to, but I do expect the person in front of me to answer my questions or at least state their disinterest in talking to me in clear words. If this was what dating meant, then I was glad I wasn't dating anyone.

We left the place at three in the morning. Later that morning, Kanika texted me that she had fun and we should do it again. Yeah, right. Next time I feel like dating, I will make sure that I go out with my phone.

27

Aisha Paul

It was a great day, wasn't it! Yes, of course it was.

The picture Vibhor uploaded of him and me that morning already had seventy-two likes. People were congratulating us for looking good together. Because that's what matters—looking good together. He was so kind to do that, parade me as his girl in front of the entire school, branding me like a cow, shouting to the world that he was now officially off the market. He was committed. The bad boy had settled down and I was the one who'd managed to make him do that.

That's got to count for something. I spent the last evening with Vibhor Rana, captain of the football team. My brother vouched for him when I told my mother about the impending date. She frowned, complained, asked a gazillion questions about him, his family, his interest in academics, talked to him on the phone, and then finally let me go.

How was it? Well, it was different from what I had learned from my practice date with Danish.

'You're late,' Danish said as I knocked and entered his room. He looked like he hadn't slept in a while, a little haggard, and a bit angry.

'Vibhor caught me in the corridor. Sorry,' I said.

'Oh yes. Big date yesterday? What did you do? Was it fun?' he asked.

'It was great! What did you do last night? You seem like you didn't sleep.'

'I just went out with my brother on a double date.'

'Great.' Words dried up in my mouth immediately. Someone had fun, like I did, and I wasn't happy about it. I continued, 'He took me to this really nice terrace restaurant. It was beautiful.'

Danish asked me, 'So did my training date help?'

'Yes, most certainly. Thanks,' I lied.

I was glad I wasn't dating Danish. He knew nothing about dating.

*

Last night, Vibhor picked me up in his dad's Skoda Superb and we drove to Hauz Khas Village while he blasted his favourite songs, and told me how pretty I looked. He had dressed up for the date. He looked gorgeous, almost like a movie star in his crisp white shirt, which strained against his veiny forearms, blue trousers and light brown Oxford shoes, a sharp contrast to my pyjamas. I had thought from my practice date that it was okay to go to a date in pyjamas. But Vibhor stopped at a mall near my house and bought me a beautiful yellow dress, saying it was more appropriate. He couldn't take his eyes off me when I emerged out of the changing room and even winked at me when I twirled in my new, little yellow dress. I blushed so hard it felt I would melt into a little puddle.

'See, so much better. We will steal the show,' said Vibhor. 'No one's going to look at anyone else today.'

'Are you sure we aren't dressing up too much?'

'This is Delhi.'

We left the mall and resumed our drive, his hand constantly on my right thigh, giving me goose bumps all over my body. No one had ever touched me like that before.

'Can I ask you something?'

'Sure, Aisha.'

'Vibhor? How did my brother react when you told him about us?'

'He didn't. He was pretty chilled about it. We have known each other for years now.'

'Okay.'

'You seem disappointed. Isn't that a good thing?'

'Yes, it is but—'

'Damn! Look at that car,' he said and pointed to a red Gallardo at a distance. 'I asked one from Dad but he said it will be an open invitation for the tax guys to mount a raid.'

Vibhor even brought a gift for me, a perfume. The price tag was cut out but later I Googled and found it was quite expensive. It was so sweet of him; he really knew how to be with a girl. He then held my hand during the entire drive, my clammy, sweaty, nervous hands, and never complained once. Sometimes, he would drive with his eyes on me, glittering in the reflection of my yellow dress, tell me how great I looked, and it would totally freak me out. He was a bad-ass in a traffic violation sort of way. Megha would have really liked him. The restaurant was beautiful and despite my feeble disapproval, he bought me a large cocktail which was so pretty and colourful and fruity that I couldn't help but taste it. It was very alcoholic too and I almost spat it back into the glass. He goaded me into having another sip, and then another one, and I finished the drink. I was then what I guessed people call 'tipsy'. He ordered my food as well. I really wanted to have biryani but he wanted to share food so we ordered for a pasta for me instead. He told me again that I looked pretty.

'She will have another one,' he said.

'No, I won't,' I said. The tipsy feeling had given way to a slight nausea and it was getting worse. But he remained adamant and another tall drink came flying to our table. Luckily, a little later he went to the washroom and I drained the glass into a flower pot. 'It was the last drink I am having today! I think I'm totally sloshed,' I said brightly when he came back.

'You don't look sloshed. You must have an amazing capacity.'

'I come from a family of alcoholics.'

He took it seriously and said, 'That's so cool. Usually girls are so drunk after just one drink. But you're quite something. I like you.'

His words went like a bolt through my body. This time he sat a lot closer to me, his muscled shoulder rubbing against mine. God. I have to admit I did feel a little tingly. This was the farthest I had gone with any guy. A shoulder rub and a hand on my thigh. Namrata would have to know about this, I thought.

'I always noticed you,' he said, tucking a stray strand of hair behind my ear.

'Then why didn't you ever talk to me?'

'I always thought you had a boyfriend. Do you always go on dates in pyjamas?'

'If I can help it. They are super comfortable.'

'So who was the last guy you dated?'

'An older guy. Quite older,' I said, imagining Danish.

'Must be a bore,' he snapped immediately.

'Ummm . . . he didn't ask me to drink.'

'Bleh.'

I got to know during the course of the night that he was the only son of parents who ran the biggest floor tile manufacturing unit in all of north India. Also, he had an extensive knowledge of all the newest clubs in Delhi, the wine shops that are open till three in the morning, and he gushed about this one time a young Bollywood starlet was hitting on him.

'So . . . that boring, old guy and you? Were you guys serious or was it just a fling?'

'He was important to me,' I said.

'Did you do stuff? Like you know?'

'Yes, it was fun,' I said, still thinking about Danish.

Since that day, I had spent innumerable hours trying the perfect combo hits of Katarina on my desktop. Next time, Danish would have a tough time getting a decent punch in. I would go all Rounda Rousey on him before he could say K.O.

'So you have had sex before? Ummm . . . with that guy?' he asked, his eyebrows burrowing.

'Ummm . . . do you need to know that?' I asked, a little embarrassed.

'Yes, I think I do,' he said. 'If we are dating I think we need to be honest with each other. You can always ask me whatever you feel like.'

Fair point.

'No. I didn't have sex with *that* guy. Now should we exchange our Facebook passwords as well?'

'Let's have some boundaries, okay? Checking Facebook is so last decade. I'm sure you and that old guy did it. Didn't you?' he chuckled.

'Why don't you try stand-up comedy? You're funny.'

'Hmm . . . I will think about it,' he said and put his arm around me. I felt the hair stand on my arms, and my body suddenly felt warm.

'You? Have you had sex before?' I asked.

'Of course I have.'

'With?'

'Been with a few girls here and there. A girl from Ramjas, someone from Springdales, another one from Delhi Public School. A couple of other girls I think.'

'You liked them?'

'Yes, a bit. But I like you more. You're amazing,' he said and kissed me on my cheek as I burnt with the warmth. He pulled me closer and nuzzled my neck. It felt fantastic. I giggled.

'Do they have names?'

'Their names aren't important any more. I told you already I like you more. They are history. Now don't be jealous.' He winked at me.

I felt a little bad for those girls. I knew their secret but didn't know their names. I didn't prod him further.

'Did you love them?' I asked. Vibhor was too busy kissing my neck to answer my question. 'Did you love them, Vibhor?'

'Naah, they were whatever. I'm done with them.'

He said while nibbling at my ear (and the nibbles were making me lose my shit—who knew teeth and earlobes can give someone so much pleasure?). I swayed out of the path of his jaws and asked, 'Do you want to do something else?'

'What? It's fun here.'

'Can we play video games?'

'What? Why? Who does that?'

He started necking me again. Now I was confused. He made me change out of my pyjamas and now he didn't want to play video games with me. My training date wasn't helping at all. It seemed like dating meant being nibbled on, and I would have to admit it felt wonderful.

I pushed a slobbering Vibhor away. 'People are looking!'

'You're hot. Why shouldn't they? Come here,' he said and grabbed me playfully.

'Let's go somewhere else?' I said and waved for the cheque.

Just before leaving, he ordered another drink and gulped it down in one go. He paid the cheque and we were back on the road again. His hand was on my thigh, rubbing it slightly, giving me little brain aneurysms. He looked rather handsome, and a part of me wanted to kiss him long and hard.

Soon, we left civilization behind and he parked the car in an empty parking lot of what seemed like a construction site.

'Is this better?' he asked.

'For what?' I asked.

'You will see,' he said and smiled.

He unbuckled his seat belt, bent over to my side, then slyly pushed the lever of my seat, which in turn pushed down the backrest in a flat position, and just like that he was on top of me. He pushed my hair away from my face and his lips hovered over mine. His breath smelled of alcohol but I wasn't sure any more if I wanted to kiss him because I was more scared than turned on. He came close and before I could say anything he jerked back and stumbled out of the car. I got out from the other side and found him on all fours, vomiting pasta. I said a little prayer and thanked God none of it was over me. Fifteen minutes later, we were on our way back, staring at the road wordlessly. He smelled of bile and vomit.

'Are you going to be okay?'

'Yes,' he said, burping. 'I didn't eat anything since the morning. So . . .'

He dropped me home and drove away, knackered.

Namrata had called me later that night once I was tucked into bed. 'How did it go? Did something happen? You kissed him?'

'I wanted to.'

'And you didn't? Chickened out?'

'No. He was nice. And so gorgeous. But I snapped out of it. I got a little confused.'

'So you're not going to see him again?'

'Of course, I will see him. He was nice to me most of the time. I still want to kiss him, I guess.'

'Make up your mind, girl.'

'I'm trying,' I said. 'Oh, I totally forgot. What about you and Norbu?'

'I can't tell you.'

'Is that the code for *ask me again*?'

'Okay, fine, I will tell you. I didn't give him a blowjob but something else happened and it was OUT. OF. THIS. WORLD.'

'What happened?'

'He went down on me.'

'He did what? Wait . . . *Shit*. Did he?'

'He totally did. It was like he was looking for a treasure down there. Well, to think of it, it was like a treasure hunt because he didn't know where to look for it for the longest time. *But it was the most amazing thing ever.* Do you know what he was digging with?'

'Please, no—'

'With—'

'Please, no—'

'His tongue!'

'Don't give me details, Namrata.'

She laughed. 'I came about thrice and I slept. He was so scared before he started. He asked me about a dozen times before he started.'

'Stop laughing. Poor Norbu,' I said and she laughed.

'He was so tired, he couldn't even talk. So much for the tongue being the strongest muscle in the body!'

'So unfair!'

'Oh c'mon. I will make it up to him the next time around. I'm practising it in my head already.'

'Okay enough, I need to sleep now and I don't want images of your lips around Norbu's whatever. Goodnight.'

'Goodnight. And hey, drink a lot of water before you sleep or you will wake up like a shrunken raisin.'

'Goodnight.'

I disconnected the call and I texted Vibhor.

AISHA: Reached home?

VIBHOR: Yes, just got in bed. I think I'm missing you.

AISHA: Ditto.

VIBHOR: Sorry for the puking thing.

AISHA: Hmmmm . . .

VIBHOR: I messed up our kiss.

AISHA: I would have still kissed you after you puked.

VIBHOR: Despite being potty-mouthed?

AISHA: Yes. If you would have asked I would have.

VIBHOR: Damn.

AISHA: But I wouldn't have kissed before you puked.

VIBHOR: Why?

AISHA: You didn't ask whether you could kiss me.

VIBHOR: I assumed . . .

AISHA: Hmm. ☹ ☹ You shouldn't have. I was scared.

VIBHOR: I will ask the next time.

AISHA: Sweet.

VIBHOR: You're hot.

AISHA: You're nice.

VIBHOR: Do you sleep naked?

AISHA: Always.

VIBHOR: Damn.
AISHA: Do you?
VIBHOR: Yes. Always.
AISHA: Damn.
I imagined Vibhor naked and looking for treasures between my thighs, got off in like a few seconds and slept like a baby.

28

Danish Roy

The day was finally here.

Tonight was the big party. Aisha's eighteenth birthday, and I was looking forward to not being a paedophile any more. After she turned eighteen, the only little technicality between me telling her how kind and awesome she was, was the student–teacher thing. So now, it was only illegal. That and Vibhor, the tree.

She seemed happy the days following her and Vibhor's first date. She didn't give me any details of her date or their ensuing relationship, which the entire school was talking about and I didn't ask. I had seen the guy come to school in four different cars, heard he had plenty of experience with girls, so I knew for a fact he knew how to show a girl a good time. Such was my life, being insecure of boys half a decade younger. But I had an important role to play in their relationship. Early that morning, Aisha had called to ask me to come with her to select a dress. I had no idea what made her think I was an expert on birthday dresses.

'So? What are we aiming for?' I asked as she dragged me to Forever 21.

'If this were the last time I was stepping out in public, what should I be in? That's the theme. It's a strictly no-pyjama party,' she said and she walked swiftly through the racks, rejecting reasonably beautiful clothes. 'What about this?' She picked a sparkling silver dress and put it front of herself.

I wanted to tell her she would look beautiful in anything she wore because it wasn't the clothes or the make-up or her hair which made her attractive, it was her heart, it was who she was, smart and fun. Of late, she had been telling me of all these books she had been reading, and my heart had jumped because the books she liked the most were my favourites too. Maybe that's what love should be about; two people who love the same books. But what struck me was her understanding of the characters, their problems, their stories—it all affected her in a way that she wanted to change herself, apply it in real life. That's what a good book should do. Make you reflect and make a positive change, and she followed this like a religion. Far better than I have ever done.

'You will look beautiful,' I said.

She disappeared into the fitting room with that dress.

'I don't know what to say. Vibhor would fall in love with you today if he hasn't already,' I said when she emerged, twirling in that little dress. She smiled that smile of hers which I had so come to love.

'What do you think? Not Vibhor, you!'

'Does it matter?' I asked, not wanting things to get awkward.

'It does.'

'Why?'

'What you think of me matters to me. You made parts of me. Take some responsibility for what you created and tell me what you think?'

I was tired of being always put in a spot by a seventeen-, going on eighteen, year-old girl.

'Ummm . . . you look like sunshine to me, well, technically you are more like moonlight because you are wearing silver but I don't think anyone's going to notice the dress or your body, and if they do, it's their fault because it's what's deep inside that body and that face is what people should see, something I have seen and come to like so much in you. You're like a slate, Aisha. You learn every day and write stuff on yourself, trying to be better, and wipe it clean and learn some more. Yes, I love your eyes—they are black and deep and almond-shaped but I see the kindness in those eyes I have never seen before, and yes, I love your lips but not because they are the most perfect grape-toned lips ever but because of the words you choose, the things you say and the ones you don't. And that face, that beautiful face, it radiates happiness and love and generosity. So I don't really know how the dress looks on you, but I do know that you're beautiful.'

I said and waited for her to realize, rather embarrassingly for herself and for me, that I was in love with this eighteen-year-old girl. She just stared at me and I could feel a sexual harassment suit hang above me like a naked sword.

Finally she spoke, 'You're awfully good at your job. Do you say that to every loser student of yours?'

It was an escape route and I took it. I nodded and smiled. I wasn't sure whether to feel happy or sad at her complete misreading of the situation so I played along. 'It's in all the training books.'

'Come, let's get you something!' she said and grabbed me by my hand. We paid at the cashier's and she kept wearing the dress while we looked for what I was supposed to wear.

'I have something to wear,' I said.

'My birthday, my rules.'

'What do you want me to wear on your birthday party?'

'You always ask the right questions. Your girlfriend must be the happiest in the entire world.'

Yeah, right. My girlfriend is probably staring at her phone in some part of her world, unmindful of my existence.

*

Thanks to my pathetic driving, I reached back home late, already dreading going to a kids' party. Just as I stepped out of the car, I felt a fist land square on my face, my jaw shattered, and I doubled up on the ground in pain. My head rang and I think I almost passed out.

'Fuck you!' a voice shouted in my ear. My blurred vision cleared and I saw a face I recognized from somewhere. I wanted to dole out my wallet, my watch, the car keys and surrender but the guy said, 'Stay away from Aisha, do you hear me?'

And that's when it struck me. He was Sarthak, the estranged brother, the thrower of parties.

'What the hell are you talking about?'

'Sir, I know you have been going out with my sister.'

'That's a hell of way to introduce yourself to your *Sir*?' I said and staggered to my feet. My jaw alternated between being numb and on fire.

'Sir, stay away from her or I will inform the school authorities. Vibhor and Aisha are good for each other. He will take care of her. So just *stay off her*.' His hands were up again, and he resembled an impoverished Sylvester Stallone from the early *Rocky* movies. I was in no doubt that he could hit me again and this time I would flatline.

I put my hands up in surrender and spoke, 'Hey? Sarthak, that's what your name is, right?' He nodded. 'There's nothing between us. If anything, I'm helping out in her relationship with Vibhor.' I added after a pause. 'As a student counsellor.'

'But you were out—'

'She asked me to. He's her first boyfriend. No experience.'

'Oh.'

He lowered his hands, the rage on his face changed to guilt and he helped me to the pavement, checked my nose, offered me his handkerchief and apologized profusely. 'I didn't know. I'm sorry. I didn't know what I was doing. I won't be around for long so I thought I would . . .'

'Won't be around?'

He thought before speaking. 'Is there something as a student–counsellor confidentiality like lawyers?'

'Yes, of course there is,' I lied, remembering what Aisha had mentioned once.

'And counsellors follow it?'

'The rules are very strict about that kind of thing. I could lose my job,' I said, still struggling for my breath. I needed to get myself checked for a concussion.

'I'm leaving Delhi for further studies.'

I wanted to say 'So what?', but I remembered they shared a dying mother. 'Oh. Where are you going?'

'Poland.'

'What! Poland? How—'

'It's a scholarship. Don't tell her.'

'I won't. But why aren't you telling her?'

'They won't let me leave. I mean they will but I wouldn't be able to leave them.'

'So you're eloping for further studies? That's a first.'

'Yes, sir.' His phone beeped. 'Sir, I should go. Some last minute arrangements. And I'm sorry. I didn't mean to hurt you. I . . . I just acted out.'

'You need to tell her, Sarthak. And you need to talk to your sister,' I said.

He nodded though it didn't seem like he would follow through on it. We shook hands, he apologized a few more times, and I waved down an auto for him. He left.

My nose still bled.

29

Aisha Paul

Right then, my brain was like Stephen Hawking's, doing a million little calculations, trying to figure out the innumerable reasons why Danish said what he did. The words he had said made me float outside my body, look at him say those words to a girl in a sparkly, silver dress and go, *Such a lucky girl*. I knew it wasn't student counsellor advice from a training book. Could he possibly like me? God. But why would he? He's like . . . well, I never thought about him that way, and then I did.

It was like the Neville Longbottom centrefold that broke the Internet. One moment, he's the cute dork you take for granted, the next he's stripping in your dreams and gyrating to a dirty song, eliciting emotions you didn't know you could have. Megha and the rest of the college were right—he was cute in an older boy sort of a way. Like if Brad Pitt constantly winked and chewed on gum.

I had taken that silver dress and walked out with him maintaining a circle of sanity around me. I didn't look at him or even breath the same air as him. He was my counsellor and I should not have been thinking about him; there are rules against that kind of thing, I believe.

'I will see you tonight then?' I had asked as he waved down a rickshaw for me.

'Sure. Is something wrong? You seem a little unhappy,' he said.

There he was again with his supersensitive antennae working overtime.

'No, not really. See you tonight, Danish?'

'Sure.'

'Sir.'

'What?'

'No, I called you Danish. I missed adding sir. So, sir.'

He had chuckled.

'Bye, Aisha.'

As the auto drove away, I waited uselessly for him to suffix 'the woman of my dreams' after taking my name.

*

My phone rang. 'Hey!' I said brightly, pushing Danish out of my head, which was easier said than done. Every time I looked at that dress, his words knocked the breath out of me.

'Are you ready yet?' asked Vibhor.

'I was just getting into the shower.'

'Take me with you,' he said.

I giggled awkwardly for he didn't know there was no shower in my washroom. There was a tap and there was a bucket and that's how you rolled in the Paul household.

'I'm serious! Send me a picture!' he said.

Wow. Why?

'I'm looking really bad right now. There's oil in my hair.'

'Oh! C'mon! You always look great.'

'I don't want to right now. Let me get ready and then I will send you one? I got this really nice silver dress.'

'Okay, fine, let's cut a deal. Send me one without your face in it? That you can do, right?'

'I seriously can't right now,' I said. I didn't want to send it. I don't know why I didn't say that. I should have just said I don't want to rather than I can't. This is, I realized, where all the problems start.

'Fine. Send whenever you like. Bye.'

He cut the call. I sat and stared at the phone. Maybe it wasn't passive aggression and he meant it genuinely. *Without my face?* I started considering it. But how good would that picture be without my eyes, lips, face? Clearly, Vibhor wasn't interested in the same things as Danish.

It took me fifteen attempts to click the picture. The mirror in my house was stained, and no matter what angle I used, the room behind me looked like a disaster. I edited the photo as best as I could and sent it to him. I switched off the phone in embarrassment. The more my phone stayed off, the more I thought he would be laughing at the picture.

Twenty minutes and a hurried bath later, I switched it on to a surprise. There were twenty-three messages from an excited Vibhor, all asking for more pictures (HOTTTTT! SEXY!!! FUCK!! FUCKING SEXY!!!! Etc.), and sixteen missed call alerts.

I'm all dressed up, I texted him. He sent a single smiley and my phone remained barren.

I dressed up, put on my make-up, clicked a picture and sent it to Namrata who told me she was reconsidering her sexuality seeing me in the dress that supposedly fitted me like dream. I told her how Danish had helped me pick it.

'He's a man,' she said. 'He knows things.'

She told me Norbu and she might try out a few things after the party and were staying the night with me and the rest of the guest list. I talked to her mother and pleaded to let her come over and help me understand calculus.

'You're the best, I am blowing a thousand kisses at you,' she said.

'So are you going to return his favour?'

'What favour? Oh? That! Actually, I want to go all the way today. I feel like it.'

'Are you ready?' I asked, nervous as if it was me. But with best friends I guess sex does become a group activity in a totally non-perverse way.

'Yes, I am. I'm going to lose my virginity today to Norbu! He will be the guy to get it. At least, the date is going to be easy to remember, right?'

She said she had to go and that she will see me tonight and cut the call.

I kind of hated how Namrata used that word—lose; I had been guilty of using it as well. What's there to be lose? Sex should be an experience, and experiences are gained. And why lose? There's nothing to be lost here. Nonsense! I decided to not use 'lose' from then on.

That's when my brother walked in, just in time to not see me click myself in a provocative pose. He smiled. He smiled?

'Happy Birthday, again,' he said.

'Thanks.'

What I really wanted to do was cry, and lunge at him, and spend the rest of the evening hugging him and talking to him and catching up on all the years we had lost. Instead, I walked out of the room to show my dress to my mother.

'How do I look?'

'Isn't it too short?' said my mother. I frowned and she hugged me. 'I was joking, baba. You look great, so beautiful.' Her voice quivered. 'Happy birthday, Aisha.' She was about to cry now. 'You're so beautiful.'

Mothers. No matter how broken or fucked up, we are beautiful enough to make them cry.

'Come with me, Maa,' I said and kissed her on the forehead.

'Shut up, Aisha. It's a young people's party. What would I do? You and your brother have fun. He has been planning it for so many days now. Please go. And call me from whichever friend's house you will put up at, okay? And make sure you take Namrata along, okay?'

'I don't want to go,' I said and didn't leave my mother who tried prying herself out of my death-claw hug. 'I want to be with you.'

'Be with your brother. He's acting strange these days. Don't you think?'

'When does he not?' Maa frowned at me. 'Okay, I will.'

'And call me every half an hour.'

'Okay, Maa.'

My brother walked in wearing a white shirt, blue jeans, nicely shined shoes, and he had even bothered to shave. He must be attractive to girls his age. I wondered if it's a family curse. Not being able to find someone to date. I made a mental note to try and set him up tonight with someone.

This note was amongst the other notes I made in my head: Have my first kiss. Yes, today was the day I was going to *lose(?)* my kissing-virginity, if that's a thing. That didn't sound right, so I decided to use the word *share*. I was going to be the kind of woman who shares things like kissing and virginity. We should all share our virginities with guys, not lose it to them. Losing means it's coveted, like it's valuable, and can be wrested away for some kind of good. *Share* felt more right— like we are being benevolent with our virginities and allowing ourselves to experience some of our awesomeness.

I already felt better about my birthday.

30

Danish Roy

I walked into the party, head bowed, hoping no one would notice, walked straight to the bar and ordered a large vodka and Red Bull. The students looked at me, pushed their drinks away from them, and quietened for a bit before they realized I was harmless and went about their ways. Aisha wasn't there yet. I was hoping to make it a swift in and out, like a wedding, stand in the line, hand over the gift, shake hands and move out. I kept refreshing my Twitter and Instagram timeline and looked busy for the students who never looked at me once as I ordered more drinks.

A little later, everyone shouted and cheered as Aisha walked in, looking like she always did, in the dress we had picked out earlier. Vibhor walked next to her, his arms around her waist, and I heard the girls go, 'Aw, they look so good together.' They did look like they had just walked out of a glamour glossy. They ushered her towards the three-tiered pink cake with little baked versions of Louis Vuitton and Gucci bags.

'I didn't know she was into bags,' I heard a boy say behind me. Next to the boy was a girl I recognized from before. I was still squinting while looking at her when she looked straight at me and smiled. She spoke, 'Namrata!'

'Oh right, of course I remember you. And yes, she is not interested in bags,' I said. 'What did you get her?' I pointed to the gift she carried in her hand, nicely wrapped in a newspaper and a red ribbon.

'It's a book,' the boy said who now I recognized as Norbu. 'It's our favourite book.' He looked at Namrata who blushed. '*Book Thief* by Marcus Zusack. We are sure she will like it.'

Before I could laud their choice and tell them how much she would love the book, she started cutting the cake and people sang the birthday song. For people who weren't even friends with her, they were awfully happy on her birthday. I walked back to the bar while about a hundred people made her take a bite off their pieces of cake. Vibhor stood right by her, smiling for pictures, cracking jokes everyone laughed at, and being the charmer he was always known to be.

'What happened?' I asked Norbu who walked up to the bar with the demeanour of an alcoholic and ordered two Red Bulls. He looked shattered.

'He gifted her pumps from Todds, a clutch from Chanel, and shades from Gucci. On that table lies his gifts worth over 1 lakh rupees, and next to it lies our book. Three fifty rupees.'

Namrata stared at her glass of Red Bull as if trying to drown out years of sorrow and pain.

'If it means anything, it's not his money, it's his father's.'

'Still,' said Namrata. 'What did you get her?'

'I forgot to get her anything. I didn't think people still gave each other presents.'

'What fun would that birthday be?' Norbu said, throwing back the Red Bull down his throat. I didn't tell them I had bought the exact same book as they had and it was lying in the dustbin behind the bar counter. I knew I should have got her the Kindle. I could have slyly downloaded *Lolita* on it, the love story of an old pervert and a young girl.

That's when I heard the sound of clacking heels rushing towards me, and I turned to see Aisha with her arms outstretched. I got up and hugged her, and wished her, 'Happy Birthday!'

'Did you watch me cut the cake?'

'I was here the whole time,' I said.

Vibhor joined us. I shook Vibhor's hand and he smiled widely at me. 'Great party, nicely done,' I said.

'Anything for her,' he replied and almost scooped her off the floor with one arm and kissed her on the cheek. 'Though she's not drinking tonight. I have tried but she's too stuck up!'

'Let her not if she doesn't want to,' I said.

'It's her birthday!' he protested playfully, and before I knew it, there were twenty kids near the bar shouting '*Drink*' '*Drink*' '*Drink*' '*Drink*' at us.

'*Fine, fine*!' she said. 'If Danish gives me the permission, I will.'

People looked at me like I was the party pooper, the old boring teacher. I stuck my ground for what seemed like a million years.

'Fine,' I conceded. 'One drink of my choosing.' I chose a Daiquiri. Light. Almost non-alcoholic, with a huge piece of lemon dipped in it.

'*Bottoms up! Bottoms up!*' shouted the kids and she did so and scrunched up her face. And they cheered and got back to their dancing. I don't understand this evangelistic zeal of people who trick or force people into tasting alcohol or chicken or whatever they have chosen not to eat or drink.

'Come, dance!' said Aisha and started to drag Namrata, Norbu and me towards the dance floor.

'I need to smoke,' I lied. 'I will just be back. No. No. Of course I will come back and dance. How can I not?'

And I left the dance floor so that I would not embarrass myself any further. I could have left for home but I wanted to stay, to look at her over and over again, to talk to her, and it was strange because she would come to school the next day anyway. Outside, I found Sarthak sitting on the pavement, a lit cigarette dangling from his fingers, scrolling through his phone.

'Nice party,' I said, and sat next to him.

He apologized to me again.

'We have put that behind us. Although I do think my nose is permanently damaged.'

He passed the lighter to me and we smoked in silence.

'Vibhor is a nice guy,' I said.

He nodded. 'She's lucky,' he said. 'And so is he. I'm so happy they hit it off. He will take care of her.'

'You seem to have a lot of trust in him. Old friend?'

'No. But he's the only one who knows,' said Sarthak.

'Knows what?'

'Nothing.'

'You can tell me, you know that. The student–teacher confidentiality thing. I don't want to lose my job, remember?' I said.

He stayed shut. Troubled, but shut. 'Okay, let's make a deal. I will tell you something about myself and then you can tell me something about you.'

He shrugged, smiled pitifully, and put out his cigarette. 'Why are you doing this?' he asked.

'Doing what?'

'Fixing us.'

'That's my job,' I said, reflexively.

'Fine, tell me yours, sir.'

'Fine,' I said and rummaged my mind for an embarrassing aspect to share. 'I'm quite a bit of a failure. My brother is a start-up genius and I'm pond scum. My parents are sort of ashamed of me. I'm the black sheep, the prodigal son, the wastrel of the family who will still inherit their property and live off it.'

'Hmmm.'

'Your turn.'

He laughed.

'So? So what? That's not something to hide,' he snapped angrily as if I had cheated him.

He tried lighting his second but his fingers trembled and he dropped it. He stomped it and shouted, 'Fuck!' His face was flushed and he took deep breaths to calm himself down. I gave him my cigarette and he pulled a long drag.

'It's okay,' I said. 'You don't have to tell me. Take care, okay?'

I got up to go inside.

'I'm gay.'

I turned.

He looked me dead in the eye and said, 'I'm gay.'

'Not to stereotype, but from now on you're going to pick my clothes,' I said and turned again towards the door of the club.

'That's all you have to say?'

'What's there to say? You're gay, and that can only be a good thing. There are only 940 girls for every 1000 men. More men should be gay. India would be a lot safer for women,' I said and went inside.

I walked to the dance floor, to see Aisha kiss Vibhor, amidst a group full of cheering youngsters, shouting *'Kiss' 'Kiss' 'Kiss'*. They separated from the kiss and she saw me standing at the doorway. She smiled and raised her cocktail glass at me. She motioned for me to join her at the dance floor. I pointed at my watch and mouthed, 'I have to leave.' She frowned and then smiled and I left the party, leaving a drunk, happy Aisha behind.

*

Research shows that people were in general happier in the 1930s and the 40s than they are now and for good reason.

There was no Instagram or Facebook or Twitter to keep you updated on how other people's lives are so much better than yours. Last night, Instagram and Facebook wrecked my life and left me suicidal. I had left the party to ensure I didn't have to see Aisha and Vibhor rub their perfectness in my face, but I hadn't accounted for Instagram and my penchant for hurting myself. I was still there at the party. I wasn't missing anything because I kept getting constant updates, and I refused to log out and sleep.

They had left the club and gone to Vibhor's house. There was a picture in the car, and one outside the house. They were playing Truth or Dare. There was a blurred picture of the spinning bottle. And here, she was wrapping herself around Vibhor like a little puppy. The updates stopped at 3 a.m. and I slept at 7 a.m. after I was done imagining what would have happened afterwards.

'Crazy night, haan?' Ankit asked me at the breakfast table. I intended to take my cornflakes back to bed and watch TV and cleanse myself of the images of Aisha with another boy.

'Feeling better? Did you drink a lot?' Maa asked and kept a tall glass of lemonade in front of me. She ran her hands through my hair and kissed me.

'No, Maa. Just one beer.'

'We have been hearing good things about you from the principal.'

'Yes, it's cool there,' I said.

'But you're not going to go from tomorrow,' Ankit said, brightly. 'You're coming with me.'

'What? Where?'

'We are expanding. We have started hiring people for the HR department now and you're going to be a part of it,' he said and punched my arm.

'But—'

'What but? You're coming and that's final.'

'And you're telling me like this?'

'What? You want an appointment letter or something?' he asked and laughed. 'No questions, man. You're coming with me. You can choose a fancy designation as well.'

'I will think about it.'

'Maa? Look at him.'

Maa said, 'Just go naa, baba. It will be good for you.'

My mother looked happy with this new opportunity so I nodded. Maybe it wasn't such a bad thing. It wasn't going to be easy to be in the school with Aisha and Vibhor around.

'I will call the principal. They will have a month's notice period.'

Ankit hugged me and my mother smiled. Maybe I wasn't going to be a failure after all.

31

Aisha Paul

I woke up hurting. My head hurt, my body hurt, my legs hurt and I felt dehydrated and sick.

I got up from the bed, pulled up my pants which were bunched up near my ankles, wore my T-shirt, which lay crumpled near the bedpost, stumbled and fell on the floor. My head spun and I felt like I was dying. My stomach retched and I vomited all over the carpet. Carpet? My room didn't have a carpet. I vomited again and staggered and propped myself up against the bedpost. I dragged myself to the washroom, washed my face, and then vomited a little more in the pot. For the next hour, I sat next to the pot, dozing off and vomiting. I called out but no one came.

After about another half an hour of dozing off and vomiting, I heard the door click open.

'Shit!' said Namrata and ran to my side. 'Are you okay?'

I nodded. So I was at Namrata's place. It looked a little different, a little richer. She helped me up, grabbed me from behind, walked me towards the bed and sat me down. Norbu watched silently, unsure of how he could help.

'You drank a little too much,' said Norbu.

'Please don't talk. My head hurts.'

Norbu and Namrata brought me soup and juice, nursed me to health for the next hour and I felt a little better. No one talked for while. I liked the silence.

They told me we were at Vibhor's house. They were surprised I didn't remember anything.

I wanted to sleep a little but every time I closed my eyes, the world spun and I would start feeling nauseous again.

Norbu charged my phone and I called my mother and told her I was fine, just a little tired, nothing to worry about. She told me she was worried sick because I hadn't called after I reached Vibhor's house. 'Namrata called me to say you had fallen asleep and that she was with you,' she said. Sarthak had gone back home since he had an assignment to complete and submit the next day.

A little later, the door flung open and Vibhor walked in. 'There you are,' he said. He walked to up to where I sat, took my face in his hands and kissed my cheek. 'You look beautiful,' he said. I flinched a little. 'Now, all of you, come down. My mother has made breakfast and she's waiting downstairs.'

'How did we get here?' I asked.

'You seriously don't remember?' asked Norbu. 'We drove here from the party? Played Truth or Dare? You passed out?'

I shrugged. Vibhor laughed. 'You seriously don't? Man, now that's a blackout. Now come down, everyone is waiting.'

'I need to take a shower,' I said.

'Okay, then. The towels are on the racks,' said Vibhor, wrapped his arms around me and kissed me on my lips. They felt raw and chapped.

I stood beneath the shower for quite some time, trying to wash away the alcohol and the cigarette smell from my body. I felt a little different. My body ached and there's was a little bruise on my inner thigh. I felt a little burning sensation in my vagina but I didn't think too much about it. *Too much alcohol*, I thought and tried smiling it away.

I washed my face in the mirror. I found my handbag lying upturned on the bed, fixed my hair and my face quickly and walked out smiling and pretending my body was not broken into pieces. Vibhor welcomed me at the table and made me sit right next to him. There were three other people apart from

Namrata and Norbu who sat at the table with us, all of whom were at the party last night, and they smiled at me and wished me good morning.

'I hope all of you had a good night's sleep,' said a voice from behind me. 'Did you sleep well?' I turned to see Vibhor's mother addressing the question directly to me. 'They told me you vomited a little.'

She had a kind face and she touched my face in a way she wouldn't touch any other girl's face on the table. It was clear she knew about Vibhor and me.

She addressed me and then the rest, 'I hope all of you like *aloo puri*.'

Then, she instructed the maid to ask us if we needed milk or juice or tea. Just then, a man appeared at the door in front of us, dressed in an expensive-looking suit, threw us a cursory look, walked right past us, then sat on the sofa in the living room and opened the newspaper. Vibhor's mother brought his briefcase and his cell phone, and he left the house soon after.

The food was served and everyone ate quietly, battling their own hangovers.

'Quite some night, *haan*,' said Vibhor as he leaned on to me. He shoved his phone into my face as he scrolled down pictures from Instagram.

'When were these clicked?'

'You don't remember? It was so much fun. You were a riot,' he said and showed me more pictures. They were all clicked at his house. I was told the party moved from the club to his house where we drank some more. 'We played Truth or Dare and you killed it. Of course, I just wanted to kiss you more and hence we played it.' He winked.

The others who were listening in giggled. I had no memory of any of this so I took the phone and swiped through the rest of the pictures. In most of them, I was clinging on to Vibhor for dear life. There were a few pictures in which my tongue was buried deep inside his mouth. I cringed. It wasn't how I had imagined my kisses would look like.

'So I passed out?' I asked, pointing to the last few pictures. The others were still drinking, posing, while I seemed to be sleeping on the couch, mouth open, drooling all over my dress.

'You were shit-housed!' said a boy at the table. I nodded, embarrassed. The others giggled some more.

'Now, stop embarrassing her,' ordered Vibhor. He put his arm around me and kissed me thrice on my cheek.

I finished my breakfast, bathing in embarrassment and left to wash my hands and the shame away. *You shouldn't have got so drunk,* I told myself.

'So? How was it?' A voice said from behind. I turned to see Namrata and a girl I didn't recognize stare at me.

'How was what?'

'Oh c'mon! We know!' they said.

'You beat me to it! So stop acting and tell me everything,' said Namrata.

'Tell you what?'

'Fine,' the other girl said. 'I will go if I'm the problem. I will ask Vibhor.' The girl washed her hands and left.

'What was she talking about?'

'Oh, shut up and tell us. Vibhor has already told us!' She held my hand. Her face had lit up like Christmas. 'You did it last night, right? Lost your virginity? How was it?'

'I . . . I . . .'

'What?'

'I don't remember, Namrata.'

'Oh, shut up. How can you forget that?' she asked.

'But . . .'

'Stop acting, now.' She rolled her eyes. 'If you don't want to tell, it's fine. I just thought we weren't hiding anything from each other.'

I stood there trying to recall the last night. I had no memory of leaving the club, or coming to Vibhor's house, or playing Truth or Dare, no memory of posing for those pictures or kissing him, or having sex with him . . .

'But I had passed out, Namrata,' I said. 'You saw the pictures.'

'Yes, you had and Vibhor put you to bed. But you must have woken up and felt horny?' said Namrata, winking and nudging me.

'I *didn't* wake up!'

'Maybe you did.'

The tears came and so did the shame.

'Nothing happened, Namrata.'

'Then why is he saying that it did.'

'I don't know why!'

I ran to the stall and locked myself in. I buried my head in my knees and cried while Namrata stood outside and kept calling out my name.

'Aisha?'

'. . .'

'Aisha?'

'. . .'

'Are you okay? Are you okay, Aisha?' she said. 'Talk to me. Talk to me.' She kept knocking at the door. I kept hitting my head against my knees hoping it would all come back to me.

'What . . . did he tell people?'

'Ummm . . . that you guys did it,' said Namrata.

'But I didn't.'

'Aisha?'

'. . .'

'Aisha?'

'. . .'

'Stop crying? Listen to me?'

'Yes?'

'You were wearing your T-shirt inside out today.'

'But I didn't take it off—'

No. No. No.

And then I remembered. When I woke up this morning, my pants were bunched up around my ankles and my T-shirt was lying upturned near the bedpost.

'Aisha? Did you take off your T-shirt yourself?'

'. . .'

'Did you?'

I mustered up the courage to say the words, 'I have been raped, Namrata. I have been raped by my boyfriend.'

'Aisha?'

'. . .'

32

Danish Roy

The meeting with the principal was brief. He wished me luck and hoped I could stay for a little bit longer. The board exams were nearing and the students could really use some help, he told me. It felt good to be wanted. I told him it was a great experience and he could still send students to me if they needed help though I knew he would hire the next person available.

Back in the room, I dreaded seeing Aisha again. The first two students came to me worrying about their class ten results. They cried, and I told them stories about people who had made it without excelling in stupid standardized tests, and they stopped crying and talked about issuing the biographies of those people. I offered to talk to their parents and they took down my number.

Once calm, one of them updated me on the latest rumours. Usually I would ask them to shut up but today they talked about how the entire school was abuzz with Aisha and Vibhor *totally doing it* in his house.

'Are you sure about it?'

'Yeah, of course. Everyone knows that,' said the kid brightly.

When he talked about the rumour, it felt like someone had ripped out my heart with a butter knife. On a scale of ten, if the hurt from her falling in love with Vibhor was a ten, her sleeping with him, right now, was Taylor Swift. I felt petty and small for thinking the way I did and forced myself to be happy for her. Easier said than done.

That day I decided to eat my lunch at the cafeteria instead and hoped to bump into Vibhor and Aisha. The heart gets what the heart wants. If it wanted more pain who was I to deny it that?

The cafeteria fell silent for a few brief seconds as I took a seat at the corner table. I pretended to read a book on my Kindle while I stole glances at the table Aisha and Vibhor sat on. Namrata and Norbu were there too, and they were laughing all too loudly, and so was Aisha. She caught me staring a few times and walked up to me, smiling.

'Hi,' she said.

'Nice party that day. I wanted to stay—'

'Why did you leave early?' she asked. Before I could answer she said, 'You shouldn't have.'

She wasn't smiling any more. Why was she angry with me? I wasn't the one who was putting up snuggly Instagram pictures.

'I'm sure you had fun,' I said in a tone befitting a friend, and not a jealous boyfriend.

She shrugged as if she didn't. Who was she kidding? Of course she had fun.

'You shouldn't have left,' she said again.

Her eyes were on me but were some place else.

'Maybe I will stay for longer the next time and play Truth or Dare with you guys. That seemed like fun.'

'Who told you about that?'

'I saw the pictures. _Everyone_ has seen the pictures,' I snapped.

'Glad you have,' she said dryly. 'I don't need you any more.'

'Excuse me?'

'You heard me.'

'What's this about, Aisha?'

'I have talked to the principal, Danish. He said I was well enough to stop going to your sessions.'

'Why would you do that?'

'How does it matter? You're leaving the school anyway. I thought you would tell me before anyone else,' she said.

'I would have told you today.'

'Anyway, it doesn't matter. Nothing you said matters.'

'Is something wrong?' I asked.

'Yes, I was wrong. What you told me, taught me? Everything was wrong,' she said, her voice steeling up. 'I was foolish to listen to you. You encouraged me and look what happened.'

'What are you saying?' I stood up and reached out but she jerked back.

'STAY. AWAY.' she shouted. A few students looked at us. She lowered her voice and said, 'What did you tell me? To be my own person? To do what I want to do? Experience everything? That's not what a girl does.'

'Of course that's what a girl—'

'Shut the fuck up, Danish.'

'Excuse—'

'You were wrong. I should have never listened to you. Who are you after all? A failed psych major. You know nothing about anything.'

'Can you just tell me what happened?'

'Life happened, Danish.'

She bolted and left the canteen.

33

Aisha Paul

I was sitting in a bathroom stall crying for what I believed was a couple of hours because I heard the bell ring. I had just shouted at Danish in the canteen for *no* apparent reason, for something that w*asn't even true*, something that I was *overthinking* and *wasn't much of a big deal*.

But if all of it were true, why did I want to slit my wrists and die?

I woke up today morning feeling the simultaneous need to shower, vomit, and to stay in my bed and never get out. I told my mother I was sick and would not go to school but of course she insisted that I go and got my breakfast to bed. Since the last two days I hadn't been able to keep food down. My body rejected everything. I threw the paranthas out of the window as soon as my mother left the room. For the longest I thought it was a side effect of the iPill Namrata had made me swallow the day after but it wasn't. Why did my mother let me go to that party? Why? I should have just stayed home and nothing would have happened.

'Aren't you going to get ready?' asked Sarthak when he saw me in bed this morning. 'You will miss the bus.' None of this would have happened had Sarthak not planned the party. 'And why aren't you picking up Vibhor's calls? He called me twice today. He told me to tell you he misses you.'

Why was Sarthak still talking? Why was he talking? Why did he have to leave for home that night? How was his assignment more important than me?

'Call him, okay?'

The mention of Vibhor's name made me gag. I got up, washed and scrubbed myself till my skin turned red and burned. The mirror fogged up and I was glad not to see myself in the mirror.

I dodged the glances of my curious school mates who by now had heard of me losing my virginity to Vibhor on my birthday, reached my class, and settled at the last seat. Yes, I lost my virginity. I didn't share it. I didn't experience it. I lost it. It was snatched away from me.

Namrata entered the class a little after me with Norbu walking close by. My eyes met Norbu's and he looked away, probably in shame. Yesterday, he had texted me to enquire if I was fine and I knew it was a courtesy text. I didn't blame him. What was he to do? He probably didn't believe me anyway. Even if he did, he wouldn't have known what to say or how to behave.

Namrata came and sat next to me. Other boys in the class looked at me and smirked, almost as if me having had sex with one boy meant they had a shot too. Maybe they did? What stops them from having sex with me right now? Vibhor never asked. It wouldn't be any different. I felt their eyes on my skin like little crawling spiders. I could barely keep from crying.

'Are you okay?' asked Namrata. I shook my head. 'Do you remember anything?' I shook my head. 'We all drank from the same bottle. I'm sure there was no sedative. Are you sure something happened?' I nodded and showed her the text Vibhor sent me.

VIBHOR: Last night was great, we should do it again sometime. You took an iPill no?

My stomach retched. 'Are you sure you didn't want to do it?' asked Namrata. 'You really liked him, Aisha. And you were kissing him all the time.' I had nothing to say. 'Are you sure you're not overthinking this? Are you sure it's a big deal? You don't even remember it. Can't you try to forget it?' asked Namrata. She rubbed my hands trying to calm me down. 'Can't you get past it?'

'No.'

'He was your boyfriend. And he really likes you. Doesn't that matter? He still dotes on you.'

'But I didn't want him to do it—'

'But it had to happen, didn't it? Some day or the other?' asked Namrata. 'Are you sure you're not saying this because you don't want people to think you willingly had sex with him?'

'What—'

'I'm just saying.'

'What are you saying, Namrata? Please tell me, what the hell are you saying?'

'I am just—'

That was it.

I ran from the classroom, through the corridors, bumped and crashed into people, away from her and from everyone else, and didn't stop till I reached the roof of my school building. I walked towards the edge of the roof and looked down; my head spun. I knew I wouldn't jump. I slumped on the ground and the tears came all at once.

My best friend was supporting Vibhor, asking me to get past it, telling me that it had to happen some day. He had raped me. Hadn't he? Did he not? Was she right? Could it be even called rape? It had to happen some day? He likes me? He was my boyfriend? He still doted on me? Namrata was an intelligent woman, way more intelligent than I am, so could it be that she was right? Maybe the decision was his to take? But why did I feel powerless? Betrayed? Or this was how it was supposed to be? My phone rang. *Vibhor calling.* I switched it off. I stared at the phone, scared, as if he wielded the power to hurt me even through the phone.

'There you are!'

I turned. A cold shiver ran down my spine as I watched Vibhor walk towards me, smiling. I wanted to tell him to walk away from me but lost my voice. He came near, and with one swoop, he took me in his arms and nuzzled his nose against my neck and told me I smelled great.

'Where have you been?' he asked, putting me down. 'I got something for you.' He rummaged through his pockets, took out a few old parking receipts and threw them away, and then found a little Swarovski pendant. 'This is for you. To celebrate you know . . . *that.*'

We were alone. Was this why he was there? I felt like running. I felt like jumping off the terrace. Would he try doing it again? He held me tighter. Words dried in my throat and I felt my body go limp. What if I screamed? What would I tell people? He came to my room when I was asleep and had sex with me without my consent? He raped me. Who would believe that? I was the school slut for everyone anyway. And those Instagram pictures? The pictures at the party? I was the loose cannon and Vibhor was the nice boyfriend who had gifted me things.

Namrata's words rang clear in my head. *It had to happen some day. It had to happen some day. It had to happen someday. It had to happen some day. You were kissing him all the time. It had to happen some day. It had to happen some day. You were kissing him all the time. It had to happen some day.*

I didn't fight back. He held my hand and we walked to the canteen together, hand in hand, like lovers. He smiled at his friends and they smiled back at him and at me. I felt the sickness take over my entire body. I was afraid, but most of all I felt alone.

People looked at us in the canteen with envy. We were the IT couple, the couple other couples would choose to emulate, we were in love, we had had sex, we were happy and smiling, but I was so alone, so fucking alone.

As I sat in the canteen, I decided I was done trying to find the woman I wanted to be. It was all a lie. All that Danish told me about experiences, about learning through mistakes, about forgiveness, about truth, about being your own person, about trusting people, everything we read together in the books, everything we talked about in those countless counselling sessions was a big fat lie to make me feel better about myself. Women can't make mistakes. One false step and you're done. No second chances. I had made my chance when I decide to drink at that party and now everything is ruined.

I was raped and it was my fault. I was raped and it was my fault. I was raped and it was my fault. I was raped and it was my fault. I was raped and it was my fault. I was raped and it was my fault.

I had no reason to cry foul. It was my mistake.

34

Danish Roy

That's why the Internet is a good place, a safe place, and no one's disappointed or rejected on the Internet if you just manage to lie right.

Right now, Mohini, a girl I found on Tinder was sitting next to me after she sat through a boring movie with one expression, and told me categorically that she thought video games were for children. She was training to be a doctor, and had had five boyfriends (though none for the past one year), read a lot of books, so she wasn't to blame for why we got bored that day. It was probably me. It was mostly. Fine. It was me.

'I'm sorry,' I said. 'This date isn't what you expected, is it?'

'You come to expect these things when you go out with faces and not people,' she said, referring to Tinder.

'Do you do this a lot? Try to find love like this?'

'It's pathetic and desperate, isn't it?'

We kind of felt bad for ourselves, and then giggled and then laughed. This was the first moment of our date which wasn't excruciating, and things turned for the better after that. Suddenly, nothing was at stake. We didn't try to impress each other by being funny, or knowledgeable, or ambitious, or fun any more. We admitted being different and that's when we could finally talk and get to know each other better. She told me how much of an asshole her ex-boyfriend was, and I told her about Aisha.

'So you really love her?'

'I think it's the closest I will ever get to love,' I said.

'Are you crying?'

'Me? No. Maybe a little bit. On the inside.'

'That's sweet.'

'I miss her so much, like there is an empty cavity inside my ribs, funny as it may sound, it is painful and it's embarrassing.'

'She must be perfect,' the girl said, her eyes lighting up.

'She is full of beautiful little flaws. And she gets excited whenever she discovers one. It's so cute and noble and amazing.'

'Not flirting because that hasn't clearly worked for our date today, but you look amazeballs when you talk about her,' she said.

'Well, she's someone else's now,' I said and shook my head.

'Never mind, at least you felt love and that's a rare thing,' she said and held my hand.

'Have you felt love?'

'Maybe, maybe not. I'm not sure. I will keep you posted though.'

We laughed. The rest of the date wasn't half as bad. We talked about her college, her proud parents, her nosey relatives, and I told her about my brilliant brother, my sceptical parents, and we had a nice time. She dropped me home and we promised to keep in touch.

The next day at school, I heard rumours floating around in the school like harmless dandelions. I walked slowly through the corridors, spent more time at the urinals eavesdropping on students talking about her.

'*Such a slut.*'

'*She begged him to let her give him a blowjob.*'

'*Did you see the pictures? She would have fucked an electric pole.*'

'She hit on me as well.'

'She's an actual whore.'

'She's fucking lying. She must have slept with someone else as well.'

'She's not hot enough to be . . . you know what.'

'How's that even possible? She must have been turned on for him to push it inside.'

'She deserves it. Look how drunk and slutty she got.'

After a point, I knew I had to stop or someone would have had their skull crushed. I decided to get to the bottom of this. I looked around for Aisha but she hadn't come to school that day. Neither had Namrata. I got hold of Norbu who was nestled in the far corner of the library.

'What the hell is going on? What are these rumours about? And where's Aisha?'

He looked up. His left eye was bruised and his lower lip was cut and crusted with blood. The top three buttons of his shirt were ripped and the shirt pocket with the logo had been torn off. He started to cry a little.

'Come outside,' I said, held his hand and led him outside. He sat on the stairs and adjusted his shirt. 'What happened to your eye?'

'I didn't mean to—'

He broke down in little sobs.

'Who hit you?'

'I can't tell you.'

'You will. Or I will find out.'

'The guys in the football team.'

'Why?'

'For what I said about Aisha and Vibhor.'

'Please tell me you had nothing to do with all the nonsense that I have been hearing about Aisha.'

He stared at his shoes.

'Norbu? What did you do?' I banged my fist on the table. He cowered. I counted till ten and calmed myself down. 'Fine, tell me and we will fix it.'

'I told someone what Namrata told me,' he said.

'What did she tell you?'

'Aisha claims she had been raped that night, that she was—'

'Wait? What? What are you saying?'

'I'm just telling you what Namrata told me!' he said, covering his face with both his hands. Norbu told me that Aisha had lost (what Aisha would call 'shared') her virginity in her sleep and hadn't consented to it. She had no memory of it.

'Are you sure that's what she told Namrata? That she was raped?' I asked.

She had no reason to lie. Namrata was her friend, her only friend, and she would never lie to her.

'I'm sorry,' said Norbu.

'You did no wrong. You can leave now.'

'But sir—'

'JUST. FUCKING. LEAVE.'

'They . . . they will hit me again,' said Norbu, clutching to his seat. 'Please don't tell anyone.'

'I'm sorry for shouting. I won't tell anyone. Where is Namrata?'

'She's not talking to me since I—'

'It's fine,' I said. 'I will talk to her. No one's going to hit you again. I will make sure of that. Does anyone else know? Has she told her parents yet?'

'No.'

I wrote Norbu a sick note and he was allowed to go home early that day. I felt sick myself and threw up thrice. How the fuck did it happen? Why didn't she tell me anything?

I called Aisha but her phone was switched off. Sarthak was visiting his father and was unreachable. I saw Vibhor later in the school and he seemed normal, even happy, so I asked the peon to get him to my room.

'Sit, Vibhor,' I said to him when he appeared at my door. He sat and leaned back on his chair. 'Is there something you want to tell me?' God knows what it took for me to restrain myself.

'What?'

'The rumours. Is there any truth in them?'

He laughed uncouthly. 'Of course not, sir. I expected better out of you. She's just acting out. You know she's a little crazy, right? Things are fine between us.'

'She hasn't come to school for a couple of days.'

'I know. But that's because Sarthak is out of town and her mother's not well.'

'Are you sure there isn't anything else? Because if there is—'

'Of course, I'm sure. Can I go now? Because the more time I spend inside this room the more people will think I'm a nut job. No offence.'

'Okay, leave.'

He got up to leave. 'And sir, it's a personal skirmish between her and me. It's better if you don't make it into a big thing.'

'Listen, you asshole. If I find even a sliver of truth in this, I will thrust my hand into your mouth and rip you in half.'

'Whoa. Sir. Chill. Nothing happened.'

'For your best interest, I hope so.'

He smiled like he didn't give a fuck, and left whistling.

35

Aisha Paul

I ran a fever for three days. I had switched off my phone.
Sarthak wasn't around so I curled up in bed with my mother's
arms around me and cried all day. I felt guilty. What would
my mother think when I tell her this? My father? They
would die knowing I exposed myself to such a risk. They
had placed their trust in me and I had betrayed it by getting
drunk and allowing this to happen. It was a lesson, and I
deserved it.

The bell rang. 'Let me get that,' my mother said. I clutched
her tighter. 'I have to, baba.'

She tucked me in and kissed me and left to get the door.
Minutes later, I heard a few voices from the living room and
then the shuffling of feet.

'Look who's here!' exclaimed my mother, her arm
interlocked around Vibhor's. He was smiling, and in my
house, in my room with my mother by his side.

'Beta, she's been sick for three days. Sit, sit, I will get
something for you to eat.' My mother left me with him in
the room.

He came and sat next to me and he wasn't smiling any
more. I pulled the blanket over myself. He held my hand
softly, like the nice boyfriend he was, and kissed it softly. I
jerked my hand back and it was wet with his saliva. I rubbed
it on my bedsheet and tucked my hands beneath my thighs.

'I missed you so much,' he said. 'A strange thing happened
today in school.'

'What?'

'Norbu told a few people that you were sleeping when we had sex,' he said as a matter of fact. 'Why would you say that to him?'

'I didn't—'

'Of course, you didn't,' his voice down to a murmur. 'He told me you said that to Namrata.'

'I was just—'

'We had a little fight, Norbu and me. I know you said it because he took the beating.'

I gasped.

'All I want to understand is why you said it.' His eyebrows burrowed. He got up and paced around, scratching his forehead.

I stared at the wall behind him.

'TELL ME.'

'I was sleeping . . . I didn't know you—'

'SO WHAT?' he shouted and punched the wall. 'You wanted it as well. You know that!'

'Vibhor, I'm sorry.'

'You are sorry? YOU FUCKING GOT DRUNK THAT DAY! IT WAS YOUR IDEA TO STAY OUT! YOU KISSED ME AT MY PLACE! And you accuse me of rape—' he yelled. 'Are you out of your fucking mind? Do you know what people would think of me? That fucking teacher of yours called me into his room like I was a goddamn mental person. He fucking threatened me.'

'I'm sorry, Vibhor. I just told her I was sleeping.'

'THEN WHY IS THE WORD RAPE HANGING IN THE FUCKING AIR. What do think others will think about me, huh?'

'I just—'

'You didn't say anything the next morning. You sat at the dining table with my mother and you were smiling. You were smiling and holding my hand, damn it.'

'But you didn't ask me before—'

'Ask you? You were piss drunk, Aisha.' He unbuttoned his first button. 'This! You gave me this before you passed out!' He pointed to a love bite a little below his collar bone. I was crying now. And so was he.

'Vibhor?'

He spoke again, his face was flushed red, 'I should have known better. I should have listened to the others. Everyone called you a slut and yet I dated you. It was a damn MISTAKE!'

'I'm sorry,' I mumbled.

'Sorry? You're sorry?' he said and came close to me. 'I'm sorry to have not known that you're a bitch! Not that anyone would ever believe you, but I can't have people looking at me strangely.'

He held my hand and squeezed it till it hurt. 'You're going to come to school and tell everyone it's a sick joke, okay? Or I'm going to the principal tomorrow!'

'But—'

'Tomorrow! And I will show all the pictures to him of me and you and all your friends drinking! They will all tell the principal you were drunk out of your mind and were all over me,' he said, angry and teared up.

'But—'

'TOMORROW!' he shouted.

My mother walked in with a tray with two glasses of Coke and steaming pakodas and placed it on the bedside table.

'Thank you, Aunty, but I need to go,' he said. He bent and touched my mother's feet, waved at me and left the room. My mother left after him to close the door, asking him to stay a little longer.

'But I was sleeping and you didn't ask. That's rape,' I finally mumbled as I heard the door slam close. It sounded ridiculous. Obviously, he was right. I was asking for it. How would he know I didn't?

I didn't even say no.

I had to go to school the next day and apologize for the ugly rumour I had spread. It was all my fault. I called Namrata that night and told her about the lie, and she screamed at me because it was my fault Norbu got beaten up and called me the worst friend ever. She cut the line. But she texted me seconds later.

NAMRATA: I'm sorry. You're lying now. I just thought about Norbu and acted out.

AISHA: Let's not talk about it. I will clear it out tomorrow morning.

NAMRATA: Are you sure?

AISHA: Yes.

NAMRATA: I'm sorry.

AISHA: It's not your fault. I would have said the same things. Goodnight.

NAMRATA: Goodnight.

NAMRATA: ?

NAMRATA: ?

NAMRATA: Are you there?

NAMRATA: Pick up my calls?

NAMRATA: Aisha, call?

NAMRATA: Don't scare me? Are you there?

NAMRATA: ??

NAMRATA: ??

NAMRATA: ??

AISHA: I'm okay. Night.

36

Danish Roy

I saw her the next day in school, smiling. She was right there, with Vibhor and his friends who talked like she was trash yesterday, and she was giggling at their jokes like they were Russell Peter's spawn.

I literally saw her cut my call from fifteen feet away. I dropped in a text for her to see me at my office post lunch. Having read all about how to deal with rape survivors, I knew I would never make it in front of her without breaking down but I had to try. It was eating me up inside to think what she must have gone through. It was seventeen hours since I'd slept a wink. How many hours would it have been for her?

Later that day, she walked into my office with Namrata in tow, the same smile pasted on her face.

'Oh, it was just a joke,' she said after the pleasantries were exchanged and I told her why I had called her. 'I told Namrata that it felt like rape because he was that good!'

She seemed extra happy telling me this.

'That's nothing to joke about. It's insensitive and crude. I thought you were better than that,' I said.

'I'm sorry,' she said and laughed inappropriately.

Namrata laughed, too.

'Are you sure there's nothing to worry about?' I asked.

'Unless great sex is a cause for concern!'

'And you will tell me if anything's wrong?'

'You're overreacting, Danish. Can I go now?'

'Yes.'

She didn't feel like the person I knew and was in love with when she laughed almost caricature-ishly. She left the room without a worry in the world. I felt pathetic to have killed myself over someone who was really happy without me.

*

'I checked your search history, Danish,' said Ankit, half-drunk, with Smriti almost dozing off on his shoulder. 'You're in love with her!'

How is he so productive when he's always drunk or with women?

'No, I'm not,' I said. 'I'm just concerned about her.'

'Is that why you keep opening up her pictures? Over and over again? Every day?'

'That's a dick move, Ankit,' I said. 'Let this be the last time you touch my computer.'

He winked and dismissed my anger.

'You can join me as soon as possible if you want to get away from her. It will be a change,' he said, suddenly sober.

'I don't need to get away from her.'

'Can I at least meet her? I need to see the girl who has you wrapped around her little finger.'

'No, you don't.'

'Of course I do. I'm a little jealous I'm not the person you love the most any more.'

'Shut up, man. Don't you have a million to make?'

'Already done that for the day. I had this deal—'

'I wasn't serious.'

'Oh. Is it your sense of humour that drew her towards you?'

'She was never drawn towards me.'

'How's that possible. You're the most dateable twenty-three-year-old ever.'

'Is it your sense of humour why Smriti is drunk and in your arms?'

'Repartee? I like that. Okay, screw that. When are you coming to office?'

I left the room without answering, leaving the two of them alone. I cried myself to sleep that night like a three-year-old, cursing Vibhor and punching my pillow. I needed to grow up. I decided I would bail on the counsellor's job, skip on my notice period and start working with my brother if the going got any tougher than it already was.

37

Aisha Paul

I was my mother.

No matter what I did, it was what ran in my veins, there was nothing I could have done to fight genetics. But at least she was brave. Every day I would sit back in the washroom for hours at end, playing with the razor blade, marking where I would slice my wrists. Sometimes I would miss my class and sit on the roof thinking about whether jumping off and having my brain splattered on the sidewalk would solve anything. It would be worse on some days when I felt like doing it more but never gathered the courage to do so because it still felt like a selfish choice. A couple of weeks had passed and I hadn't talked to Danish. We crossed each other in the corridors almost every day; we would acknowledge each other but never stop and talk.

Namrata kept a strict watch on me. She knew I had lied to Danish. But she kept her mouth shut. She never told anyone about it. It would be for nothing. No one would believe her or me, and Norbu would be beaten up again. No one had anything to gain out of it.

And why would I complain? Vibhor was good to me. He was nice, he always called, told me he loved me, and never misbehaved. He did kiss me a few times a day, more when his friends were around, probably to prove the rumours wrong, and at those moments I felt like dying. Just stop breathing. I closed my eyes every time his tongue went inside my mouth and I wished I would never wake up. But I always did.

I was dating my nightmare.

'Here, she is,' my mother said as soon as I got home. I saw my brother first. He was back from his science symposium trip and with him sitting on the sofa was Vibhor. I smiled weakly. 'So Vibhor told me he has a get-together at his place tonight and you weren't going because I wouldn't give you permission?'

Yes, that's what I'd told him.

'And I have homework. There's so much to do,' I said.

'Can't you do it tomorrow?'

'No, I have to give it tomorrow. It's important. It's 10 per cent of the total evaluation.'

'You can go,' said my mother and held my hand. 'But only if Sarthak goes with you too.'

My mother looked at Vibhor.

'Everyone's invited, Aunty. I will drop them back by ten,' said Vibhor brightly. Words choked in my throat. 'I better be going now. I need to get some stuff.' He bent and touched my mother's feet, shook my hand followed by Sarthak's, told us he would see us in the evening, and left.

My mother asked me what I wanted to wear to his house today. I ran to my room and closed the door behind me. Later that evening, Sarthak and I were in the auto hurtling towards my boyfriend's house.

'Is there something going on between the two of you?' asked Sarthak.

'Us? No!' I said, putting on the smile and the brightness in my voice I had perfected over the last few days. A month or two and it would start coming naturally.

'You know you can talk to me if there's anything.'

'I just wanted to stay at home and do my assignment, okay.'

'I will help you complete that later.'

I nodded. By the time we reached there, Sarthak had nodded off with his head on my shoulder.

'We are here.'

He woke up with a start and noticed my smudged kohl right away. Yes, I put on kohl. I wasn't raped. What happened to me had to happen. So why wouldn't I put on kohl? I fixed myself up.

'HEY!' Vibhor hugged us both, and welcomed us.

His friends were already there, drinking. Some of the faces I knew, some were new. He introduced me to them and some of them hugged me. I wondered if they had imagined me with him as well, if they would use me tonight as well if I pass out again. I felt nauseous. Both Norbu and Namrata had skipped.

Drinks were served and I was coerced. *Drink*, they said. It will be fun, they said. *Don't be such a bore*, they said. *Life's great when you drink,* they said over and over again. Making a girl drink had replaced charm. All the charm comes in a bottle full of vodka.

I told them I had loose motions and alcohol makes it worse. They backed off, making faces. Vibhor kept getting drunker as the evening progressed. His hands kept wandering, sometimes caressing my thigh, sometimes on my shoulder, Sarthak looked away every time he saw that happening. It took me all my might to not burst into tears.

A little later, Sarthak left with a friend of Vibhor's to get more alcohol from the neighbourhood liquor store. Vibhor sat straight and addressed the rest of his friends as soon as he left.

'I was waiting for her brother to leave,' he said.

My heart jumped. What was he going to try?

'We have a really funny story to tell,' he said and took my hand into his. 'That rape story?' He looked at me and

I laughed. That's what he wanted, I guess. 'Tell them!' The story I had told Danish had stuck. It was the official story now.

I told his friends the story and they listened in rapt attention.

'. . . and because he literally ravaged me, I used the word rape and Namrata misunderstood. It was all a big misunderstanding.'

I finished narrating the story; every word that escaped my mouth seemed to burn it. Everyone laughed and with them laughed Vibhor.

Sarthak came back and more drinks were poured. Sarthak stared at his phone for the most part of the evening. He knew about that night, the ugly rumour, and the official story but he didn't say anything about it to me. I felt sorry for him. His sister was a PMSing slut.

One by one, our friends started calling it a night. Every time someone left I felt like screaming and asking them to stop. Save me, I wanted to shout and run. A few of them winked at us. Have a good night, they said. My hands felt cold. Sarthak was the last one to leave.

'Dad called. I have to take Mom to the hospital for a check-up. Nothing serious though. Aisha, you can stay and come back later. But be home by ten, okay?' said Sarthak.

'What? What check-up?' I asked, dialling Mom's number.

Sarthak stopped and told me it wasn't anything serious.

'I will come with you?'

'No, it's fine, Aisha. Nothing to worry about. Just routine,' said Sarthak.

'I will drop her home later? In about an hour?'

'Thank you, Vibhor.'

Sarthak's head hung low.

'I should really go, Vibhor. Please. I also need to do some homework.'

'I will take care of that,' said Vibhor, fished out his phone and called my mother. 'Yes, Aunty. Aunty, can I drop Aisha home in a couple of hours? Of course, Aunty. Yes, sure, Aunty. And Sarthak just told us you need to get a check-up done? Should I send a car, Aunty? Okay, okay. No, Aisha was getting worried here. Yes, Aunty, I will ask Sarthak to go. Don't worry, Aunty.' He cut the call. 'See? All handled.'

Sarthak wished us a good night. His eyes couldn't meet mine as he left; his night wish hung in the air.

Once Sarthak left, we sat in front of the TV because I told him I wanted to watch a movie. A little later, Vibhor's elder sister walked in. She had just had a kid a month back and still carried the extra weight.

'It's so tiring,' she blurted out and sat next to me. 'Never have a kid unless your in-laws love children.'

She showed me pictures and videos of her daughter who was as cute as a button.

'I always wanted a daughter,' she said. 'There are so many clothes to choose from. Shopping for little boys is so boring.'

'Please, haan?' interrupted Vibhor. 'A boy would have been so much better. At least I could have played with him.'

'You can play with her as well, Vibhor. She's your niece.'

'Yeah, whatever,' he said and peered into his phone.

His sister looked at me and took my hand into hers, 'So, you two? I heard you guys are very serious, are you? I have never seen Vibhor dote on someone so much.'

I nodded.

'Didi!' protested Vibhor. 'Can we not talk about this?'

'See, he's blushing so much,' said her sister and laughed. 'You look great together. I checked your pictures online. He doesn't tell me anything.'

'Hmm.'

Vibhor switched off the television. 'Can we please stop this conversation? Didi, stop embarrassing her.'

'Arre, what embarrassing her? I can't talk to her or what?'

'Let's go, I'm too sleepy,' said Vibhor, stretching his hand to take mine.

'Can't we stay for a while?' I said. 'At least finish your drink?'

He wasn't drunk enough to pass out and leave me alone.

'I'm done,' he said.

He pulled me up from the couch, waved at his sister and led me towards the flight of stairs towards his room. I wanted to resist, stand and wrest my arm free, but couldn't find the strength. Her sister winked and smiled at us from the couch.

And then, we were in his room, the lights were off, and he disappeared in the washroom for a few minutes. I sat on the bed, my head spinning, thinking of scenarios I could create to save myself from this. I felt nauseous, powerless, trapped. A voice shouted from inside of me—you can run away from this. RUN. RUN. But I couldn't. A darkness came over and I couldn't move. I felt bound. A little later, he emerged from the washroom, shirtless, with a little box in his hand.

'Here,' he said. 'It's for you.'

He ripped off the wrapping paper and thrust it in my hand. It was a little blue velvety box.

'Because I love you so much,' he said and kissed me on my cheek like he really did love me. But if he did, why did he do what he did that night? *People were right*, I thought as I opened the box, I was overthinking. I had passed out, he was drunk, I was his girlfriend, and he did what he had to do. And who knows, maybe we would have done the same thing if I had been awake? So why the fuss? Why was I acting so pricey? I should feel lucky I had him. I had no reason to be a cranky bitch. It's not as if I could have got someone better to date me and fuck me. It was a favour he had done me. *I am such a fool*, I thought. I smiled.

'Do you like it?'

'This is so sweet.' I told him and he hugged me again. It was an iPhone with my name engraved on it in pure gold. Now who would have matched that? I hugged him back despite my body not wanting to touch his.

He kissed me, this time full on the lips, and I tried kissing him back but it didn't happen. I closed my eyes and willed my tears to stay. He pushed me onto the bed. He slipped his hand in. The silent tears came. I swallowed hard.

His hand was awfully warm; his breath became ragged as he nuzzled at my neck, I opened my eyes and watched the lamp at the side table. I thought if I stared hard enough, maybe nothing of this would register. He took his remaining clothes off and came over me. Never have I been so aware of every inch of my skin. His body was warm and sweaty. I waited for everything to be okay. *Nothing is happening. Nothing is happening. This is all okay, Aisha. This is all okay. He loves you. He really does.* I wanted to howl. I squealed instead. Nothing was wrong here. He loved me. He brought me gifts. His mother knows me and yet I mumbled, 'I don't want to do this, Vibhor.'

He shut me up with a kiss, a foreign tongue inside my mouth and he whispered, 'It will be fun,' and took off my clothes.

'No,' I mumbled again. He didn't listen. His kissed me again. I saw him fumble with a condom and he put it on. I cried a little more. I felt weak, defeated. I tried pushing him away but his body was too heavy, he was too strong. *Why is this happening?* He pushed himself in. Even I couldn't listen to myself over his grunts. He grunted and moaned and bit me and sucked me. I lay there staring at the lamp telling myself it's okay, it's okay, its normal, at least he loves me, at least he loves me, and cried.

Once done, he rolled up, pulled up his boxers, kissed me and said, 'See, I told you it will be fun.' And smiled. He kissed me again. 'Hey? Do you mind if the driver drops you in a bit?'

I shook my head. He rolled over and went to sleep.

*

I wrote a note for him. Initially, it was four pages long but by the time I kept it under the new phone he had gifted me, it had only two sentences.

I'm breaking up with you. I don't deserve this.

I came back home, took a shower, slipped next to my mother, hugged her, cried and went off to sleep.

38

Danish Roy

I was pathetic, unintelligent, and lived off the power and position of my folks, but even I outdid myself. That day I was eating the same salad, and the same amount of alcohol as I had on my date with Aisha to mourn my unrequited love for a girl who was busy living it up with her boyfriend. It was a new low for me, which is saying a lot. I missed her, we hadn't talked in weeks. It was my third straight hour of Tekken 3 when I ran out of coins and cash. I went all around the mall to withdraw cash from an ATM and by the time I was back, someone had taken my place, and she was *good*. The combo hits were all in place, the flying kicks were precise, and she blocked perfectly well.

I put in a coin into the other slot. The game screen beeped 'New Challenger.'

Aisha looked at me. 'You? Here?'

'Same question,' I said, and told her I was getting bored at home. 'You come here often?'

'I might be addicted.'

'You're winning,' I pointed out. 'Then why are you crying?'

'I'm not crying,' she said, wiping her face with her sleeve. 'It's just condensation. I came from a cold place.'

'I'm sure that's a thing. Oh, here's my player. You're so dead.'

We played through 35 coins without talking. There was no place for words when two Tekken champions faced off. Way too much was on stake. She was good; it went down to the wire, and she beat me 16–19. I had to pay for the coins.

'I broke up with him,' she said. 'I wrote a note and left it on his side table.'

'Still better than a text.'

I wanted to jump up and down and shout and dance a little.

'Are you doing okay?' I asked.

'I'm fine,' she said. 'Relationships are not for me.'

'Everyone says that after a break up,' I said, not wanting the future Aisha to never be with me.

'No, really, I'm done. I better leave now. Mom must be waiting for me. She's undergoing some tests.'

'Is everything okay?'

'Yes. They are routine. Happens once every year. Nothing to worry about.'

'Okay. Haven't seen you in a bit. So thought we could hang out a little more,' I said in the most non-sorry, undesperate tone I could manage.

'I can't. I have to go.'

We walked towards the exit of the mall.

'I'm leaving the school soon,' I said to make her stay as she turned to get an auto. 'There will be a new counsellor coming soon.'

She nodded and tried waving down an auto. 'I don't need one any more. I plan to stick to the rules. No point trying to be someone else.'

'Of course, there's a point,' I said. 'I think you were doing great.'

An auto finally stopped in front of her and she asked the man if he would go to Pitampura. The man nodded and switched on the meter. 'There's my auto,' she said and jumped into it as if actively trying to get away from me.

'Bye.'

She left. I had to stop pursuing her, the reluctance on her face was far too evident for me to miss.

39

Sarthak Paul

Everyone knew I was gay.

I stepped inside my classroom and I could feel the hatred claw into my skin. My secret was finally out there. I didn't know how it happened or who did it, but I knew everyone believed it. We tend to easily believe things like these. A few guys smirked and looked at me from top to bottom and shook their heads. It felt different from what I always thought it would feel like when I came out of the closet. Though I hadn't walked out of the closet—I was pushed out of it. But I didn't want to run and hide as I thought I would, instead I felt defiant, and I stared back at them.

So what? What the fuck will you do if you know I'm gay? Try anything and I will knock your fucking teeth out.

I took my seat. The guy I used to sit with had taken a different seat and was gossiping raucously with three other classmates of mine. My past behaviour was being scanned with the gay lens on it.

'Oh, he asked you to be a partner in your laboratory experiment?'
'Shit. I didn't know. He used to be in the locker all the time!'
'I had caught him staring quite a few times.'

Suddenly, I was not only gay but a gay slut who stared and leched and touched people inappropriately. By the third period, I had been spat on by a guy, ignored by my lab partners, and called to the principal's office.

'Sarthak,' said the principal. 'What am I hearing?'
'What are you hearing, sir?'

OFFoff

The wall of defiance was crumbling, and behind it I was weak; I knew I wouldn't be able to keep it up for long.

'That you're gay, Sarthak. I am sure you know about this,' he said.

'I have heard the rumour, sir.'

'And? What do you want to say about it?'

In the split second I had to answer the principal's question, I wondered which way to go, towards freedom and sadness, or hiding and happiness. I chose to lie.

'That's it . . . it's a rumour.'

'Fine. I'm getting calls from all the parents and I don't want to hear about this from anyone else. Do I make myself clear?' I nodded. 'You can go now.'

'Thank you, sir.'

I got hammered on the football field that afternoon. I was pushed, trampled on, called a girl/pussy/wimp, and punched in the gut. If it were any other day, I would have crawled off the field but not today. I had to stand up and run, to prove I was nothing they wanted me to be. They tried hard to run me over, have me beg for mercy, concede defeat and walk off, admit I was weaker. Because gay is weak. It's feminine. 'Well, fuck them!' I said in my head and ploughed through the match even as my heart pounded and I tore at least a couple of ligaments. Back in the changing room, I got out of the shower and saw the entire team standing in front of me, still in their gear.

'What?' I said, my guard up again.

Something bad was about to happen.

Vibhor stepped up. 'You're gay, dude. You stayed in our midst and didn't tell us the truth. You're a fucking traitor, man,' he said murderously.

The others nodded.

He continued, 'We can't compete with you on the team. We can't have a gay defender in our team and get laughed at. You have to leave.'

'Why don't we let the coach decide that?'

Vibhor laughed and mimicked a girl's tone, 'Why don't we let the coach decide that? Fuck the coach. I decide what will happen on this team.'

And then at his command, the guys stripped me. They were too many of them. I connected a few punches, broke a couple of noses but they overpowered me soon enough. Five of them held me down, one of them stuffed an underwear in my mouth, and Vibhor and the striker, dug their studs repeatedly on my knee and my ankle till they were satisfied I was damaged enough. They took my clothes and peed on me, asking me if this was what I liked. Before leaving, Vibhor spray-painted the words 'GAY' on my chest and my back. He clicked a picture and threatened to make it public if I didn't drop out of the team quietly. He whispered in my ears just before leaving, 'That's what you get for dumping me. I fucking love her. Ask her to call me back.'

They locked the room and they left me, bleeding and writhing in pain on the locker room floor.

*

I heard Aisha scream outside.

After fifteen minutes of trying, she managed to break the lock with a spanner she'd borrowed from the guard.

The door opened. She stood there, aghast. I staggered towards her, leaving footprints of blood behind me, and took the clothes I had asked her to bring. I quickly wore the clothes and cleaned up the wound on my knee the best I could.

'Can you take me to a doctor?'

An hour later, my wound was stitched up and tended to, and we left the clinic. The doctor had given me a crutch to use for the next three weeks. We stopped at the Haldiram's close to our house. She stood in line and got two plates of *papdi chaat*s for us; back when she was younger she used to drag us down here every Sunday for it.

'Why did they do this?' she asked, her face white as a ghost's.

'You know why.'

There was no point in hiding it from her any more.

'We need to register a complaint against the entire team. We need to do something about this. This is *not* done, Sarthak. They can't do this to you.'

'No, they can. I'm gay.'

'Don't you feel like doing something? We need to do something.'

'Did you listen to what I said? I'm gay, Aisha,' I said.

'We need to—'

'I'm gay, Aisha.'

'I will talk to—'

'ARE YOU LISTENING TO ME, AISHA? I'm gay—'

'YES, I AM! I HEARD THAT!' she shouted.

A few heads turned.

She whispered, 'I know that! I have always known that. So what if you're gay? The President of Ireland is gay!' She banged the table.

'Wait? You have known? Since when?'

'Since the time I knew what being gay meant.'

'Then why didn't you talk to me about it, ever?'

'I didn't think it was important,' she said. 'And you never talked about it so even I stayed shut.'

'. . .'

'Why didn't you tell me?'

I laughed and she thought it was the trauma.

I said, 'You remember a boy in your class? Eighth standard? Ramit?'

'Yes, I do, the guy who was a little—' Her voice trailed off.

'The word you're looking for is *gay*. Yes, he was effeminate and you used to proudly bully him, call him names,' I said.

She stared at the glass of water, guilty.

'How was I supposed to tell you I was like him? I didn't want you to hate me.'

'I'm sorry. I . . . I just bullied him . . . I wanted attention. I didn't mean any harm,' she said, started to cry and threw herself at me, mumbling apologies.

'I didn't mean to—'

'It's fine.'

'I was just stupid and—'

'It's okay, it's okay.'

Having her in my arms was unequivocally the best thing ever. Just then, her phone rang. It was Vibhor.

'Are you going to pick that?'

'No.'

'Good. You can do without him,' I said.

I didn't tell Aisha about Vibhor's threat and him asking me to tell her to call him back. It was for the best that she stayed away from him. How wrong had I been about him?

We ate in silence.

40

Aisha Paul

My voice didn't matter.

Who would listen to me? I wasn't strong enough to fight the rumours. It was *they* who had all the power. Who was I but a slut? The sister of a gay brother who had jerked off the entire football team. That's what they said and everyone readily believed it. Victims of assault remain victims for long even after the assault is over, their wounds are constantly picked on. Accusations and fingers hover over them like flies over a septic cut.

'You should complain,' said Namrata.

The school corridors were hostile, littered with little landmines in the form of vicious teenagers and their caustic words, so we spent our lunch breaks in the basement.

I just laughed.

Just the day before, Vibhor had shared the picture I had sent him in my towel (amongst others) to a few of my friends, and of course, they hadn't kept it to themselves. Word went around that even though we had broken up (because I was a *temperamental, high-maintenance, moody bitch,* I think that's what women who don't want to get raped any more are called), I still had the hots for him, and that I gave him secret blowjobs in dark alleys, behind dumpsters, and in movie halls.

Namrata would cry a lot for me during those times, because unlike me, she had a flickering hope for her voice to matter. But of course it didn't. None of us mattered. We were of the wrong gender and the wrong orientation.

'How's your brother's preparation going?'

'Good. He doesn't come out of his room.'

We went back to class.

Luckily, my brother was shielded from all the humiliating insults and rumours dished out on a regular basis. He had deleted his Facebook and Twitter profile during the preparatory leave for his board exams.

I rarely saw him during those days. He would only emerge from the room to go to the washroom. He filled pages after pages in his beautiful handwriting, committing everything to memory.

The board exams started and he was probably the most well prepared student in all of history. He was always the last person to enter his classroom during the exams. He would make sure he was the first person to leave after the exam as well. After every exam, he and I would go to KFC and have the chicken bucket, and it was a sort of purging for the nonsense he had to learn for every exam. The dysentery which followed was quite annoying though.

We got back home after the last exam to see a big cake with candles lit up in the living room and my father standing there, eyes twinkling, arms wide open.

We hugged our father. He said to Sarthak, 'You will do great.'

We cut the cake and ordered Chinese food like we used to whenever Dad was in town. Our order always remained the same—American Chopsuey, chicken fried rice, garlic chicken—and as usual, my mother pretended to be full and ladled most of it in our plates. I remember it to be one of the happiest days of my life. We clicked a few pictures though my mother pretended to be busy clearing the dishes. Once full, we settled in front of the television and watched a re-run of an old comedy show, and that's when I told my parents about Sarthak's decision to study abroad. Sarthak hadn't told me about it but I had seen the brochures and the acceptance letters.

'What? When?' my father gasped.

Sarthak was clearly not ready for the conversation yet so I butted in.

'They give full scholarships to only three students every year. He doesn't even have to wait for the board exam results! It will be so good for him. He was waiting for the right time to tell you.'

My mother was already crying. She took Sarthak's face in her hands, cradled it, and kissed it over and over again.

'You did it all by yourself. We are so proud of you,' she said and disappeared into the kitchen where she cried in peace. She wouldn't see her son's face for months at a time. First our father and now the son.

My father read through the acceptance letter, the boarding facilities, and his scores on the scholarship exam, and smiled proudly. He was crying too, well okay, his version of crying, which was to have his eyes filled with pools of tears while denying that he was crying.

'This is good,' he said. 'But—'

'It's so far,' my mother said, emerging from the kitchen, devastated. 'How will I see you?'

'Skype, Maa. We will Skype every day.'

'As if he talks, Maa. You can keep a picture and talk to that. It would be more communicative for sure,' I said and my mother slapped me on my back.

'And you're leaving in a month. There's so much packing to be done. We will have to buy so many things . . . it will be so cold there . . .' her voice trailed off. She stared at her feet and tried hard not to sob.

My father, usually not an expressive man, shook Sarthak's hand and told him how proud he was of his achievement. My mother said she needed to make kheer to celebrate it and disappeared into the kitchen again. I followed her and saw her crying more than she had done when I had found her in the bathroom, almost dead. I patted her back for around five minutes before she gained control of herself.

'I'm happy for him,' she said. 'So happy.' I nodded. 'Finally he will be happy to be away from here.'

'Mom, don't say that. He's happy here too,' I said and hugged my mother from behind as she kept working.

'He's not,' she said, and gave me one of those looks only mothers possess, the one that says I know what you're hiding, I always know what you're hiding.

She finally said, 'I know he likes boys.'

'What! Are you crazy? No, Maa.'

'I know. You don't have to lie,' she said, and kept working like it wasn't her or any parent's biggest nightmare ever.

'How . . . how did you know? You're okay with that?'

'I'm okay with whatever makes him happy. I know why he's going to that side of the world. I read the newspapers.'

Yes, she does, and to think of it, she couldn't read a single word of English when she got married. She learnt it when my father taught Sarthak. We didn't even notice when we went from ordering an English newspaper and a regional newspaper to just one newspaper.

'It doesn't matter to you?' I asked.

'His happiness matters to me. It's uncomfortable but I love him and I will get to see him. That's what matters. What would I get in being angry with him?'

'Since when have you known?' I asked and kissed her on her cheek and she swatted me away like a fly.

'Ever since he was little. I waited for him to tell me. It's okay though. He must have been scared.'

'Does Dad know?'

'I told him last year.'

'. . .'

'He was way angrier than I was,' she said and smiled a little. 'He stopped calling. But you know your father,' she said and giggled, 'he Googled and searched everything about being gay. He called me one day and said, "Our son is all right, he's just unhappy, and that's our fault, not his." And since then, we have been waiting for him to tell us.'

'Maa, you two are too cool for your own good.'

'YOLO. And I'm dying anyway.'

'Maa? What are you watching these days? And please, you're not dying, stop being dramatic,' I said, and wrapped myself around my mother who knew what YOLO meant. Like what else can you ask for in life?

We, sons and daughters, we underestimate our parents' capacity to love us the way we are. I felt ashamed and so would Sarthak if he knew. Maybe that's what it was really like to be a woman, to have the capacity to love and sacrifice and learn and change and stand up for the right, and maybe that's what I should have aimed to have. I should have become my mother. She had done everything right.

The kheer made, we went outside where my father and my brother were going through maps on the Internet and Sarthak showed him pictures of his college, the football grounds and the libraries.

We all had the kheer, and I whispered into my mother's ears, 'Why don't you stop him? He has family here.'

My mother smiled like I was a seven-year-old, ignorant about the ways of the world and said, 'It's time he makes some friends. We love him and he knows that but he needs to be loved by a great many more and who are we to take that away from him? We will love him, and he will love us, but there's more to him than just us. He's finally going some place where they would accept him, applaud him, and embrace him.'

I slumped on the sofa and imagined my brother being greeted by other gay brothers who knew what he had been through, a mystical land of equality and love and acceptance, and wondered if there was any place on earth where women received the same warmth. My Google search yielded nothing. A women is raped every minute even in the US and the UK.

Where's that country for women?

A month later, my brother left, looking for happiness, friends and a voice, leaving my mother behind who pretended she was dealing well with it, my father who had never spent enough time talking to his son, and me who had to go back to school in three more days and face everyone.

Where could I run to?

41

Danish Roy

It was in the newspapers first.

Both my parents stayed at home that day, frantically calling Ankit who kept cutting their calls. They called his hotel in Mumbai as well without any luck. Furious, my father threw his phone, which landed on my mother's favourite vase, smashing it to pieces. My mother kept reading the newspaper article repeatedly. It said in bold letters, *'TranferB.com CEO asked to leave the company over irreconcilable differences over company policies. Resignation expected today.'*

Not having built anything on my own, I didn't know what it felt like to lose anything. The way I saw it, my brother still owned 15 per cent of the business valued at 80 crores, which meant he still got to pocket 14 crores which wasn't bad for a twenty-one-year old. The only casualty in the whole ordeal was me—I would no longer get the HR job he had promised me.

'I have got you the tickets,' my father said, tapping on his phone. 'I have sent you the address of the hotel he's staying at as well. Go and talk to him. Ask him not to resign. Ask him not to let go of his company.'

'Ummm . . . okay,' I said.

I checked the tickets he had just sent me—business class. I tried not to feel happy about it. I was the worst brother ever.

'You have to leave now! The flight leaves in two hours,' shrieked my mother.

Five hours later, I was knocking at my brother's door. I knew he was inside because I had checked with the hotel staff. 'Open the door, Ankit.'

'Fuck off.'

'You have to know that I travelled business class today and it was fun. I got at least three forced smiles from the flight attendants.'

I heard the door click. My brother opened the door, hair in disarray, shirtless and definitely hungover. Smriti was there, too, wearing his shirt, and she waved at me.

'Hi.'

'Hi, Smriti. Aren't you supposed to be working somewhere? Running a company? How are you always with my brother?'

She rolled her eyes. 'I should be leaving,' she said, got dressed, kissed Ankit and left.

The hotel room was rather opulent and over-priced. I took a ridiculously expensive coke from the minibar, settled at the lounge chair near the wall–to–wall window overlooking the pool and said, 'Mom and Dad sent me and asked me to tell you to not resign.'

'I knew they would do that,' said Ankit.

'And you don't want to.' He nodded. 'So what do you want?'

'I want to start over. Work on a new idea. Do something exciting!'

'Why would you want to do that? Why would anyone?'

'See, this business was fun in the beginning but then the money came in and they started dictating what should be done. Those fuckers—' He took a bottle of Absolut vodka and drained it into the commode. 'They are paying for the hotel room. Anyway, it got really boring, Danish. I'm so glad they want me gone. I want myself gone.'

And then he opened his laptop and showed me a few business plans he was working on, all with complex, incomprehensible graphs and projections. Though I didn't understand anything, I knew now how Ankit got the funding for his businesses—his excitement was palpable and I could feel his passion course through my veins even though I didn't understand a single word of what he said.

'I think you should resign.'

'Right? Right! Mom and Dad would never understand,' he said.

'You do own the equity, right? That's a lot of money.'

'Dad would want my name in the papers again and that's a long journey, Danish. They will have sullen faces till the time that happens again, if at all it does.'

'You're overthinking this, Ankit. They are usually too busy being disappointed in me to be disappointed in you,' I said.

He laughed.

'Wait. Why don't you tell them you had a nervous breakdown? That you were overworked! They would totally freak out . . .'

'That's not a bad idea, Danish. You could tell them that you found me on the floor, frothing from the mouth or something. That will scare them,' he said.

'And mention the equity to them over and over again,' I said. 'Fourteen crores is a lot of money.'

'Thanks, Danish,' he said. 'And sorry for the job loss.'

'Don't mention it.'

'Do you want to drink?' I asked.

'No reason why we shouldn't.'

We drank and drained what we couldn't into the commode.

Our parents threw a fit once we were back. Things settled down once Ankit told them fake stories about his deteriorating health, the nervous breakdowns, the irregular heart activity, and the recent deaths of three overworked entrepreneurs, which totally freaked them out but got them off his back.

I called the principal and he told me my job was still there if I wanted it. I was reinstated.

'Seems like you get to spend more time with Aisha, bro?' said my brother.

'Yeah.'

'It's time you make your move. Didn't she break up recently?'

'Yes, she did but I don't think she likes me that much.'

42

Aisha Paul

I was in a good space.

Keeping quiet was working out quite well for me. There were still a few hours in a day when I felt violated, assaulted, depressed and suicidal, but the feeling would pass soon enough. I hoped it would die with time. I had designated corridors for myself where I was sure of not bumping into Vibhor who had not stopped calling and texting, telling me alternatively that he loved me and thought I was a prostitute.

Despite everything, Vibhor still reigned, walking with his pack of minions, the boys who had hit and spray-painted my brother. Sometimes they booed me, or pinched me in the alleys of the library, but I didn't retaliate. It would only bring me more pain. I had put myself in the position I was in. I had made myself vulnerable.

And life was good otherwise. Sarthak and I would talk over Skype for hours every day. His college was beautiful and so were his friends. He couldn't stop smiling and telling me about all the crazy nights and awesome places he went to every day. I started living a little through him.

There were times when I thought of telling him or my mother about what Vibhor had done and was still doing to me, but I felt that would be selfish of. It happened to me and they didn't need to go through it. I had brought it upon myself and I needed to deal with this pain on my own.

I had started going to the counselling sessions again. Of course, I just lied and hid everything from Danish, but seeing him every day for an hour, even if it was in his office, made me feel as if nothing had happened. It was a little time capsule that I could sit in and travel back in time when we discussed books and movies and argued like he was Danish and not Danish sir. He never pried and just let me be. I would talk to him about Sarthak and how happy he was and he listened to every word I said, nodding and smiling.

Sometimes I cried and he would just offer me a tissue and get back to reading his book. I had wanted to tell him as well, but I was always afraid of the repercussions. He would bring in a shitstorm.

I could already hear people saying, 'Who would believe you?'

That day while I was in the washroom stall hiding out a free period, I heard a few girls walk in and talk in hushed tones.

'Are you really dating Vibhor?' asked a girl.

'Yes! It's going to be so exciting!' answered the girl. The voice sounded familiar. 'He's taking me out tonight.' I opened the door ever so slightly to confirm my suspicion. It was Megha. I closed the door.

'So lucky! I don't know what he saw in that bitch,' said Girl 1.

'Such a slut she was,' said Girl 2.

'I know,' said Megha.

'Did he kiss you yet?' asked Girl 1.

'What are you wearing?' asked Girl 2.

'Are you going to do it?' asked Girl 1.

'I haven't decided yet,' said Megha.

'He won't listen to you,' I thought. I opened the door and walked out. They shut up and pretended to check their lips in the mirror.

'Megha,' I mumbled. 'You need to cancel the date. He's not what you think he is.'

Megha looked at the others and then at me. 'Don't tell me what to do.'

'He ra—'

Words dried up. I tried to mouth the words but they failed me.

'You lost your chance, Aisha,' she said, 'now back off.'

And saying that, she left the washroom.

*

'I need to talk to you about something.'

'Come in,' said Danish ushering me in, and closed the door behind me.

I sat on the chair, and picked at the skin of my fingers. He pulled a chair next to me, crossed a leg over the other, and scrolled through his phone while he waited for me to talk.

'Something happened,' I said, my tongue still wanting to retreat into my throat, choke me. 'I didn't have sex with Vibhor.'

'Okay,' he nodded, kept his phone on the table, and looked directly at me, his eyebrows burrowed.

'I was raped.'

'When?'

'It happened twice. Once on the day of the party and once later,' I said and broke down in little sobs.

'Tell me everything.'

I narrated the entire incident, breaking down and howling in between, and he kept listening to me intently, offering me tissues and water.

'Does anyone else know?' he asked. 'Your parents? Your brother?'

I shook my head.

'Why didn't you stand by your story?'

I didn't have to tell him why.

'You were scared no one would believe you?'

'Do you?'

'I do,' he said, and got up from his chair. He started to stuff his files into his leather bag. He switched off his computer and locked his drawers. 'Come. We need to tell your parents.'

'NO,' I cried. 'WE CAN'T DO THAT!'

'Your parents would understand,' he said, sternly. 'Didn't you tell me they surprised you by how openly they had accepted your brother?'

I shook my head.

'You were assaulted. It was a crime, Aisha. You can't just shut up about this. You *have to talk*. We need to inform the principal as well.'

Tears flew abundantly and I clutched my chair just in case he thought about dragging me out.

'Listen, Aisha. It wasn't your fault. That guy is a rapist and he needs to pay for that.'

I shook my head and kept crying and telling him I wouldn't go, I would die but I would not tell my parents.

He sat down, took my hand into his and asked, 'So why did you tell me this today?'

'Megha,' I said. 'She's going out with him today. I was just afraid he would do it again.'

'And whose fault is that?' he said.

I didn't answer. He sat down and asked me to look at him.

'Aisha, you getting raped isn't your fault but keeping shut about it is your fault. What can potentially happen to Megha is your fault. Do it before it's too late.'

'I can't do it,' she said. 'He's powerful. He will ruin me. He . . . beat up my brother.'

'What!'

I told him about the incident in the football locker room. Angry, he threw the paperweight that lolled on his table against the wall and it shattered to little pieces.

'That fucking bastard! You need to fight this. We need to tell your parents. What are you scared of? And stop thinking about how powerful he is. We will figure that out.'

'What will my parents think? They will never love me again.'

'That's the stupidest thing I have ever heard, Aisha. There's no one who knows you and doesn't love you,' he said. 'Trust me.'

43

Danish Roy

Before leaving the school, I talked to the principal about the incident and he told me all necessary action could only be taken after an FIR was lodged and the investigation proved Aisha was telling the truth. Also, Vibhor's name could not be let out because he was not eighteen yet, and his parents were not the type who would take this lightly. He told me I had his support in whichever way I wanted.

I felt pure, raw anger while we hurtled towards Aisha's house. I had to close my eyes and imagine myself slowly torturing Vibhor, picking out one tooth after another, skinning him alive, to temper it. An hour later, we were sitting on the couch in her house, her parents in front of us.

'What's the matter,' her father asked, scared. 'Did she fail her exams?'

Her mother came and sat next to her and took Aisha in her embrace. She wiped her tears.

'Calm down, Aisha, you can take the exams next year. There's no need to cry,' she told her and Aisha burst out into more tears.

'It's not her exams,' I clarified.

'Then, what is it?' asked her mother.

I narrated the incident with as much objectivity as I could manage. Once finished, her mother covered her mouth with her saree and cried into it for a few brief seconds before she wiped off her tears, and asked Aisha, '*Are you okay, are you okay, why didn't you tell me! You tell me everything! Why did you hide this?*'

'I thought you would not love me any more. You trusted me and I betrayed that trust. You let me go out with him and this happened,' Aisha kept repeating.

'I am here, beta, I'm here,' she said and kissed her all over.

Her father sat there, stunned, and then with trembling hands took out his phone and called his friend, asking him to come over. He sat there, unmoving with his head in his palms. Half an hour later, his friend, a doctor, came home and we sat with him in the living room. Things weren't looking good.

'It's been too many days. She has showered since then. If there was any tearing it would have healed by now.'

'There should be something we can do,' said the father, holding his friend's hand, begging. 'Something. Something that proves it. *Kuchh to hoga, yaar. Aise mat bol, dost.* You can't tell me there is nothing we can do.'

The doctor shook his head. Mostly to humour her father, he took Aisha and her mother to the adjoining room, ran a few diagnostic tests, and found nothing. Before leaving he hugged Aisha's father and offered his help if he needed anything. Her father cried openly now.

Aisha and her mother came out of the room, Aisha clinging on to her for dear life, both wiping their tears.

'We should inform the police. He has to pay for this,' said her father.

I nodded.

Aisha looked on, horrified. 'No! I won't be able to go to school!'

'I will be there,' I said.

'NO! JUST NO!'

She threw her hands up, stomped her feet, and stopped only after her mother restrained her.

'Aisha, think about Megha and all the others. If he gets away this time, he will repeat it,' I said.

'I just want things to go back to normal,' she said, and slumped on the sofa.

She dug her face in her knees and cried.

We left for the police station in about an hour. It took another painful retelling of the incidents from Aisha. The cops looked at her in disbelief, already blaming her for what happened in their heads, scorning at the parents for being irresponsible while they listened. Had there not been a kind lady police officer present during the time Aisha talked, they would have thrown us out of the police station. The FIR was registered and the statements of Namrata and Norbu, who had joined us at the police station, were taken down.

That evening, Vibhor was arrested. He got out on bail within fifteen minutes. Three days later, the summer vacations started.

*

'Should we get him picked up?' Ankit said later that night.

'And do what?'

'I don't know. Beat the bastard up,' he said. 'Should we put up a picture on Facebook with all the shit he has done? Why don't we run a Facebook campaign? I will sponsor it. It will get a million hits in a day.'

'No.'

'Why the fuck not? We will destroy him. No matter what happens in the court, he will be a rapist for life. Everyone will know he got away because he's rich.'

'Innocent till proven guilty, Ankit.'

'But you know he did it, right?'

'Yeah, I know. But let's not encourage mob justice. How different will that be from those people who lynch a guy because he's a suspected rapist?'

'But he's not suspected. You know—'

'You get my point.'

'Whatever,' he said. He put his arm around me. 'But I'm proud of you. You handled it right.'

'What handled it, yaar? There's no hard evidence. Everything points against her. The pictures, the students, everything. No one is going to believe her.'

'You believed her.'

'. . .'

'I wish more people did,' he said. 'You should make them.'

*

We didn't stand a chance in court.

Despite Ankit's support and his money and my parent's lawyers, we got decimated in a fast-track court, and things got really ugly once the pictures and the texts surfaced. Their lawyer went on a carefully rehearsed rant about young drunk girls regretting their wilfully made choices the morning after. We had no case.

Vibhor got off scot-free. He mouthed the words, *fuck you bitch,* before he left the courtroom. Aisha didn't leave her house for many weeks after the case ended. The summer vacations had started before anyone got to know about the court case and that saved Aisha a lot of grief. But slowly, the case and the result was common knowledge amongst the students. Anonymous accounts on Facebook and Twitter called Aisha a vengeful slut. The boys of the school started to throw facts about fake rape reports filed to harass young men, and the girls started to project her as one of the reasons why even *real* instances of rape aren't reported.

'Do you think we should tell Sarthak?' asked the father.

'No,' the mother said. 'Let him be. He has just joined college.'

Her mother served Ankit, Namrata, Norbu and me tea and biscuits. She had held herself better than Aisha's father in the past few days, shuttling between meetings with lawyers and psychiatrists and comforting Aisha.

'Sir, what did you decide on the school?' I asked. 'Did you get time to go through the brochures?'

Her father shook her head.

'New Era is a good school,' said Norbu. 'Great academic programme. Their principal is quite nice too. I considered it when I was shifting schools.'

'Even BBPS,' added Namrata.

'I went through the brochures,' said the mother. 'I don't think she should shift to another school. I don't want her to run from this.'

'But I talked to the principal. Vibhor is staying on in the school. He told me it's not in his hands. He's helpless—'

'I think Aunty's right,' said Ankit.

'Are you sure?' asked her father.

'She shouldn't change her school, the boy should. A new school won't change anything. She will spend her life being scared. I don't want that,' she said.

'But she's not even taking psychiatric help, how do you think she will agree to go back to school? It would be so hostile,' her father said, close to tears.

We looked at Namrata and Norbu. Namrata stammered and stuttered before she could say anything intelligible.

'They still think she lied. The sympathy is with him . . . I don't think—'

Ankit rolled his eyes. We slumped.

'Danish will be there,' said the mother and looked at me. I nodded to reassure her.

'She has to fight this.' She held her husband's hand. 'And she will. We will help her. If she changes schools, it will look like she was at fault. She's not. We need to constantly tell her that.'

'So, it's decided,' said Ankit. 'She's going back to school.'

'Should we ask her?' I asked.

'If that's what Maa wants, I will go back to school.'

We all turned to see Aisha standing at the door. Her hair was dishevelled and she had dark circles from sleepless nights. 'I will go back.'

Her mother smiled, and rushed to hug her.

'That's like the Aisha I know.'

44

Aisha Paul

My parents booked a cab for me the first day.

Norbu and Namrata sat by my side, holding my hand the entire way, telling me that it wouldn't be as bad as I thought it would be. Did they know how I imagined school? How I imagined myself standing at the edge of the roof, staring down, wanting to jump and end it all and yet not find the courage to do so? Did they know anything? I walked into the school nervously, my eyes stuck on the marble pattern on the floor, Norbu and Namrata constantly whispering assurances in my ear.

When I looked up, I saw friends of Vibhor huddled in the corner. They booed, surrounded me and called me a slut, threatened to beat up Norbu, gag Namrata's mouth and fuck her skull. I tried not to cry, be strong, keep my chin up, just as my mother had asked me to. They spat on me before leaving for class.

We ran to our own class once they left, and took the last seats as usual. Our physics teacher taught us Fission, and never once looked in my direction. Clusters of students talked in hushed and accusatory tones, throwing sidelong glances and rolling their eyes, calling me an actress.

The class ended and I collected my books. A little chit fell out from the desk. I took it and walked to the basement, somewhere I knew I could hide, head hung low. Namrata and Norbu stayed back to catch up on assignments.

I prepared myself for an insult as I opened the chit with trembling fingers. Before my mother made me delete my

Facebook account, it was inundated with messages which said
more or less these things:

Slut.

Fuck you.

You got what you deserved.

You should be gang-raped.

Did you and your brother together fuck the entire team?

I read the note. The handwriting was beautiful, and the note
said, *I believe you.* I smiled for the first time in days. This
wasn't someone from my family. Or Namrata or Norbu
or Danish. It was from a stranger, and that somehow
mattered.

I ate my lunch alone. When the bell rang, I went and sat
in the class for the next three hours wondering who amongst
the students had sent that chit. My desk had SLUT scrawled
on it. But inside the desk were two more chits with the same
message, *I believe you.* I folded them and saved them with
the other note. I spent the rest of the period rubbing out the
word SLUT on my desk.

'How's your first day going?' asked Danish when I entered
his office.

'I could see you standing outside the class. Thank you.'

He pulled up a chair next to me.

'You tell me if anyone says anything to you, okay?'

I nodded.

'You have to remember that you have been wronged, and
he should pay for it.'

I nodded again.

'Someone wrote the word "slut" on my table,' I told him.

'Then we have to do something about it,' he said.

'What?'

'We will think about it,' he said. 'Did you manage to take notes today? Concentrate on the teacher's words.'

I shook my head.

'Oh. Never mind, my brother is a sort of genius and he never studied in class either. He will teach you when the exam time comes.'

'They also abused Norbu and Namrata,' I said.

He pushed a pad in front of me and asked me to write the names of the students who did it.

'But—'

He asked me to write out those names and I did.

'What are you going to do?'

'Namrata had an idea,' he said, got up and rummaged through his desk.

He took out a few printouts and laid them out in front of me. I read through the pages. They were prints of all the nasty stuff the students had either messaged me or wrote on the bathroom stalls or scribbled on blackboards about me, Namrata, Norbu and my brother.

'Norbu helped Namrata hack into their Facebook and Google accounts to fetch these. We are going to mail these to their parents so that they know the kind of language their children use.'

'I see no point . . .' I said, scared of what their parents would think of me, but he interrupted me and asked me to read them again. I did so.

Sahil Chugh: Aisha is a fucking slut, man! A train can pass through her pussy without a groan.

Arunee Mehra: Norbu? That gay asshole? He should get down on his knees and suck my dick, man. And his girlfriend surely would love to eat my cum.

Shrikant Gupta: I think Sarthak became gay because he knew he wouldn't get anyone hotter after fucking his own sister.

He continued, 'Their parents should know. It should teach them a lesson.'

'But—'

'Don't worry. I will have people keep an eye on them. They won't touch you. And the minute they say anything, let me know. Their parents would be notified and I have a feeling this time people will believe us,' he said, his eyes fiery embers.

'Why are you—'

'Because their voices need to be snuffed. Only then will our voice be heard.'

The bell rang.

'You should head back to your class now. Don't be weak.'

I nodded. 'Thank you, Danish.'

'Thank Namrata and Norbu. This is my job. What they are doing is great. You're lucky to have them.'

*

I thanked Namrata and Norbu and they asked me to stop embarrassing them. We were still waiting for our chemistry teacher to come when the door was slammed open and Vibhor walked in with four of his most hateful cronies. My heart jumped and I dug my nails into Namrata's hands.

'Just stay quiet. Don't cry,' Namrata whispered.

They jumped and stomped on the tables and walked straight towards us. Vibhor sat on the table in front of us and the cronies sat on the chairs, all of them cocking their heads, hissing.

'We will see you later,' said one of the cronies to Norbu who was trying to wriggle past and leave the class.

Norbu looked at me apologetically and I managed to smile back at him as he stood at the door, watching helplessly.

'What do you think you were trying to do, bitch? Did you think you would fucking beat me?' snapped Vibhor.

My classmates dropped everything they were doing and looked in Vibhor's direction.

'You're nothing but a fucking jealous slut.' He stood up on the bench and faced the class.

'She lodged a complaint against me. Imagine her fucking guts! She came to my party, got drunk on my alcohol, spent my money, went to my bedroom, fucked me, not once but twice and then shouted rape! Poor, poor Aisha, that's what you wanted people to think about you? Why don't you tell them what the lawyer said about you? Huh?'

'Vibhor—'

'I can't hear you. Let me tell them if you're being too shy. He told everyone that she's a slut who sends her naked pictures to boys. That she had always wanted to gag on my cock and fuck me. He read texts in the courtroom. Wait wait wait. Where are you going, Aisha? Stay here and let me read them out to the class?'

He scrolled through the texts.

'*Are you naked, Vibhor? Damn!* This is what the slut sent me days before she fucked me. And all this is hard evidence, Aisha. Now say, what were you saying again?'

'Vibhor—'

He addressed the class. 'I came here for you guys. To tell you to be beware of these middle-class, attention-monger bitches. Talk nicely to them and what do you know? They fleece you off your money, drink your alcohol, talk sweetly to your mother and then cry rape.'

'You raped me—'

'Blah blah blah. SHUT THE FUCK UP. I know what she would have done if we didn't have a strong case against her. She would have asked for settlement money! Wait, wait, it just struck me. Oh my God. It makes sense now. Is this how your brother got the money to go to Poland? Threaten someone with a gay rape case? Because your shitty-ass father couldn't work for a thousand years and get the money!'

I got up, stumbled and fell on my face. I cut my lip and it started to bleed. I tasted metal in my mouth. Vibhor laughed.

'Look at the slut go.'

I got up and ran past them crying, and heard Vibhor and the cronies laugh behind me. A girl whispered into my ears just as I ran past her, *Be strong.*

45

Danish Roy

'How did it go? You look angry,' asked Ankit as I entered the house.

He was furiously typing away at his laptop, chewing a pencil. The white board behind him had gibberish written on little post-it notes stuck haphazardly. I tried to read one and he slapped my hand away.

'Don't spoil the order.'

He gets that way whenever he's working on a new project.

'Quite awful. It might be the worst day of my life,' he said.

I told him about the letters we had sent to all the students' parents. The principal's phone had been ringing off the hook since then. Most of the parents didn't budge, didn't want their kids to apologize, called Aisha names and told me to concentrate on throwing Aisha—a girl with no character—out of the school. They fought with me for hours on end, even told me they thought their kids were being noble by supporting Vibhor against a false rape case, and whatever slurs—*cum guzzling slut, randi, prostitute, whore*—Aisha was being subjected to by their kids was fair. They told me they would move court if their kids were asked to apologize.

Thankfully, a few of the parents sounded angry and apologized for their sons' and daughters' behaviour, and assured the principal it wouldn't happen again. They asked me to apologize on their behalf.

'What did you tell them?'

'I have asked them to come in person and apologize to the aggrieved parties. A few of them are coming on Monday.'

'Aggrieved parties? Is that how you talk these days?' he laughed and I rolled my eyes. 'I'm just kidding, but it's a great idea. You're like her knight in shining armour.'

I told him it wasn't really my idea, and that Aisha wasn't a damsel. It was Namrata who was the knight, if anyone.

'And what about the parents who are not coming? Nothing about them?'

I shook my head. 'They abused me, threatened me, and told me it was Aisha's fault and that their kids were right in supporting Vibhor.'

'What? I . . . I don't know what to say that. Did they even read what kind of messages their kids were sending out? The language?'

'They did. But as they say, like parents like kids. Out of the twenty-three students whose parents we had contacted, fourteen took the fight to the school and wanted me gone. But the principal has been extremely supportive. He even fetched CCTV footage to support our claims. So that's really nice of him.'

'I still can't believe some parents can be such assholes!' he said.

'Yeah, I was kind of taken aback too. Remember the first time you said *bhenchod* when you were in the eleventh? Mom brought the entire house down and didn't talk to both of us for a month. A month! And these parents will do anything to shield their kids. If their parents are okay with the kind of sexist language these kids use, what else do you expect from the kids?'

'Yeah. God knows what the fuck is happening to people. Anyway, come and see this. It might cheer you up,' he said, and motioned me over.

I peered into his screen which looked straight out of the Matrix movies.

'You expect me to understand this?'

With a few quick clicks and commands he made it all disappear, leaving behind a little empty dialog box and the little button on the right side which said, *'TALK TO ME, I'M LISTENING'*.

'What is this?'

'This is you, Danish, a faster, omnipotent work in progress version of you.'

I told him he had lost it.

'Let me explain how. Now suppose Aisha didn't know you, or scratch that, if I needed someone to talk to in that hotel room in Mumbai, who would I have turned to? Or Sarthak for that matter? Who could he have talked to?'

With a flourish of a hand he pointed towards the screen.

'Write anything and you will have someone to talk to. It's totally anonymous. So if you have a problem you can't share with anyone, this website will come to your rescue. Write your problem and it will guide you to anyone who can help you, talk to you and be there.'

'Like a suicide helpline? Only online and for every kind of problem?'

'Sorta.'

'And anyone can join and start helping other people?'

'Yes, anyone. You can just sign up and start posting your problem or start helping people. As simple as that. Anyone can sign up!'

'You do know that if it's *anyone*, people can be easily misguided, right? What if I write fuck-off to someone's genuine problem?'

'There are two fail-safes for that. First, anyone registering will have to first write an essay on why they want to help people, and secondly, they will have to get verified with a photo-ID. Also, I'm working on an algorithm where the answers can be screened for profanities. And last but not the least, every problem will be sent to at least ten people, so even if one of those ten is naughty, nine will be nice!' he said. 'So as I said, it's an updated version of you.'

'You're giving me way more credit than I should get.'

'Am I? I found those little chits you're making for her, and I'm guessing you are going to drop them in her bag or her desk,' he said.

'She needs to know there are people out there who believe her.'

'I have another idea,' he said, and turned back to his laptop. 'I can send out ten emails every day to her from IDs that don't exist. You can say whatever you want to and she will never know these people don't exist.'

'Can you—'

'Of course I can.'

'How are—'

'How am I not rich, successful and adorable? I actually am.'

'When was the last time you got some decent hours of sleep?' I asked.

'Sleep is immaterial when you have cracked a big idea, bro,' he said and asked me to mail him whatever I wanted to say to her so that he could forward them to Aisha.

He got back to his laptop, tapping furiously at what I thought was a brilliant idea. But that's what I always expect from my genius brother.

*

The next day, the parents of the boys and girls were already waiting in the principal's room when I got there. Out of the twenty-three kids whose parents we had reached out to, only eight had found this issue pressing enough to visit the school. *Just great.* Why did the other parents even bother to send their kids to school if they were okay with them being raised as savages? Why get teachers to teach them when all you do is threaten them when they voice their opinion or act harsh with the kids?

I took my seat. The principal introduced me to the parents and the parents hung their heads. 'He's Danish, the teacher who caught them using bad language while addressing their fellow students.'

'Hi. I'm Danish. I would like to thank all of you for coming there. You took the trouble to listen and try to address the issue unlike the parents of other kids who didn't think it was important enough to chide their kids who were openly harassing their fellow students. I'm glad to see you here.'

The parents nodded. I passed out the printouts of what their kids had written or said to Aisha, Namrata and Norbu. They read it and looked murderously at their kids.

I continued, 'I think we should call the boys and the students they humiliated.'

The parents nodded reluctantly.

Fifteen minutes later, eight kids and their angry, repentant parents stood in front of Aisha, Namrata and Norbu. Aisha's mother was there too and she was the first one to speak. Her voice quivered, and her fingers, which were wrapped around Aisha's hand, trembled. 'Namaste. Thank you for coming here. It means a lot to me and to Aisha. As you know by now, the court says my daughter wasn't raped and Vibhor, the boy your kids are friends with, is innocent. We have accepted the court's order. What else could we do? We can't change that. But what we can expect is for Aisha to come back to school and attend her classes like everyone else. Without anyone calling her a . . . without anyone calling her names. Is that too much to ask for my daughter? What did my daughter do to your sons and daughters that they hit her? Spit on her? Write words like "slut" on her desk? Or her bag? Why?' Aisha's mother looked up at a few of the women who felt ashamed. 'Can't they let her study in peace?' Aisha's mother rummaged through her bag and brought out mark sheets of Aisha, right from the second standard to the eleventh. 'Here. Here. Here.'

Aisha's mother smiled weakly at the old, yellowed mark sheets. I took them from her and passed them around. The parents stared at them because they couldn't meet Aisha's mother's eyes. 'She's has always been a scholarship student, always among the top three students in her batch. When she was younger, the class teachers even made weaker students sit with her so they could learn. And now the same students . . .' Her voice trailed off. She clasped her hands as if to beg. 'I'm requesting your kids to leave her alone. Can you do that for her? I'm not asking you to believe her. Just leave her alone?' It looked like she would burst into tears but she didn't and instead held Aisha, who was crying now.

There was silence. The parents shifted in their places, angry and ashamed.

'Apologize to them,' a few parents said to their boys. Things happened in quick succession from then on.

A mother slapped her son and waved the printout in his face. 'Is this what we have taught you, huh?' The mother looked at Aisha's mother and said, 'I don't know where he learnt all this. We are sorry.'

A father cried for her daughter. A couple of boys apologized before their parents got hold of them.

Aisha's mother was consoled by a boy's parents. 'We are sorry. We had no idea. We will make sure our boy stays away. We know Aisha. He would often get Xeroxed notes of her copies home. We are so sorry.'

A girl cried and hugged Aisha. They muttered their apologies and swore they would never do it again. Aisha stared at her feet. The parents apologized to Aisha as well once the kids were done.

Finally, Aisha spoke, her eyes pools of tears, 'Can you ask them why they called us names? Why they spat on me? Why they called Namrata—'

The parents looked at their kids. They didn't answer.

'Your parents are asking you something,' I said.

One of the boys finally spoke, 'She filed a rape complaint against our friend, Vibhor. And he won. We knew he was lying and—'

The boy was interrupted by a tight slap that resounded against his cheek. His father heaved in anger.

'But she went to his house—'

His father slapped him again. The other parents looked at their sons like they were pond scum.

'Don't hit them,' mumbled Aisha, behind the tears. 'He's right. *I* drank. *I* went to his place. *I* thought he loved me. He was *my* boyfriend. *I* stayed quiet. It's *my* fault, is it?'

Aisha's mother continued, 'I had given her the permission. It was her eighteenth birthday.'

'Mom, she was drunk,' argued Kunal, one of the boys.

'So?' snapped his mother, and stared down her son.

'The boys made her feel she deserved it, or that she was lying,' I said.

A father slapped his son and held him by his collar. 'You have a sister, Karan. What if this happened to her? Haan? Would you doubt her too, you asshole? And whatever happened was between the girl and the boy. Why did you have to butt in? Is that why we send you to school?'

He looked at the principal and then at me, helplessly.

'I don't know where we went wrong. We are so sorry,' he said and threw his hands up in the air. The boy muttered another apology.

Sumit's mother shouted at her son as he cowered in the corner, 'Who would lie about such a thing? Are you a fool? Her life is destroyed. Why would she lie?'

'No, Aunty, it isn't destroyed. She's still an intelligent, kind girl. Nothing is destroyed here,' corrected Namrata.

A couple of parents walked to Aisha and her mother's side and made her sit down, offered her a glass a water, ran their hands over their heads and comforted them.

The boys were given a week's suspension but Norbu came up with a better idea. The boys were supposed to wear a placard around their necks for the next week that read **'I'm sorry, Aisha'** if their parents were okay with it. The parents nodded in agreement; it was a fit punishment, they said. Aisha's mother thanked the parents who asked her to feel free to reach out if she needed anything. I collected their cards on her behalf.

I saw Aisha and her mother smile after a really long time, and realized that it didn't take all twenty-three kids to apologize for them to smile, just a little bit of support, that's all they needed.

Later that day, Norbu designed the **'I'm sorry, Aisha'** placard and got them printed. For the next one week, the eight students wore them around the neck all through the school day. A few people scoffed and called it a bullshit measure of the school while others took it more positively. The incredible thing it did—something that we hadn't expected at all—was people now talked about it from both perspectives rather than just raging about how a girl reported a *false* rape case. Often, I would pass students in the corridor to find them aggressively debating the case, questioning the attitude of people who lynched Aisha right after the trial, and raised fingers on their behaviour as well. One day, I heard a boy passionately argue Aisha's case with his dissenting friends in the men's washroom. He said, 'It's not about who won the case or who lied. It's an apology for the kind of behaviour we meted out to her. That's the point of the placard. If I wear it, it's not because I believe that she was raped but because it's an apology for me calling her a slut before and after she reported the case.'

I think he nailed it.

46

Aisha Paul

A week had passed since my return to school and it was getting as easier as it was getting harder to be there every day—to return the smiles of people who had somewhat started to believe in me, or at least were trying to understand that there might be more to the situation than Vibhor's side of the story, people who wrote little messages for me; to continue to bear the caustic looks of many who still labelled me as an attention-seeking slut or whore.

Norbu's placard idea had worked. No one abused me openly any more and a *few* people who had bothered me earlier even came up to me and apologized. But still quite a few of them found ingenious ways to hurt and humiliate me.

Boy 1: So this girl totally sent me naked pictures and asked me to rape her! Must be some fetish.

Boy 2: Yeah, same thing happened with me dude.

I would try to ignore them, think about the other wonderful people who were by my side but I couldn't push these incidents out of my head.

Vibhor would still stare me down in the hallways, spit on the ground when he would see me, flash his middle finger, thrust his pelvis towards me, which would often reduce me to tears. His posse of faithful men had decreased though. They were scared they would have to carry that placard again for a week.

Every day, a few new girls would tell me that they were with me. The number of chits I started to get in my desk every day started to increase. Sometimes the assurances ran into

224

paragraphs, some of them recounted incidents from their own life when they had been judged and poked fun at in the past, and I often cried reading them. I had a little scrapbook at my place with all the chits pasted on them and I would read them whenever I felt low. Just having people believe me was half the battle won. I didn't feel choked any more, just sad and scared.

Namrata and I were sitting in the canteen when Norbu came running to us. He told us there was a surprise and he asked us to close our eyes.

'Just tell us!' exclaimed Namrata.

'No, close your eyes!' he said.

We closed our eyes. He made us open our palms and kept something in each of them.

'Open.'

It was a little round badge that said in bold white lettering on a black background, 'I AM SORRY, AISHA.' He spoke, 'I have two hundred of them. We are going to give it for free.'

I don't know why but I started crying again and Namrata tried to quieten me. It happened a lot those days. I tested their patience by breaking down every now and then. It was amazing that they were still friends with me.

'You don't like it?' asked Norbu, scrunching up his face into a little ball. 'I know the colour is a little dull.'

Between little sobs, I said, 'I like it but—'

'This is awesome, Aisha,' said Namrata, thrusting my face into her bosom to shut me up, even as Norbu pinned one on his shirt and one on Namrata's.

'But who will wear them?' I asked, still crying into Namrata's chest.

I wasn't crying because I felt no one would wear them, but to see my friends believe in me so much. In those moments I felt so loved, so normal.

'People will,' said Norbu. 'Eventually. Here, put one on!'

'Won't it be odd if I put one on?' I asked, now wiping my snot and tears on my shirt sleeve. 'It's in third person. I would be apologizing to myself?'

We all laughed. Norbu made the canteen guy, a buddy of his, keep it at the counter and give out only one to every person who asked for it and to keep it off limits to Vibhor and his friends. The canteen guy nodded, wore one himself and flashed a thumbs up towards me. I smiled back at him.

Till the end of the day, not one badge was picked up.

*

But the next morning, the entire canteen staff was wearing the badges, and by lunch time, a few kids from the junior section sported them, and by the time the day ended, one in every thirty people had a badge pinned to their chest, 'I'M SORRY, AISHA'. Never had I been smiled at so often. The corridors of the school, once a hostile, thorny place, was now suddenly a happy place. People would smile at me and point to their badges and some of them would even wink at me. It would be so hard not to cry every time someone picked up a badge and put it on their chest. They didn't need to come out and apologize. It wasn't a compulsion. But they chose to pick it up and that meant the world to me.

I hugged Norbu so many times he almost regretted his decision. I felt like the most loved person in the entire world.

*

Later that day, my mother and I were sitting in the living room in Danish's house. His brother had insisted, made his parents call my parents, and assured them that they would be keeping a watch. I knew it was just Danish and Ankit, people I trusted with my life, yet my body revolted, and it wasn't well into the night that I finally decided I would go. My mother came along.

Ankit made all of us sit on a couch and showed us what he called the 'beta' version of his site. It's going to be the next big thing, he had said, which I assumed he said about every site he made and not for no reason. He looked every bit the genius Danish had made him out to be. He explained the workings of the site, how to log in, how to access the account amongst other things, and answered all our questions. He told us 1500 people had already registered for this beta site.

'Anyone can register?' asked my mother, with childlike enthusiasm and Ankit showed her how to make an account. 'Once your account is created, you can browse through all the different problems people have shared. You can click on "Reply" and reply to their problems. You wouldn't know the real names of the people who are posting their problems and they won't know you! It's completely anonymous.'

Ankit showed my mother the list of problems people had lodged under anonymous names.

Username	Subject
Broken498	I don't feel like living any more . . .
Smriti	I have had enough. I want to run away.
NoName	Do we always need to do what our parents tell us?
DDDDDD	Lost. I'm totally lost.
HD	A friend is depressed and I think she might be . . .

'Teenagers have a tough life,' she remarked. 'Look at this girl, Broken498? She found out that the boy she loved was also with three other girls? Horrible. She's crying every day now. Can I reply to her?'

Ankit showed her how to send across her message. Sarthak had taught Mom how to WhatsApp before he left for Poland so it didn't take her long to pick up typing on a keyboard.

It was the happiest I had seen my mother be. Even while we ate, she kept tapping on the keyboard, one letter at time, typing out page-long answers to people looking for help.

'You have a very talented son,' my mother told Ankit and Danish's parents even as she cried and typed out solutions like a godwoman to the troubled people.

Uncle and Aunty nodded, and Mom kissed Ankit who beamed. Aunty then told us how Ankit had built a company and then sold it after the evil investors drove him to a nervous breakdown.

My mother responded, 'If Ankit would have shared his problem on this site, I would have helped him. That's the problem. Kids don't go to their parents with their problems.' She smiled at her own joke and everyone laughed seeing her so happy.

'He had his brother to take care of that,' Ankit's mother told her.

Aunty had to pull my mother away from the laptop to make her eat. My mother remained distracted on the dinner table, throwing glances at the laptop where the list of kids writing about their problems kept growing.

After we were done eating, my mother made Uncle and Aunty go to bed since they had office the next day and got back to answering questions, one key at a time. She cried and she laughed and was also shocked, reading the problems and issues the kids came up with.

'My brother is good, right?' Danish asked.

I nodded.

'Why don't you try and answer some?'

He thrust his laptop in front of me.

'I can't.'

'I know it's hard. But you have us, Aisha. We all love you. Think of someone who doesn't have a mother like you? Just try it out. You can share your experience as well. Maybe it will make you feel a little lighter?'

It was really hard to turn down anything Danish requested. The kid-like earnestness in his eyes was hard to ignore so I nodded and took the laptop from him.

Within the next fifteen minutes, all four of us were feverishly tapping out our responses to the questions that came in, answering the cry for help of people without names.

'My boyfriend broke up with me after three years. What should I do? I don't think I can go to school any more. We even had sex. I feel so used!'

'My mother is asking me to get married. I don't want to! I'm only seventeen. All my friends are going to college, I want to do that too, how should I do that?'

'I was molested by my father's cousin, my own uncle. I want to die! I want to die!'

'I broke up. He cheated on me. I want to kill myself.'

'My board results are awful. My parents curse me every day. I didn't get through DU. What should I do?'

'I'm a girl. I like girls. Is something wrong with me?'

I realized soon enough that I wasn't equipped to solve their problems. Ankit noticed that when I threw my laptop away on the sofa, held my head and paced around in a little circle.

'What?' he asked.

'THIS IS SO FRUSTRATING! THIS IS A BAD IDEA!' I tried not to choke on my words.

'There are people getting molested, cheated on, broken, forced to do things that they don't like and all we can do is give reassuring suggestions? How will that help them? This website is crap. It's shit.'

Ankit spoke, 'It will—'

'It won't. We will sound like ceremonious assholes who don't know anything about the pain they are going through.'

'But—'

'What? Ankit, what will you tell someone who's suicidal about his results? You have been an ace student all your life. This website won't work.'

Mom placed her laptop carefully on the side, made me sit, calmed me down and gave me water. No one said anything for a while.

'Why don't we get them to help themselves?' said Danish, looking up from his laptop.

'Is that a riddle?' asked Ankit.

'Ankit? Suppose a girl mails to us about being molested when she was a kid. Sure, all of us aren't professionals so the most we can do is guide them and be there for them. But we can send them the numbers of NGOs and professionals along with that mail. And a copy of their mail can be sent to the NGO. We can tie up with a bunch of NGOs. They can step in and make a real change. We can be the bridge for these troubled kids.'

'What if they don't want to talk to anyone from an NGO?'

'If they don't, we can connect people with the same problem. Like, for example, I failed my exam and I put up a cry for help. And you failed your exam as well. The website will connect these two people and they can talk about it and help each other out. We can reach a higher level of empathy by doing that?'

We all looked at each other.

'Okay, I might have been excited about a stupid idea,' conceded Danish and peered back into his laptop.

'It's a great idea,' said Mom.

I nodded.

Ankit hugged Danish and laughed raucously.

'My brother is the shiznit!' he said out loud, and got back to his computer, tapping furiously. 'Give me until tomorrow.'

47

Danish Roy

It was one in the night and we were still typing out our responses when Mom woke up and asked us if we needed anything. We shook our heads but she still made us coffee.

'Danish,' she called out as she was leaving the room. 'Your father wanted your help opening a cupboard. It's stuck. Can you come?'

Okay. Now that was our code for when they wanted to take me away from a public setting and talk to me. I nodded and followed Mom into her room. My father was reading a hardbound book under the lampshade, his spectacles perched precariously on his head. They didn't look like they had slept a wink. He kept the book on the side, and brightened the lamp. I sat on the bed and waited for them to talk. Usually, it was to chide me but it had been years since I had been last summoned to the king's bedchamber for a sounding.

Mom kept a hand on my arm and smiled.

Dad looked at me and spoke, 'We are very proud of you. Ankit told us what you did for the girl and we are so happy to hear that.'

What? What? What were they saying? *Where's my fucking phone when I need it?* I needed to record this.

'You were so supportive to her. It really takes a lot of grit,' said my mother. 'I told everyone at work about you.'

It looked like she would cry.

'Even the principal called and praised you. The parents of the kids love you as well. Maybe this is the right career choice for you,' said Dad.

I nodded. I knew if I were to say something I would cry. I had waited for this moment for years, literally years, for Mom and Dad to tell me I was worth something. And then it came. Like a little schoolboy I burst into tears and Dad hugged me, and then Mom hugged me and she cried a little. I told them how much it meant to me, how much I wanted them to be proud, how much I wanted to be a little more intelligent, a little smarter, get a few more marks, be praised by a professor or two, be famous or popular, and it killed me every day to know that I had disappointed them. I totally regretted it once the words left my mouth. It was embarrassing.

Dad laughed.

'You have never disappointed us, Danish. We just pushed you like we push our students in college. We knew you were made for better things. We just didn't know for what until now. Yes, we were a little impatient. But that's how parents are. They want their kids to be the best in the world. We wanted the same for you.'

'And you're the more handsome of the two,' said Mom.

'Will you say that in front of Ankit?'

'Of course not. I will say the same thing to him,' she said with a smile. 'Now go, your friends are waiting.'

She kissed me on the forehead.

'We are really, really proud of you.'

'Do a good job,' said Dad and shook my hand.

I walked out of the room, locked myself in the washroom for fifteen minutes and cried and laughed, and then wiped my face and joined everyone like nothing had happened.

'Did you manage to open the cupboard?' asked Aisha.

'Yes, I did. It felt wonderful.'

48

Aisha Paul

If they ever changed Fantastic Four to Fantastic Two, since anyway their movie franchise isn't working, with two brothers, Ankit and Danish would be the star contenders. I was hooked to the website. It was four and I was still on it. Yes, it made me cry and shout, for there's no end to injustice in the world, but it felt nice and warm and fuzzy when people thanked me for saving them, like they told me I saved them. My mother had dozed off by then, and Ankit was frantically testing out codes, asking Danish for suggestions, and then going back to typing. He had emptied the pot of coffee Aunty had left us almost by himself. Seeing them, I missed Sarthak, and all those years we had lost out on.

I got back to replying to more entries when the subject line of one of the entries caught my eye: Not Important, but important to me. Not really. It's a little silly. Don't open.

I opened it.

Hi.

Ummm.

Okay, this might be a little silly. I don't know if anyone will ever read it. Maybe it will get lost like the bottles with little scraps of paper with messages that people throw in the ocean. Maybe you have already stopped reading, right? What I want to say doesn't matter to anyone, except maybe me, which is why I need to put this out there for at least someone to read or to know.

I'm in love with a girl.

She's smart, she's kind, and she's insane.
She's the most amazing, amazing, amazing woman/
girl I have ever known. And it's a complete
privilege to have fallen in love with her.

She's strong and she's beautiful and she
makes everyone feel so good about themselves.
I have never seen someone who has the capacity
to love so deeply and so passionately. She
would fall in love with someone, a friend, a
parent, a brother and then love them with all
her heart and all her life. It's a rare thing.

I stopped reading. This guy should really tell the girl, I thought,
and started typing out a response. I stopped midway. I wanted
to read the whole thing.

I had a crush on her the moment I saw her, which is
slightly shallow and it was a little pervertish
at that time because she was seventeen. But
hey! I didn't know she was seventeen. So you,
anonymous person, should stop judging me. I
thought the feeling would pass. That I would
stop thinking about her. Hah. But that never
happened. I slipped down the long slippery
slope of love and never looked back.

I'm not a great guy. I'm not even an above
average guy.

I'm a normal guy. I'm the definition of it.
I'm not successful. I don't go to the gym. I
don't cycle. I don't run marathons. I don't dance
very well or think of myself as a traveller. I'm

not a thinker or a doer. I just live. I wake up,
I read a few books, watch TV, smile at people,
hear about the great things people do, and I go
back to sleep. No one's going to remember me.
I'm quite unextraordinary that way. And I know
that because I know people who are. Like my
brother. A young entrepreneur taking the world
by storm. Like the girl I'm in love with, whose
kindness and smartness would take her some place
great. Like my parents, both overachievers.

Wait. Wait. Wait. This can't be. I got back to reading it.

But it all changed the day I met her. The love
I had for her was quite extraordinary, and
that's something I'm sure of. I can go head to
head with all the romantic heroes you might
have read about, or seen, or heard of, and I
know I will kick the shit of them. I really,
really love her.

   That brings me to the difficult question of
what really is love. Frankly speaking, I don't
know and I can't put it in words. It's like little
explosions go off in my veins when I see her.

   Just talking to her makes my day. Like I
plan my day around her talking to me. There
are boundaries between her and me so I can't
just text her or call her any time I want to.
She's like my . . . student.

What? This was not happening. Was he? Suddenly, I remembered
the things he said when we went shopping, and how I couldn't
stop thinking about it before the incident happened . . .

I started to read again.

But I love her. There's no running away from that. I will always be in love with her. If there's something I have tried really hard, it's to fall out of love with her and it didn't happen.

A few days back she got assaulted.

By someone she trusted, someone she liked and was possibly in love with. Now, I'm not a brave person. Far from it. If there's ever a fight, I wouldn't be the one breaking it up because I would be too scared to pursue it. I'm terrified of fights. But after the assault, I have had to literally restrain myself from going and strangling him with my bare hands. I even spent a night outside the boy's home, waiting for him to come out, rock in hand to bash his skull open. Such a bad idea, come to think of it now.

I'm doing my little bit for her though. Every day I write like little chits to her, to tell her I believe in her, but now she doesn't need that any more. Others have started to believe in her. Thankfully. She gets chits from others as well now.

I think that's what will happen eventually. I will be just another chit. Today, she's good friends with me, tomorrow everyone around her will know what a great person she is and she won't need me any more. But it's fine. I think I have myself resigned to it now.

But I'm glad I met her. I have never felt this way before. I have never felt so alive. People travel. They discover things. The lead. They inspire. Me? I think I fell in love. That's my calling. It sounds cheesy and it sounds weak but now that I think of it, why not? Why shouldn't finding the greatest love be everyone's purpose in life? We can of course do away with the exceptional pixel quality in our phones, or the latest tech in our cars, if we got a few more people to love us with their lives. That's a no-brainer, right?!

Well, that's not going to happen and I am not going to be awarded a Nobel Prize for being so stupidly in love.

But as I said, she would never know. And she doesn't need to. She's into great boys, not into failed men. But I do hope the best for her. I do hope she finds love in her life.

I'm sorry to have wasted your time. You can't really help me but it feels good to know that someone out there knows.

I love her. I always will and she can always count on me.

Bye bye.

I closed the laptop. It was him.

I opened it again and read through the identifying passages again. It was him. Oh God. I looked at him. He was pointing his fingers at Ankit's laptop screen, and scratching his head, and biting his lips, and he was in love with me. He was in love with me right now, right at this very moment. It felt strange. Good, but slightly threatening. He yawned and looked at me.

'I think I will just go and sleep now.'

'Danish? Have you ever been in love?'

'Yes, once. Why?'

'What happened?'

'Nothing happened. I'm still in love and will always be, I think. It's a little embarrassing. Can we not talk about it?' he asked, scratching his hair.

He walked up to me and I felt a little scared. I scrunched up in my sofa lest he tried touching me. He didn't. He bent over to talk to me. I held my breath. I thought about all those times he had held my hand, comforted me, and I thought about the worst. My body felt stiff. My throat dried.

'I'm going to bed. When you're ready you can take Aunty to the guest room and sleep there,' he said and started bunching the coil of his phone's charger around his palm.

He moved away a little. I breathed easy. I felt calm again.

For those few moments I was scared of him. I was thinking about what if he did the same to me? I felt ashamed and scared for thinking that way. He was just being kind, but I still imagined the worse. I felt terrified thinking that I would always be this way? Would I ever let anyone come close to me?

He walked out of the room and soon after Ankit did too. I woke up my mother and hugged her. Late into the night, I asked my mother, 'Will I ever be able to fall in love with someone?'

'Yes, baba,' said my mother, wiping my tears. 'You will and whoever you fall in love with will love you with all his life.'

'What if I never forget what happened?'

'The man who loves you will wait for an eternity. Don't settle for anything less,' she said, and I decided that if I ever fall in love with someone, it would be Danish.

49

Danish Roy

About a week later, I was sitting in my room in the school, testing out a few changes Ankit had made to the website when Norbu came rushing in and spoke between ragged breaths.

'Fi . . . Sar . . . hak . . . fight . . .'

'What?'

'Come with me.'

I ran behind him through the corridors, he was a little too quick for me, towards the basketball court. Scores of other students ran alongside us. We pushed through the hundred-strong crowd swarming towards the basketball court, and found Sarthak and Vibhor jumping around in circles, shadow boxing.

'Dare you fucking touch me! I will kill you!' shouted Vibhor.

'LOL,' answered Sarthak. 'Why the hell are we hopping around each other if not to throw a few punches?'

Sarthak and Vibhor exchanged threats without following through.

'I don't know how he got here,' said Norbu.

'Chill. Find Aisha and get her here.'

A few students from the crowd started to shout. 'Fight. Fight. Fight. Fight.' And suddenly, everyone joined in and pumped their fists. A few took out their mobile phones and started to record.

They still weren't fighting. I fought my way out of the crowd.

'Where's Aisha?'

'I have called her,' Norbu said. 'She's coming.'

A little later, Aisha reached there, panting and heaving. 'What's going on here?'

'Sarthak and Vibhor are in there. It's going to get bloody.'

'Sarthak? What's he doing here? Are you kidding me?'

'He flew down for this. We should let him have his day under the sun.'

'Ask them to stop. What the hell are you doing here? Do something! Stop him!'

'They haven't even thrown a punch. I'm looking forward to it actually.'

'DANISH!'

I grabbed her and took her away from the crowd. 'Danish!' shouted Aisha. 'Stop them!'

'NO. I will not!' I shouted back.

'Why?'

'Why the fuck would I stop them, Aisha? Your brother needed to know and now he's angry. Why should I stop him?'

'Did you tell him?'

'Of course I told him. How did you feel when he didn't tell you he was gay?'

'Danish!'

'I wasn't going to hide it from him forever. And you didn't tell me about what Vibhor did to him in the locker room. Vibhor deserves it. Sarthak needs to beat the shit out of him and that's what's going to happen today.'

'You called him?' she asked, clutching her head and walking around in circles.

'Of course I did.'

'But how's he here? I mean, how?' she said, crying and laughing at the same time. 'He's going to get pounded, Danish. He's going to get hurt.'

'No, he will not. Don't underestimate him, Aisha,' I said. 'Now come.'

I climbed up a few stairs in the gallery around the basketball court and gave my hand to her. She hesitated for a bit, and then climbed up on her own. Aisha chewed on her fingernails and her skin tags. We sat there watching as Sarthak mocked Vibhor, jumping in his spot, shifting his weight from one foot to another, his fists raised up to his face.

'Why? Are you scared of this little gay boy? That's what you said, right?'

He threw a few shadow punches, swayed out of imaginary jabs and hooks, the years of boxing training kicking into gear.

'No one's going to be by you this time around, dude. It's just you and me.'

'I will fuck you up,' spat Vibhor, scared and angry, and scanned the crowd for support.

Vibhor's aides from the football team, most of whom were the ones who had to carry the placards for a week wanted no trouble. They looked the other way. One or two did try to join Vibhor's side but Erskin, Sarthak's Irish boyfriend and part-time powerlifter kept them at bay, shouting Irish profanities at them.

'That's his boyfriend. He's Erskin. 6'6" and 256 pounds,' I pointed out.

'Are you serious?' she said. 'He's dating The Rock with blonde hair?'

Erskin was almost as tall as a basketball pole and very broad. If he wanted to, he could have flicked Vibhor into orbit. Finally, after three more minutes of shouting and cajoling and booing from the crowd, Vibhor threw his first punch, a wild right hook, and Sarthak effortlessly swayed out of the way. He smiled, danced to Vibhor's side, and rained a three-punch combo in Vibhor's rib cage.

'Your brother is straight out of Tekken 3, Aisha.'

'Should I be enjoying this?' she asked.

'Yes.'

Vibhor, now disoriented, threw his punches wildly in the air. Sarthak weaved out of the way every time, and landed painful punches on his jaw, and on his rib cage. The fight lasted a total of three minutes and Vibhor got knocked to the floor thrice. He bled from his eyebrows, his fists and had a huge gash on his upper lip. We could hear the painful cracking of his ribs from afar. A straight punch in the stomach had made him throw up. A kick in his kneecap twisted his leg in an odd angle.

I climbed down once Vibhor was knocked out for good, and lay writhing and moaning on the ground.

'MOVE OUT OF THE WAY!' I shouted. 'GO BACK TO YOUR CLASSES OR I WILL HAVE ALL OF YOU SUSPENDED! WHAT THE HELL DO YOU THINK IS HAPPENING HERE!'

Within seconds the crowd dispersed and I helped Vibhor to get to the sick room. 'Don't die,' I whispered in his ear as I dragged him through the corridors.

An hour later, Vibhor, all stitched up and limping, had ratted to the principal. Sarthak, Erskin, Aisha and I were summoned to his room.

'Care to explain, Mr Danish?' asked the principal, putting his angry face on.

He knew the boy deserved it but not in the way he got it. I strongly disagreed. No matter how much I was against mob justice, he deserved the shakedown and more.

'I was late on the scene, sir,' I said. 'But as I have been told, Vibhor was the first person to throw a punch. Sarthak had no choice but to retaliate. Here's a video I got from one of the students. There's no audio but it's clear that he was the one to start a fight.'

The principal watched the video with furrowed eyebrows. Since there was no sound, it was impossible to tell if it was Sarthak who encouraged the fight.

'Vibhor,' the principal spoke. 'You hit him first.'

'But—'

Sarthak cut him, 'Sir, I was just showing my friend Erskin my old school and he came out of nowhere and started abusing me.'

'Sir, believe me!' pleaded Vibhor.

'There's nothing to believe, Vibhor. You threw the first punch.'

'He abused me, sir!' shouted Vibhor. 'Ask anyone! It's all this bitch's doing.'

'VIBHOR,' shouted the principal and banged the table. 'YOU WILL NOT ABUSE ANYONE IN MY OFFICE. And I have already talked to a few students. They all corroborate Sarthak's story.'

'But—'

'You can leave now, or I will call your parents and get you suspended. Do you get that?' Vibhor, defeated, left the room mumbling empty threats, '*Dekha lunga tum sabko.*'

'All of you can leave as well,' he addressed us.

We got up from our chairs.

'Except you, Danish. I need to talk to you.'

He motioned me to sit in front of him and started speaking when everyone had left.

'I know you're behind this entire thing, Danish.'

'I don't know what you're talking about, sir.'

'I know you won't admit it. But the next time something like this happens you will be answerable, Danish. I thought you knew better than to get a student beaten up inside the school premises.'

I shrugged. I got up and was about to leave the room when he called out and asked, 'But I have just one question to ask you . . . why did the students corroborate Sarthak's story and not Vibhor's? They all saw what happened, didn't they?'

'I have no idea, sir, but my guess would be they have started to believe Aisha's story. It's time she caught a break.'

He smiled and let me go.

50

Aisha Paul

'WHAT. WAS. THAT!' I shouted and lunged at my brother. 'And what are you doing here?'

'I think that was the best day of my life!' he said. 'And before you flatter yourself, I did it for what he did to me and not for you.' We hugged each other.

He broke out of the hug and kissed me on the cheek, something he had never done before and asked me how I was doing.

'I can't believe you didn't tell me,' he grumbled.

I told him I was better now, and he hugged me again, and told me how sorry he was to hear about it.

'We could have killed him,' said Erskin, the blonde Rock, with biceps thicker than my thighs and whose head hovered dangerously close to the ceiling fan.

'Yes, seeing you, you could have,' I said.

'Come here,' he said in his one-part funny, one-part sexy accent. And I disappeared into his bone-crushing hug.

'You're beautiful. You're even more beautiful than what Sarthak had described,' he said. 'Next time, the boy tries anything, tell me and I will handle it.'

I smiled.

I addressed my brother in Hindi, 'Is he really your boyfriend? Like you two are actually like serious?'

He nodded.

'That's so unfair. Take me to Ireland as well! I need my fairy tale, too,' I said.

'You already have your fairy tale,' he said and pointed towards Danish who was talking to someone from the administration.

I blushed. Which was strange. Because I didn't get the familiar crippling feeling when imagining being close to a boy. I smiled and dismissed my brother.

He said, 'Of course you know he likes you, don't you? He always has.'

'No, he doesn't.'

I don't know why I said that.

'Of course, he does. And so do you, you just don't know that yet,' he said, and switched to English.

'Yes, he loves you,' added Erskin.

How's it that it was apparent to everyone and not to me?

*

It was the most awkward evening. Thank God my father was already back in Thiruvananthapuram. He wouldn't have known what to do. Despite my brother's reluctance, I had called Erskin over to dinner at our place. He filled up our little dining room. For the first fifteen minutes, no one talked, just drinking water and pretending to be lost in their respective phones.

'What's the password to the WiFi?' asked Erskin leaning into me.

'ITSSOAWKWARD. All caps.'

'Huh?'

'It's aishasarthak. All lower case.'

My mother served the food and everyone just smiled at each other, and ate silently. I stayed shut as well. No one gave me the set of questions or topics you could talk about when your brother's Irish boyfriend comes home. I texted Danish.

AISHA: Save me.

DANISH: What happened?

AISHA: Brother + Brother-in-law + mother + language barrier = disaster.

DANISH: Lol.

AISHA: Come.

DANISH: I'm not the best conversationalist.

AISHA: You're the best.

DANISH: Give me 15.

AISHA: You have 10.

Danish was there in ten minutes. He was still in his loose, worn-out pyjamas; his hair was ruffled and he looked rather cute. Like he was sleeping with his eyes open.

'So Erskin, what do you do?' he asked as he sat at the table.

My mother, too, heaved a sigh of relief. She was afraid Erskin may take the lack of conversation as an insult.

'I'm studying literature. I want to be a filmmaker,' said Erskin. 'But my parents don't agree with my choices. They want me to join the family business.'

'Countries change, stories don't.'

'Huh?'

'Nothing, nothing. So what do your parents do exactly?'

Danish thanked my mother for ladling his plate with rice, lentils and paneer.

'They do paint jobs for aviation companies. That's how we got the free tickets to India.'

And he put his hand on Sarthak's. My mother looked away. I gasped, and so did my brother. Danish, apparently, found this hilarious and chuckled.

'I will get more *raita*,' said my mother and disappeared into the kitchen.

I followed her into the kitchen, and found her silently sobbing into her dupatta.

'Aww, what happened, Maa?' I said and put my arms around her. 'It's okay, Maa. It's okay, Maa. He loves him.'

'I know, I know, it's just that I always thought I will get a little plump girl for him to get married to,' she said, still crying softly, 'but he's getting married to a giant.'

She started to laugh behind the tears.

'He's happy and that's all that matters.'

My mother broke away from the embrace and slapped my back playfully.

'Don't teach me, Aisha.'

She wiped her tears and mindlessly rolled another chappati.

'I know that's what matters. But it will take some time.'

'I know, Maa,' I said. 'He's so lucky he has you. Look how cute you look while you cry.'

I pinched her cheeks. She flinched and tried to hide she was smiling.

'He's nice,' said a voice from behind. It was Danish flashing a thumbs up at us. 'He's nice, he's rich, and he loves Sarthak. What else do you need, Aunty? You're lucky.'

'Don't make fun of me, Danish,' said Maa.

'I'm not,' he said and sat on the counter. Mom asked him to get down from there and he obediently jumped off. 'Sarthak's so happy.'

'I know,' said Maa. 'He's like when he was ten again.' She started to cry again. 'He was so beautiful.'

'He still is, Maa,' I said.

My mother nodded. Sarthak called for more chappatis and my mother gave Danish a little casserole. He tucked it in his arm, poured a little raita for himself in a little bowl and went to the living room.

'I will go outside and not talk again,' I said.

'Aisha?' she called out.

I stopped and turned.

'Please eventually get married to a boy?'

I laughed. 'Of course, Maa.'

'Danish?'

'What?'

She walked close, made that puppy face she always would whenever she had to convince me to do something I didn't want to do, and she rubbed my arm and said, 'He's a nice boy. He likes you.'

'No, he doesn't.'

'He's in our living room talking to your brother's boyfriend so that he doesn't feel left out. My guess is he does,' said Maa, with a naughty glint in her eye you would associate with *Gossip Girl* characters.

'I need to leave.'

A little later, my mother came with extra raita and poured it in each of our bowls. And after she was done filling both of Erskin's bowls to the brim, she touched his chin with her fingers and then kissed his forehead. Erskin might not have known what was going on, but he understood the language of love. He nodded at my mother. My mother asked me to click a picture of her with Sarthak and Erskin. She stood between Erskin and Sarthak, who were both sitting and yet were taller than my mother. Click.

'How's the picture?' my mother asked.

'Great,' I said.

Both Sarthak and my mother were crying in the picture.

'Now you,' said my sly mother, pointing to me and Danish.

She took the camera from me and waited. Both of us sort of just leaned into each other and smiled awkwardly at the camera. She egged Sarthak and Erskin to join us in the picture, too, and so we had to stand and shuffle close.

I'm sure my mother acted to work the camera as she asked us to look more natural in the picture. Yeah, right. Danish leaned in a little closer, and I thought, why not? I shifted closer to him and my hand touched his. My breath quickened, but in a good way, as I had wanted it to. My heart thumped and I could feel every nerve ending. I shifted closer and I could see him lean away shyly. Erskin pushed me a little, and my hand was in full contact with Danish's now and it was heady feeling. Emboldened, I let my hand travel on his back and rest a little over his waist. Little bolts of electricity ran through my spine as I anticipated the same from him, but he just kind of kept his hand hovering behind my back and over my waist, as if too scared to touch me. My mother clicked. We sat down. The picture was passed around. It was a good picture. Erskin was smiling the widest, Sarthak looked like he was blushing and angry at the same time and Danish was literally sweating and looked scared.

I looked at him, and Danish pretended to stare in his food. I leaned towards him and asked, 'Is the paneer good? I made it.'

He nodded, blushing wildly. And in that moment, I felt something mechanically click in my body—it was as if someone had screwed open a flap in my back, taped a few wires together, removed the short-circuit caused by Vibhor and set me right. I might have been damaged but I was still under warranty. I knew I might not go back to what I was before but I felt ready to be normal again.

51

Danish Roy

Erskin, Sarthak, Aisha and I spent all of the next week taking Erskin around Delhi. To be frank, we were taking ourselves around town. Even after being in Delhi forever, I had never done the touristy things around here.

It was fun. Often because Erskin literally never went without smoking pot for more than a few hours a day and we indulged in a lot of passive smoking, and sometimes active as well.

Erskin got hit on a lot by older women wherever we went. And was pursued even more when we told people he was gay. We almost intentionally got into a fight in Sector 56, Gurgaon but the warring party backed out after Erskin made a dramatic, calculated entry. He was rather sweet, too. Like any responsible Indian, we taught him Hindi swear words. As clichéd as it is, it worked like a charm as he greeted random people on the road with the choicest of expletives. Erskin was staying at the Taj, near Dhaula Kuan, and every day the three of us would reach the hotel right when the breakfast buffet started and only leave when it wound to a close. Aisha smiled a lot and that alone rocked my world.

Later that week, I was sitting with Ankit for four hours testing out the Android app Ankit had made for the website; *everything will be on the phone, everything*, he had said.

Ankit was right. After aching for a bigger screen, and a responsive keyboard for the first two hours, I was hooked to the phone screen and the laptop lay ignored on the side. The app was much better.

I was typing my responses when my phone beeped.

AISHA: Are you free?

DANISH: Testing out the app. It's crazy

AISHA: I'm with my brother and ER. They are drunk.

DANISH: Okay.

AISHA: They are kissing.

DANISH: Oh.

AISHA: Awkward. Bored.

DANISH: Where?

AISHA: Their hotel.

DANISH: Oh.

AISHA: Hmmm.

DANISH: Oh. Wait. You want me to come?

AISHA: Why would I tell you otherwise?

DANISH: Oh.

AISHA: You're really intelligent sometimes.

DANISH: Tell me about it.

AISHA: Save me.

DANISH: Twenty minutes.

A little later my phone beeped again.

AISHA: Where?

DANISH: Car didn't start. So took a cab. Twenty minutes more I guess. What's happening?

AISHA: They told me they are going to the washroom. It's been ten minutes.

DANISH: LOL.

AISHA: Disturbing visuals.

DANISH: There in a flash.

AISHA: My brother is giggling.

DANISH: Haha.

AISHA: Erskin is moaning. In Irish. Quick.

I found Aisha in the ground floor Italian restaurant with the table littered with dishes barely touched.

'I might have ordered a little more than necessary as revenge,' she said like a puppy who shat the carpet.

'Who's paying?'

'Erskin.'

'I'm so hungry right now,' I said and pulled the plates closer to me.

We ate in silence, making sure we tried everything. We tried playing mind games with our stomachs, telling them they still had space.

And then out of nowhere, she shot me a question, 'Why don't you have a girlfriend? You can do much better than hang out with your student, his brother and gay Thor.'

'I'm boring, I think,' I said, because that's my charm. I blurt out the truth like bile.

'You're not boring,' she said, almost offended.

'Of course I am. Look at my brother. He's smart, funny, and can dance like he's getting paid for it. He's awesome.'

'So you're not your brother,' she said. 'You're still interesting.'

I sniggered.

'Of course, you are. Otherwise which teacher would hang out like you hang out with us?'

Now that she put it that way. Though a huge chunk of the reason was that I got to spend time with Aisha, but I couldn't tell her that. At least she respected me, thought of me when bored, I didn't want to lose that. I didn't want to do anything stupid, so I just friend-zoned myself. It was better that way.

We paid the bill by signing Erskin's room number. We both burped and pretended like we didn't. We walked out of the hotel lobby. Aisha walked around the fountain of the hotel, dipping her feet in the water and splashing some outside. I walked a few steps behind her. There weren't a lot of people around and I didn't want to walk very close to her. I had noticed her flinch when Ankit or I leaned over to talk to her. The fear inside her is still bubbling, I guessed.

'Hold me,' she said and stretched out her hand as she walked, balancing herself on the ledge of the fountain. I held her hand and she walked around twice, smiling, looking far into the distance like she was in deep thought, like an artiste, a singer, a writer, someone I would never keep engaged for long.

'What do you think of me, Danish?'

'As in? And why are you asking?'

'Just like that? Tell me?'

I stammered. 'I think you're . . . great. You're really nice.'

'Can you imagine yourself with me? Like us? Dating?'

'Umm . . . that would be—'

'Don't say that again. I know you're my teacher and whatever. But if it were not the case? Would *us* be a possibility?'

'Why not?' I said as calmly as I could.

'So you like me?'

'In a way, yes.'

'Do you like Namrata like you like me?'

'No!' I shot out.

'Okay.'

Shit. I should not have said that. She jumped off the ledge and led me back inside the hotel. My clammy, sweaty hand was still in hers, and I was molten wax.

'Where are we going?'

'Anywhere,' she said, entered the elevator and pressed the button to Erskin's floor.

She still hadn't let go of my hand, her fingers were now intertwined with mine, sweaty.

'Here.'

I nodded.

We walked through the corridors and she smiled at a man from housekeeping minding his business. We stood outside a room a couple had just left from, and she rolled her eyes and said, 'Shit! Shit!' loud enough for the housekeeping guy to turn towards us. She walked towards him, made a sorry face and spoke, 'Our room is still not cleaned. Can you do it right now? And can you give us the key of any other room till the time you're at it?'

The man frowned, mumbled something about rules and guidelines but Aisha threw a cluster bomb of Please, Please, Please, Please, on him and moments later we were swiping a key to a room not yet occupied. My body thrummed.

She placed the key card into the little slot by the door, an LED lit up and then the entire room. She went and sat on the bed. Her knee shook nervously. The bed creaked a little. I stood a few feet away, near the mini bar, making sure I wasn't encroaching on her personal space. I would merge into the wall if I moved any further from her.

She looked at me, and mumbled, 'Kiss me.'

It looked like she would cry any moment.

'What?'

'Kiss me. You said *we* were a possibility,' she said, her voice now quivering. Yes, she was definitely going to cry now.

'I can't.'

'Danish, please kiss me.'

'Aisha—'

'For God's sake, please kiss me.'

'Aisha?'

'Please,' she said, and the tears came, and yet her eyes were bolted on me. I walked to her side, and sat on the bed. She clutched my arm and cried into my shoulder. I didn't say anything for a while.

'I'm sorry, I'm sorry.'

I told her it's okay.

'I really thought I could do it. You know, kiss someone again? I really thought I could do it today.'

'You will. Eventually.'

She told me she thought she could be someone else for a little while. 'I wanted to move on,' she said and burst out again. I held her till she quietened.

'I'm okay. You can leave me now. You're sweating.'

She forced a smile on her face. She stared into her little, pretty fingers.

'The housekeeping guy totally believed me though,' she said, her voice childlike, her kajal all smudged and she looked like a little girl who had been denied a toy.

I nodded and passed her a tissue.

'I want to use the washroom.'

I wanted to remind her that we could be caught but she was gone by then. I sat thinking, what if she had said the same thing without crying, or without a motive of trying to put what happened behind her and move on? But why did she choose me? Well, there was no point flattering myself because she didn't really have an option.

I waited for her.

52

Aisha Paul

I washed my face and looked at myself in the mirror. I was pissed. I was so close.

The past one week had been wonderful. While Erskin and Sarthak couldn't keep their hands off each other, the only distraction was Danish. It was hard at first to shake off his confession on the website, to be around him normally, but slowly I began to realize how hard it must be for him to like me so much and yet not tell me. That's when the little glass wall I had constructed around myself started to crack a little.

We began to go on little walks and he would talk to me about his old house in C.R. Park, how once he was punched by Jeffrey Archer's bodyguards because he got too close, about the first girl he had a crush on (she was married now and was pregnant with twins). He was really *himself*. He wasn't scared of being stupid or boring or sound repetitive while he was all of these at some point or the other. He told me a story about how he accidentally scored a goal and was the class hero for three weeks, which I can narrate better than him. I really liked him. I could throw my arm around him and walk with him and feel nice. I could lower my guard and snort out water through my nose without thinking what he would think of me. I took some really big liberties, knowing he was in love with me.

Today, I thought I would take the next step. I thought I could put it all behind me and try to be with someone who likes me as I am, who doesn't play little games, someone who's as sweet as Danish is. I thought I would allow myself a little wiggle space and stretch out my hands and not be alone. I deserved someone. And I wanted someone. After all the shit I'd gone through, it's the least one could want.

I really wanted to kiss him. Like, really. But I messed it up. And now, I was washing my face off snot with stolen face wash. I could do better. I breathed in. I will kiss him, I told myself and patted my face dry.

I smoothed out my clothes. You can do this, I told myself, you want to be kissed by him, he's a nice guy, and you kind of like him, and you like kissing and you like being kissed.

I came out, took a deep breath and hoped this yoga type shit had cleansed me off my memories. He was still on the bed, sitting the way I had left him, stiff. He was always like that with me, always measured, always scared. In the picture we clicked, his hands hovered hilariously around my waist, careful not to touch me inappropriately. Today, it had to change. I would *allow* him. And yet, my sexy time started with the words, *I'm sorry*.

'Sorry? No,' he said. 'Stop being sorry all the time. You apologize for things you don't need to.'

He needs to stop being so encouraging all the time.

'Can you come here?' I asked.

I sucked at being seductive. I weighed telling him I knew about his mail so I wouldn't have to do this and just kiss him. He walked up to me, stopped two feet away and asked me what happened. Without warning, I held his head in my hands, a bit like Mountain from *Game of Thrones* did before he crushed Oberyn's skull, and I lunged at his lips and kissed him full. It was more like my teeth hitting his lips at Mach 1. He reeled away from me, holding his bleeding lips.

'Shit.'

'I'm sorry!'

He threw me a look.

'Okay, I'm not sorry.'

His lips were bleeding. He stood unmoving like a statue, waiting for my instructions. I pointed to his lips.

'You're bleeding. Go. Go to the washroom.'

He touched his lips and inspected his bloodied fingers.

'Shit.'

He tilted his head backwards and walked to the washroom. I held out tissues and dabbed his lips. Though the sink had reddened now, I couldn't help but find myself in the middle of a grin and then started laughing out loud.

'Wait. Let me look.'

I took the tissue from him and kept it against his lips. It stopped bleeding after a while.

'Does it pain?'

He licked his lips and shook his head.

'Should we try it again?'

He looked at me, confused and wobbled his head, a mix of a Yes and No. I led him out to the room again. I held his head, softly this time and went in excruciating slow motion towards his face, like I had learned in the movies, and kissed him. His hand hung limply around his waist. They were slightly distracting and made me feel I was coaxing him into making out with me so I took them and placed them firmly around my waist. We kissed now. At first slowly, and then he took the lead and really got into it. His hands were all over my back now, no longer shy. And then, he suddenly stopped as his hand touched my bare back.

'Yes,' I mumbled, and his hand crept up my T-shirt.

I felt free, and a little like crying but thought it would ruin the mood. I kissed him all over his face, and lunged on his neck, letting myself loose. He moaned and I felt a little selfish and pushed his face at my collarbone. He may have broken his nose. He kissed my neck and tried reaching places he couldn't have without my clothes on so I helped him because he wouldn't have for all the money in the world. I took off my T-shirt and he tried really hard not to stare and failed miserably. I felt my entire body warm up. I struggled. God knows I did. It took all my might to remind myself that the boy was Danish, a nice guy who loved me, and this was what I wanted too, to prevent myself from slipping into darkness again.

I hugged him, half to not let him see me without my T-shirt, and half to feel his body up against mine. I slipped my hands inside his T-shirt and pulled it over his head. Feeling his body against mine, I almost burst into flames. I pushed him on to the bed and in a move that would impress Jason Statham, switched off the light with my leg. Full points for bravery as I unclasped by bra and threw it away. I lowered my body into his and his breathing quickened.

I paused.

'We can stop if you want to,' said Danish, almost looking for his T-shirt.

'Shut up. I want this.'

'I mean, Aisha, we don't—'

'Shut up.'

'This is probably not right—'

'It is. And shut up.'

I kissed him before he reminded me of what I was struggling with. It was my past and it wasn't going to ruin my present and my future. I deserved better and wanted to be loved and lusted for. It was obvious why he stopped but I didn't want to. I really wanted this. What happened wasn't my fault and I wasn't going to punish myself for it. I would ram the thoughts out of my head every time they threatened my sanity. And so that's what I did.

I reached for his jeans, unclasped the button and pulled it away. He crouched as if hiding from me. I got naked myself. I caught him staring. I climbed over him. For the first time I felt naked. His hands ran over my bare back. I took him in my hands and stroked him gently. He reached out for his wallet and took out a condom, which I rolled over him. I lowered myself down on him. I fumbled in the dark, but soon I grabbed hold of him and slowly guided him inside me. And then I lost sense of time and space. We were a hot, sweaty mess rolling around the bed, unmindful and hungry and relentless. It was white hot blinding pain and immeasurable pleasure. I reached places in my head I didn't know existed, waves of calm and pain washed over me and I drowned happily in them.

It was the best twenty-five minutes of my life. I felt alive, I felt beautiful, I felt satisfied, I felt human, and I wanted to do it again. I told him that.

'There's also something I need to tell you,' he said as I nibbled at his ear.

'I know. I think I might love you too,' I said and we started kissing again.

53

Danish Roy

It was my first real date with serious possibilities and I had to get it right and my brother hovering around me didn't help. I had bought myself a three-minute cucumber mask from the supermarket after hours of hanging around the racks which promised better, youthful skin, and I couldn't use it till he made himself scanty.

'You need to test out this app,' he said. 'I'm meeting investors tomorrow and it needs to be glitch-free. They are not going to invest otherwise and then it will go in the dump.'

'It's going to be awesome,' I said, as I shaved slowly. 'You're a genius.'

'Danish, I need your help here. This isn't a big money-making app. So they might be a little sceptical. Hell, they might even want to charge people for it. Imagine!'

'If you want someone's help, you should take Aisha's. But you have to get this thing to work.'

'I'm trying my best,' he said. 'And I'm going to leave now. You can put on your mask if you want to.'

He left.

I picked Aisha up two hours later, my skin still the same, a little itchy though. She wore a red dress and a hint of make-up. She looked stunning and I told her that. She joked if I were just saying that to get into her pants and laughed boisterously at her own joke.

'Where are we going?' I asked.

'Only the biggest Tekken Tournament of it all!' she squealed.

263

An hour later, we got to a rundown gaming parlour with a standee that announced the tournament. It wasn't really a tournament; it was more of an intra-Facebook Tekken community monthly shakedown. There were twenty participants in all. We were the oldest by half a decade and we got knocked out in the first round, humiliated by little kids, and that was end of that.

'That wasn't nice at all,' I said.

'Yeah, we might have been a little overconfident,' she said.

'Now what?'

'We could go dancing?' In the middle of the day, I asked.

'Why not?'

And so we did. Apparently, there were a lot of clubs in Noida that held afternoon parties for school children who found it hard to get permission to go out at night. So we danced awkwardly for an hour or two and walked out sweaty and happy after I had embarrassed myself enough.

Hungry, we drove to the closest McDonald's, ordered almost everything on the menu and argued about who was the funniest in *FRIENDS*, whether Stannis Baratheon was the one True King, and whether the second season of *True Detective* was overrated, and if she thought Indian serials would be much better if they shut down in twenty-six episodes.

Later that afternoon, we found ourselves at a little nook in one of the quaint-looking coffee shops in Hauz Khas, and we wound up cosily reading our books. We debated on which one was better. We kissed each other every once in a while, and talked about how I would have to leave my job soon because what we were doing was against school rules. 'You can work with your brother,' she told me, and I nodded. Later we spent a good hour testing out Ankit's app and replying to people who had written in. She gave me a few pointers and I noted them down and shot them across to Ankit.

We made out twice in the car, almost getting busted by a cop the second time around. Sometimes, she flinched but otherwise she fought it pretty well. She was happy. And to know I contributed to it was a solid four on ten.

*

The next day, I submitted my resignation letter again, and Aisha came to my room to rue my departure with a one-pound cake which we polished off in minutes.

'I will miss you here,' she told me.

'I will miss you too.'

We packed my stuff into a little brown box the school had provided me.

'I hope you will be fine.'

She nodded and looked away from me.

'I saw him again today,' she said.

'Did he say anything?'

'No,' she said. 'I don't think he will.'

The school had stopped wearing those badges but no one doubted Aisha any more. They would all nod at her, or just let her be, which she liked infinitely better. People would talk about Vibhor though. Last heard, the physical education teacher kicked him out of the football team. His band of followers had long disbanded and he would hang out with only a handful of loyal boys who I guessed were with him because his father was still rich and paying for his exploits.

'Thank you for that, Danish,' she said.

'You should thank your friends. They did all the work,' I told her.

'But you listened.'

We finished packing and stared at each other, wanting to do something but knowing how wrong yet thrilling it would be. But just then, the door was flung open and Megha walked in.

She lunged headlong at Aisha and said, 'I should have believed you. I should have believed you.'

Aisha calmed her down. 'Tell me what happened,' asked Aisha.

'He tried to kiss me. We were drunk and so I said no, and he fought with me. He always does that. But yesterday, he blurted out the truth about you,' she said and hid her face in her hands.

'Why didn't you tell me earlier?'

'I didn't think there was anything I could do. I felt . . . I didn't know what to say.'

'Did he hurt you?' asked Aisha.

'No,' she said and started to cry again.

Aisha held her hand and told her it was okay. She nodded and wiped off her tears.

'I'm sorry. I should have listened to you.'

Aisha told her they were friends and it wasn't really her fault, and that she would take care of her.

54

Aisha Paul

Danish made it really easy for me.

I'm sure I would have felt it sooner or later. He saved me a lot of time. I could easily list down the reason why I knew I was totally in love with him. Here they are in no particular order.

1. I stare at my phone when he's not with me and abandon it when he's around.
2. He makes me feel all warm and cuddly inside.
3. And I go from warm and cuddly to hot and bothered in a matter of seconds.
4. He kisses me a lot.
5. I can be stupid and he never corrects me. He lets me correct myself.
6. He lets himself be stupid and lets me correct him all the time. Even when he's not to be corrected.
7. He kisses me a lot.
8. He turns me on. After the incident, I didn't think it was possible but OH MY GOD.
9. He notices everything.
10. I like dressing up for him. Everything I wear is for his eyes only. And maybe Sarthak's (he has a keen eye).
11. He's good in bed. Quite giving and that's important. He shares himself with me. He puts in the work.
12. He goes down on me. Always.
13. He shares his books with me.
14. He's better than Hellboy.
15. He loses to me in Scrabble. Intentionally.

16. He taught me how to swim. Though I think we took longer than necessary but I didn't mind.
17. He helped me breathe again.
18. He's GoodReads for me.
19. He laughs at my jokes. He makes me feel like I have a career in stand-up comedy.
20. He's good at Mutliplayer Tekken.
21. He listens. He really listens. He remembers things I say better than I do.
22. He watched *Gossip Girl* on my insistence. And told me he liked it. That's a big deal.
23. He helped me drink again without having to look over my shoulder. We should all be able to drink without feeling scared or guilty.
24. He goes down on me and remains there for an eternity.
25. My mother loves him. Well, my mother loves everyone but she really loves him. Like he even gets me jealous sometimes.
26. I could make love again. Over and over again.
27. He kisses me a lot.
28. He gives a lot of attention to my breasts when we are in bed. It feels okay but I like the fact that he likes them.
29. He's older. But he's also young and wise, and young and stupid.
30. He likes me in pyjamas and he likes me in dresses.
31. He enjoys it when I come, it's not a job for him, he doesn't ask if I am coming, he does his work and prides himself when I come.
32. He prefers I pick the venues of our dates.
33. He never stares into my phone.

So, yes, I was pretty sure this was love. If it wasn't, I was sure anyone else who's in *true* love rides unicorns to dates.

Danish had stopped coming to school, which meant I had to sneak out to see him every day, something he wasn't too happy about but couldn't help either. We had promised ourselves we would behave once Erskin and Sarthak went back to Poland and that day came sooner than we had expected it would.

The day before they left, we planned a party to celebrate and drown ourselves in tears. We ate at our place because we were done fleecing Erskin and the anticipated alcohol bill was enough to burn a hole through our collective pockets.

Danish, cutely enough, tried to help my mother in the kitchen. He wasn't socially adept at bonding with mothers, so when I saw him with mine I knew he liked her. But then again, she was my mother, who wouldn't like her? And that reminded me that she was *my* mother, and Danish was butting in.

'I will help her,' I told him.

My mother kissed Danish on his forehead and asked him to wait at the dining table. He walked past me, smiling, knowing full well how possessive I was about her.

The dinner was served. It was simple *daal* and rice and mixed vegetables. We all made sure we ate a lot so none of us would throw up later. We all hugged my mother before we left. Erskin threw in a little surprise for her when he touched her feet and we were all like *What!* My mother almost cried. If you open your heart to someone you will be surprised to see how much you're capable of loving someone.

And talking about loving someone, I couldn't help keep my hands off Danish in the backseat. I would be a clingy girlfriend. I knew it. It was going to be a part of my destiny. It wasn't decided whether I was going to run Apple tomorrow or Goldman Sachs, both of them seemed real possibilities, but along with that I would be a clingy girlfriend. I was seemingly good at that.

'I can see everything in the rear-view mirror,' said Ankit who was driving.

We reached Raasta, an upmarket pub bang in the middle of Hauz Khas, a venue I had chosen, and ordered for an LIIT (the cocktail for the gods) pitcher before the happy hours got over. We all got shit-housed. Drunk and hammered, Erskin, Ankit and Sarthak took the dance floor by storm. Sarthak and Ankit were great on their feet, and Erskin was a really enthusiastic dancer, stomping the floor like Sunny Deol in his heydays. Danish was pulled in soon after and he aped their steps. I was still on my first drink, going slow at it, and was battling my libido which had skyrocketed.

'Can I borrow him for a minute?' I asked, grabbing Danish's hand.

Sarthak rolled his eyes and Erskin winked at me. I pulled Danish outside the pub. We went straight to the parking lot, paid our driver an extra five hundred to go take a walk and I let Danish please me for the next fifteen minutes. Once done, I fixed my clothes.

'What about me?'

'Later,' I told him.

His cute face scrunched up and I didn't feel sorry for him at all. I was allowed to be selfish.

'Let's go.'

I grabbed his hand and he dragged his feet behind me, still trying to convince me to having one more go at it.

We entered the club and found Erskin and Sarthak dancing together on the dance floor. *Still not used to it.* We walked the other way. Ankit had already found interesting company. He's quite charming that way.

We stood at the bar on the terrace and ordered bright orange cocktails.

'Why do you smile like that?' I asked.

'What? When?' he replied, immediately wiping the grin off.

'Shut up, you know you do.'

'I just feel lucky to have you that's all.'

'You're kidding, right?' I said.

He didn't flinch.

'Really? Oh my God, that's so cheesy.'

I kissed him on the cheek.

'I get really scared sometimes. Because in my head I get increasingly cheesy about you. Like I think how we will be when we are fifty or something and then I'm like how freaked out you might get when I talk to you about it. Oh. I freaked you out, didn't I? I did. I'm sorry,' I apologized profusely.

'You don't have to be sorry. I'm cheesy as hell. I can beat your ass sleeping. You're nothing. You don't stand a chance,' he said.

'Don't challenge me. It's going to be another Tekken.'

'Not this time. I'm the daydreaming king when it comes to you. We are getting married in Mussouri.'

'Dehradun,' I said. 'I love Dehradun. I already know what you're going to wear. A purple bowtie.'

'Perfect for someone as extrovert as I am.'

'I knew you would say that. So I decided to convince you after you're suitably drunk. Also, don't die before I do. Because I have imagined situations and they were horrible.'

'That's a tricky predicament. Because I imagined the same and it sucked. And don't you dare get married to someone else. I have imagined that too and it blew as well.'

'It seems like I have competition. Hmmm . . . I imagined an elaborate sequence of coming to your wedding and breaking it off and running away with you.'

'Insane.'

'I know, right. We are pathetic,' I said.

'Totally.'

'Please tell me you have imagined yourself as a loving husband and loving father and put me out of my misery.'

'Totally. Also imagined ourselves at poor yet crazily in love. Like five of us in a one-bedroom apartment and still being happy,' he said.

We drank to that and poured out all our cheesy daydreams about each other. I thanked God I was dating him and no one else. Who else would think up all this nonsense? That, too, when it's hardly been any time since we started dating.

We were still talking about these crazy-ass scenarios when I saw him walk to the terrace, and wave down the waiter.

'He's here. Megha is with him,' I said.

'Who?' asked Danish, and I pointed out to Vibhor who was sitting at the table with a couple of his friends, smiling and drinking. 'What the . . .? And what's Megha doing with him? Is she out of her mind?'

55

Danish Roy

'Stay, Danish. We aren't leaving or talking to him,' said Aisha before I could ask the question.

'What about Megha?'

'She seems to have made her decision,' said Aisha. 'Let her be.'

'What the hell are you talking about? So we just pretend we are not here then?' I said.

'No. We are going to party with him,' she said, steeling her voice.

She took her phone out and called Erskin, Ankit and Sarthak. Within a minute they were standing next to us, restraining themselves from beating Vibhor down to a pulp.

'Why would we not hit the bastard?' protested Sarthak.

'Because I'm asking all of you to not do so.'

She looked at all of us.

'Think of it as something I need to do before I move on,' she said.

'I don't think it's wise,' said Sarthak.

'I know some guys,' said Ankit. 'It's dangerous but they can take care of him. *Permanently.*'

We all turned to him.

'What! I know them. I have never used them,' he said.

'Please, I need you to be with me,' she said.

'Fine,' we echoed.

'I'm going to his table. You are going to join me in a bit as well. And be nice to him. I need this to go normally.'

I wasn't too pleased about it but Erskin spoke, 'If he tries anything, I will bash his head in.'

He raised his fist, which was nearly as big as my head so I believed him. Aisha held my hand and we walked to his table. I breathed deeply so as to hold the impulse to crash my mug into Vibhor's face and make him chew on the shards of glass. He noticed us and stiffened up. He looked a little scared.

'Hi,' said Aisha with a smile.

'Hi,' said Megha, a little embarrassed.

'Look, I saw you with Sarthak and his guy there and I don't want any trouble,' he said in a half-scared, half-threatening tone.

'We are not here to fight,' she said and sat on the couch in front of him.

She looked calm but her fingers were digging into my arm. Her eyes watered. Her voice was even.

'I just want to talk,' she offered kindly. 'Without them around.'

She pointed to his friends and Megha.

He motioned to his friends and Megha to give them a few minutes.

'And him?' he asked about me.

'I'm dating him now.'

'Okay, so what do you want to talk about?'

'About what happened, about what you did to me. To know if you feel any remorse.' said Aisha.

She was shaking but she didn't let him notice that.

'Look. If you're trying to record this shit, it's not going to work. And I won't say anything,' he said.

I almost caught him smiling. That bastard.

'So, nothing. No guilt whatsoever? What happened in school to me because of you? What you did to my brother?' asked Aisha, trying hard not to crack.

'What I did! And what did you do, bitch?'

'Language,' I pointed out.

'Fine. Whatever,' he said. 'You screwed me over. Everyone looks at me like I'm a fucking rapist when I am not! You were in my bed and I did it. You didn't say no! Now don't just fucking say you wanted to refuse and you couldn't. Because that's just bullshit. You had sex with me. Period. You wanted it. You were asking for it. That's why you were there. You wanted to get fucked.'

I tried to free my hand and rip his fucking throat out. Aisha dug her hands in and didn't let me move.

'I wasn't asking for it, Vibhor.'

'All you girls are the same. First you dress up like you do, then you touch the guy all over, get him all turned on, and when the guy does something, you cry rape! You fucking spoil his reputation. How fair is that? Even if it did happen to you, which I'm not saying it did, it was probably deserved. I'm not a rapist. You know who rapists are and you weren't raped. You can hardly call that rape. I didn't hit you or anything.'

'You mean to say I wasn't raped enough. Like my rape was different in some way? As if it wasn't humiliating and damaging enough?'

'Of course. How different are you from the stupid-ass girls who get married and cry rape?

'I can't believe you just said that,' she said.

I could feel her breaking down. She took my glass and sipped a little of my drink.

'Whatever, ya. I don't want to waste time talking about this. You just overreacted. You felt slutty the next day and you flipped. That's what happened. Now get over it. And leave me alone. You have ruined my school life anyway. Now don't ruin my date.'

'Yes, I did, didn't I?' mocked Aisha.

'Yes, you did. And that's why I'm taking a transfer. My parents fucking got to know about the entire fiasco and they are putting me in a boy's school. All because you were getting mood swings. You must have been having your periods,' he said and smiled.

I was breaking his jaw in my head.

'You're seriously changing your school?'

'Yes, and that's what you fucking did to me,' he grumbled. He took his mug of beer and got up. 'I'm fucking leaving now. This conversation is over.'

He had scrambled out of the table when Aisha called out. 'Vibhor?'

'What—'

'I'm sorry about that. Maybe I went a little overboard. It was just a little rape. No harm in that.'

'See. That's what I was trying to tell you,' he said and put his mug down. He sat back down. 'No big deal. Rape is what happened to the girl in that bus, not you.'

Aisha leaned back on her chair. She stared into her glass for a minute or two. Silence engulfed us for a minute or two. She smiled and leaned forward. 'I think you're right, Vibhor.'

'Are you serious, Aisha?' I said, shocked.

Aisha smiled weakly. 'Of course, Vibhor's right. He never deserved what he got. I'm deeply apologetic about it.'

'Are you?' asked Vibhor, victorious.

'To think of it now in hindsight, it was stupid and impulsive.'

'Aisha? What are you talking about? We really need to talk about this. How can you say all of this? We need to leave,' I butted in.

'I'm talking to Vibhor,' she snapped.

'See, I told you what you did was totally unnecessary and dumb.'

'I should have listened. I guess I was just a little angry, Vibhor.'

'Exactly! All is forgiven then?' asked Vibhor.

'All is forgiven. I'm so sorry and so embarrassed about the hoopla now. I'm sure in the future we will look back at all of this and laugh our heart out . . .'

'It's okay, Aisha. Happens to the best of girls. They panic after the first time they have sex. Chill.'

'Yeah, I'm sure it does,' she said. I looked at her, aghast.

Aisha raised her glass. They clinked it. I had no idea what was going on here.

'No big deal,' she said.

I looked at her.

'Just forgive him, Danish,' she said looking at me. 'You have to admit we did cross a line with him. The whole beating up thing, the badges, the labelling of him as a rapist. It was all a little excessive. We should have heard his side of the story as well.'

I shook my head in disbelief.

'Trust me. Try not to be so prejudiced. I think you, too, owe him an apology,' she said and I sat there, dumbstruck.

'I don't owe him anything. And neither do you. What are you doing, Aisha? After all that—'

Vibhor noticed and offered me a drink and asked me to lighten up a little. 'It's all done and dusted, Danish sir. Why are you angry now if she's okay with it? Chill. Have a drink. And you don't have to embarrass me by apologizing, bro. It's all good.'

'I will just be back from the washroom. You guys carry on. And Danish, chill, it's okay, I have got over it now. Let bygones be bygones.' she said.

She left me with him. Not a good idea at all. A few shots came to the table and he had two in quick succession. He peered into his phone. We didn't talk. He drank in silence. His eyes were bloodshot and he was slightly drunk now. I could drag him out, pull him behind a bush and strangle him. What the hell was Aisha saying? Was she fucking drunk?

'C'mon, have this,' he said and pushed a shot in front of me. 'I know why you are so angry. Must hurt to sit with a guy who had fucked your girlfriend, right?'

'No. You need to shut up.'

'Oh wait, girlfriend and student! Must suck for you, man. Your student fucking your girlfriend. That must have been a blow to your male ego.'

'Not at all, Vibhor. You need to stop talking to me or I will hit you.'

'Of course it was. Stop playing around, *sir*. Maybe in the matter of girls you should take a few lessons from me,' he said and winked.

'Fuck off, Vibhor. And you need to keep your hands off Megha as well.'

'She was right. You should get over it. If she's over it, you should be too.'

'What are you guys talking about?' said Aisha, having retouched her lipstick and fixed her hair.

'Hey! Hey! I thought we were cool!' exclaimed Vibhor, seeing Erskin, Sarthak and Ankit emerge from behind Aisha.

'We are cool,' said Ankit and shook hands with Vibhor. 'We just thought we will join the party. It's a good day today.'

'Ankit? We all need to leave,' I said, pointing to everyone.

But Ankit sat next to Vibhor and poured every one shots from the bottle of Absolut he had carried from the bar. Megha and Vibhor's friends joined as well.

'Aisha has a stable boyfriend, Sarthak has found the love of his life, Megha and Vibhor are together, and my app got funded! So cheers all around, and Danish you need to lighten up. Don't mess our vibe,' said Ankit.

He passed on the shots.

What the hell was happening here?

'What say Sarthak? Erskin?' asked Ankit.

Both of them took the shots and downed them. They shook hands with Vibhor as well.

'I'm sorry, man,' Sarthak addressed Vibhor. 'I went a little overboard. I heard all those things and I just had to beat you up. I'm a brother after all, right? Aisha just told me how sorry she's for doing whatever she did to you, so I thought I should mend my ways too.'

'It's okay. It still pains as fuck, bro,' said Vibhor. 'It wasn't a fair fight though. I could have taken you down. I just wasn't ready that day.'

'Of course you would have.'

Liquor flowed freely and within the next hour, Vibhor was one of us, cracking jokes, a back-slapping buddy, laughing with us, dancing with Sarthak, being a friend, clicking pictures, that fucking rapist. I dragged Sarthak, and then Erskin, and then Ankit away from Vibhor and his friends, to confront them, to ask them how they were even tolerating that guy and they all told me I was overreacting and that if Aisha had forgiven him, so should we. They asked me to lighten up, damn it. Like how?

Ankit told me, 'What are you doing, Danish? She has moved on and so should you? We are all having a good time here. Don't be such a bore and a spoilsport. The fight is over now. We have all moved on. Just chill now.'

Sarthak said, 'And don't sit there and grumble all the time. When we have forgiven him why are you so stuck up? It's all

cool now. You're with her and she's happy and everything's
fine now. So now chill.'

I snapped, 'I have no idea what you guys are talking about!
Are you out of your fucking minds?'

Erskin said, 'Just drink, Danish. Be happy!'

I didn't drink. I was seething in anger the entire time. I
was surprised how the rest were. Like how drunk were they?
How could Aisha say it was her fault after all that happened?

'Danish's not drinking!' shouted Vibhor, climbing up on
one of the tables. 'He's a little pissed about something I said.
C'mon, sir, lighten up! WE ARE ALL FRIENDS!'

'Drink, no. Don't be a spoilsport,' said Aisha and rubbed
my back.

'What are you saying?' I whisper-shouted at her.

'Just drink,' she said, 'For me. Bottoms up on the pitcher.'

'No, Aisha, I'm not in the mood to,' I said.

She insisted. And then everyone started shouting. I picked
up the pitcher, mostly because I was angry and this right here
seemed like a bad freaking dream, downed it in one go and that's
almost the last thing I remember before everything blacked out.

*

I woke up in a hotel with a bitch of a headache and rushed
straight to the washroom and puked all my internal organs into
the commode and flushed them down. What happened last
night? I stumbled outside the washroom and found Sarthak,
Erskin, Ankit and Aisha sitting calmly on chairs and the floor,
sipping on what seemed like lemonade, staring at me.

On the bed lay a naked boy. It was Vibhor.

I mumbled, 'What did you do with him?'

56

Aisha Paul

The look on Danish's face was priceless.

'We didn't kill him,' I clarified. 'He got a little drunk and he's sleeping.'

'What's he doing here?' he asked. He looked around. 'Where's Megha?'

Sarthak told him they had dropped her home in the night. Scared, Danish bent over to check if he was still breathing.

'What did you guys do? And what happened to me!'

'You drank too much,' said Ankit. 'Relax.'

'People! You need to tell me what's happening!' he shouted.

And with that, Vibhor stirred in his bed. He grunted and he moaned and he rubbed his eyes. He called for his mother a few times. When he got no answer, he sat up in his bed and stretched his arms. He rubbed and opened his eyes.

Now Danish wasn't the only one who was shocked in the room.

'Aisha? Where's Megha?'

'She's home. She doesn't want to see you any more. She came out with you yesterday so that you could meet us at the bar. Don't you dare contact her again,' said Aisha.

He laughed nervously when he found he was the only one naked in the room and there were eight pairs of eyes on him.

'What is happening here? Where am I?'

'We got you to our hotel,' said Erskin, brightly. 'You were too drunk. We just had a good time, Vibhor, that's it.'

'Huh,' he said and scrambled for his clothes.

'Oh, never mind them. You had puked all over those clothes so we have given them over to Laundry,' I said. 'They will be here any moment.'

Danish still looked at me strangely. Vibhor laughed nervously. We all looked at him and smiled. He was sweating now. Just then, Vibhor's phone rang. It was kept on the opposite side of the room. To reach for it he had to get down from the bed. He wrapped his bedsheet around him to cover himself. Now, that bastard had shame? We still looked at him, every bit of him, even as he tried covering himself.

'What is it?' asked Sarthak as Vibhor looked into his phone.

'Oh. Just likes on some pictures,' he said, smiling, almost relieved. 'Pictures of last night. God! We were drunk—'

And then, the smile was wiped off his face.

'When did this happen?'

He pointed to a picture of him with five shots in front of him. He had drunk them all.

'You were quite fun last night. We just uploaded the harmless ones on your Instagram. Why don't you check the other pictures? There are some real fun ones in the gallery,' Erskin said naughtily.

He swiped ahead. There was a picture of Erskin and him dancing, and another one of Erskin picking Vibhor up in his arms. And then the classic, Erskin and Vibhor were pouting in one, and right in the next, Erskin was kissing Vibhor on his cheek. Vibhor flushed and looked at us. We grinned right back at them.

Danish, totally at sea, took the phone from Vibhor and started flicking through the pictures.

'What is happening here?'

He was shocked. Well, I didn't blame him.

'God.'

'What!' Vibhor shrieked.

Vibhor peeked into the phone. I knew what they were looking at. The twelfth picture was of Vibhor and Erskin arm-in-arm in the backseat of the cab, Erskin with his face buried in Vibhor's neck and Vibhor giggling away. The next one was an Instagram video of every one of us raising a toast.

'BEING GAY IS AWESOME,' shouted Vibhor.

Of course, he meant it for Sarthak and Erskin who were his best friends last night but we edited the video to suit our purpose.

In the next picture, Erskin and Vibhor were sitting next to each other, hands on each other's thighs, and Danish had passed out on the ground. The next video was classic—Erskin had taken off his T-shirt and Vibhor was touching his biceps, shouting, 'That's huge!' Then there were a couple of pictures Sarthak and I had taken the liberty of cutting ourselves out of but both Erskin and Vibhor were shirtless and generally hanging out like two alpha males. The last picture had Vibhor sitting on Erskin's lap. God. *Was he that drunk last night?*

And after that Vibhor passed out and we began our work.

The next few pictures looked like after sex pictures of Erskin and Vibhor. Vibhor was splayed out on the bed, naked, and Erskin was with him, their crotches and asses strategically hidden by stray bed linen. Vibhor's chest and back were littered with love bites.

Vibhor lost his shit when he got to the end of the picture series.

'What the hell is this! WHAT THE FUCK IS THIS!' he shouted.

Danish walked up to me and grumbled, 'What's this?'

'We had sex last night. And it was good,' said Erskin and threw Vibhor a flying kiss.

Sarthak chuckled.

'Yeah, I know, I was watching. You're good, Vibhor. You should join us in Poland,' said Sarthak.

'I didn't do anything!' squeaked Vibhor.

'What happened here? What did you do, Erskin?' said Danish.

'What? We had sex! Big deal. He has a nice ass and I fucked it. It was slightly tough but we had lube,' said Erskin. 'I'm sorry, Sarthak.'

Vibhor struggled in his bed, as if to check for any physical signs and there they were. Two big purple love bites on his neck and about a dozen more on his chest. He started to cry.

'YOU DIDN'T,' said Danish, and looked in my direction. I shrugged. 'I didn't have anything to do with it.'

'You fucking raped him, Erskin!' shouted Danish.

'NO!' shouted Vibhor. 'Nothing happened to me.'

'Of course, something happened,' said Erskin to Vibhor and then turned towards Danish, 'Oh please, you should have heard him moan while I fucked his sweet ass. He wanted it. He touched me all over. Look at the pictures.'

'This is not a game, people,' said Danish, frantically. 'Why didn't you stop them, Ankit!'

'I had passed out, dude. Why didn't you stop them?'

Danish sat on the bed, and held his head. I sat next to them and patted his back.

'He wanted it, Danish. Chill. And he knew what was happening to him,' I told Danish.

'NOTHING HAPPENED TO ME!' shouted Vibhor and got off the bed, looking for his clothes.

He tripped over the bedsheet and fell face first on the ground. He ran around naked for a bit while all of us, except Danish laughed. He found the bathrobe and wore it. He was bawling now.

'I think I should upload all of these pictures. People anyway suspect you're gay. Read the comments once. They are all congratulating you for coming out of the closet. I remember the day I came out. It was awesome! Should I upload the ones in which I'm lying naked with you?' asked Erskin.

'YOU WILL NOT!' he said and laughed nervously over his tears. 'People would know you're gay. EVERYONE WILL KNOW.'

'They already do. And back home, no one really cares. They would just think I broke up with Sarthak. And then we can do this more often,' said Erskin and walked towards Vibhor who ran and hid in a corner. 'Why are you running away now? I think I need you again. You're already naked, so why not?'

Vibhor crunched up in a ball in a corner and tried swatting away Erskin like he was a common housefly.

'I wasn't raped. I didn't have sex with a boy. Nothing happened here,' said Vibhor, crying.

'And who's going to believe you, Vibhor?' asked Aisha.

'EVERYONE!'

'Erskin, why don't you upload that picture? I will share it on my wall and slowly but steadily it will reach all the boys in his new boy's school. I wonder who would they believe?'

'ME.'

'You wish. These pictures clearly say you're gay, no offence you two, and that you have been fucked by a tree, no offence Erskin, or that you're straight and you just happened to be naked in the bed with a large gay man,' she said.

'NO ONE IS GOING TO BELIEVE YOU!' he shouted, his voice cracking now. 'My father will sue all of you! I will go to the police!'

Sarthak laughed. 'I wonder how that will go. Will your father believe that his MCP son he so proudly brought up is straight? Oh, what fun would that conversation be? And with the police. What would they call you? Can't wait for that to happen to you. And wait, wait, even if you win the case, which you won't because we have pictures and stuff, the same you had, will you really win the case?'

Sarthak took the phone and tossed it at him. 'Please call your father. I'm dying to hear that conversation take place.'

Danish stood up, looked at all of us and said, 'Do you guys realize someone was raped here? No matter what he did, you did it to him. How different are we from him if we did the same thing! HAAN? WHAT THE HELL WERE YOU THINKING? YOU RAPED A GUY, PEOPLE!'

I didn't want to lose it but I did. I didn't want to shout at Danish, but I did.

'HE WASN'T RAPED, DANISH! JUST LIKE I WASN'T RAPED. HE WAS ASKING FOR IT. HE WANTED IT. HE PROVOKED ERSKIN. HE GAVE OUT ALL THE SIGNALS. HE DESERVED WHAT HE GOT! HE HAD SEX WITH HIM. THAT'S WHAT HAPPENED HERE. JUST A LITTLE RAPE. WE DIDN'T HIT HIM. HE'S OVERREACTING!'

Danish threw his hands up in the air and slumped on the bed. The bell rang. Ankit got the door.

'Here's your laundry and should I get your luggage?' asked the bell boy.

Sarthak guided him to Erskin's and his luggage and the bell boy took it away.

'Here,' said Sarthak and threw Vibhor his clothes.

Vibhor wore them hiding behind a curtain, quietly sobbing.

'We need to go, Aisha,' said Sarthak. He held my hand and tugged at it.

'One second,' I said and stepped a little closer to Vibhor. He didn't look up to meet my eye. He was scared and he was sobbing. I felt no pity for him. 'Vibhor. You raped me. That happened. Believe it. Know it. You raped me. It was real and you're to blame for it. Only you. It wasn't my fault. It was yours. You should feel guilty about it. Have some damn remorse. It was all your fault. You're a bad person. You have no place in our society. Do you get that? Haan?'

'But—'

'Do you know now how it feels to have your voice taken away from you? To be powerless. Like this. Remember this when you try anything like what you did to me with anyone else the next time,' I said, held Sarthak's hand in one, Erskin's in the other and left the room.

Erskin paid the bill. A little later, Ankit joined in. Danish was with him but he didn't say a word. We took a cab to the airport. Danish sat in the front and no one said a word for the first twenty minutes.

Finally it was Ankit who gave it away. He laughed so hard, he started to cry. He tried to shut up but he couldn't. The rest of us tried restraining ourselves but we couldn't hold it down any longer and we burst out laughing again.

'That's cruel. You guys know what you did. It was horrible,' said Danish.

And we laughed again.

'What's wrong? Have you guys totally lost it? You guys are goddamn criminals,' said Danish and turned to us.

Sarthak literally had tears in his eyes from all the laughing. He said, 'Vibhor wasn't raped. We faked it.'

'What?'

'I wouldn't touch that thing!' said Erskin.

'And I would break up with you if you did,' said Sarthak.

Danish looked at me for an explanation. I held my ears and mouthed a sorry at him.

'Thank you,' I said. 'For playing the bad cop. I'm sorry but it was essential to our plan.'

'What plan! What fucking plan, Aisha? You were all in it? Ankit too?'

I nodded. 'Yes, they were.'

'FUCK,' he said and slapped his head even as the rest of us laughed. 'But didn't he know he wasn't . . . like his ass?'

'That's a little trick we played. We gave him this medicine—'

'Shut up, Sarthak, I don't want to know! And those love bites?'

'It's a simple vacuum, Danish,' explained Ankit.

'NO. You could have told me. I was being a fool all this time? At the bar? In the hotel room?'

For the rest of the ride, Danish kept trying to wrap his head around the whole thing, and cursed us for not letting him in on the secret. The car stopped at the airport and we unloaded their luggage.

'Why didn't you tell me?' he asked, holding my face and kissing me, knowing now that I wasn't part of a gang rape.

'You wouldn't have acted so well if you knew. We wanted someone to support him and we knew you would do it.'

'What if I hadn't?'

'You're a nice guy, Danish. Nicer than all of us. We could count on you. None of us would have supported him,' I said.

He rolled his eyes. I kissed him.

'I'm right here. Can you not do this in front of me?' said Sarthak.

'Says my brother who's dating Giant Gonzalves. No offence, Erskin,' said Aisha.

A little later, Aisha's mother reached the airport too. The time for their flight approached and we hugged them endlessly and countless tears were shed.

Aisha's mother kissed Erskin's forehead and said, 'You're the best boyfriend I could have hoped for Sarthak.'

And I thought I saw the giant almost cry. I knew how much it would have taken my mother to say that so I hugged her and winked at my brother. They got their documents checked and disappeared behind the airport gates, and we waved at them till they were out of sight.

'I will drop Aunty home,' said Ankit. 'I'm sure you two have somewhere to go.'

Both Danish and I blushed. My mother kissed me and then Danish on his forehead and asked us to come back home early. Ankit took her away.

'So,' asked Danish. 'That was interesting. What's the plan now?'

'Want to go somewhere and discuss the names of our kids? Of course we have to make sure no one overhears us because who does that?'

'I have also seen some flats on Housing. Do you want to go check them out?'

'Pose as a married couple? Sure. I'm down for that. Should we tell them we have a little girl?'

'Aren't I too young for that?'

'We can fake it,' said Danish.

'And later we will go to a family restaurant like an old couple whose children have left them?'

'Shhh. Who does that?'

'We do that.'

'Shhh.'

'I love you.'

'I love you.'

'Danish?'

'Yes?

'Thank you for listening.'